THE DEAD
GO TO SEATTLE

stories by

Vivian Faith Prescott

Book design by Selena Trager

Library of Congress Cataloging-in-Publication Data
Names: Prescott, Vivian Faith, author.
Title: The dead go to Seattle: stories / by Vivian Faith Prescott.
Description: Pasedena: Boreal Books, an imprint of Red Hen Press, 2017.
Identifiers: LCCN 2017011412 | ISBN 9781597099042 (softcover: acid-free
paper) | ISBN 9781597095822 (ebook)
Classification: LCC PS3616.R465 A6 2017 | DDC 813/.6—dc23
LC record available at https://lccn.loc.gov/2017011412

The National Endowment for the Arts, the Los Angeles County Arts
Commission, the Dwight Stuart Youth Fund, the Max Factor Family
Foundation, the Pasadena Tournament of Roses Foundation, the Pasadena
Arts & Culture Commission and the City of Pasadena Cultural Affairs
Division, the City of Los Angeles Department of Cultural Affairs, the Audrey
& Sydney Irmas Charitable Foundation, Sony Pictures Entertainment,
Amazon Literary Partnership, and the Sherwood Foundation partially
support Red Hen Press.

First Edition
Published by Boreal Books,
An imprint of Red Hen Press
www.borealbooks.org
www.redhen.org

ACKNOWLEDGMENTS

"A Boat Named *Coffin*" and "Escape from Planet Alaska" appeared in *Cold Flashes: Literary Snapshots of Alaska*, edited by Michael Engelhard (Fairbanks: University of Alaska Press, 2010); "Alien Stories," appeared in *Cirque: Journal of the North Pacific Rim* 2, no. 2 (Summer 2011); "The Man Who Married a Tree" appeared in *Weird Year* (August 2010); "Salmon Woman" appeared in *Tidal Echoes* (2010); "Daughter of the Tides" appeared in *Altered States: Sci-Fi and Fantasy Stories about Change*, edited by Amy Locklin (Charlotte, NC: Main Street Rag, 2011); "Men's Stories" appeared as a poem in *Punkin House Digest: Family Issue* (2010) and as a short story in *Cirque: Journal of the North Pacific Rim* 2, no. 2 (Summer 2011); "House Falling into the Sea" appeared in *Alaska Sampler 2015*, edited by David Marusek and Deb Vanasse (Running Fox Books, 2015), and read by Frank Katasse on 360 North's Writers' Showcase (November 13, 2015); "52-Hertz" appeared in *13 Chairs: A Literary Journal* (#1); "Can I Touch Your Chinese Hair?" appeared in *Building Fires in the Snow: A Collection of Alaskan LGBTQ Short Fiction and Poetry*, edited by Martha Panschar Amore and Lucian Childs (Fairbanks: University of Alaska Press, 2016). "The First Assimilated Sámi in the World" and "The Girl Who Paid Attention" appeared in *13 Chairs: A Literary Journal* (#2); "Deadmans Island" appeard in *Cirque: A Literary Journal of the North Pacific Rim* 8, no. 1. (Winter 2016).

Although these stories are works of fiction, I would like to thank my father, Mitchell Prescott, for contributing his stories (fictional retellings of family stories) to the characters Nillon Hetta, Isak Laukonen, and Charlie Edwin. Several other characters are historical people: John R. Swanton, John Muir, S. Hall Young, and my great-grandfather, William Binkley. I would also like to recognize my sisters, Joy Prescott and Tracey Martin, and my daughter, Vivian Mork, for their input and insight into the Wrangell myths and thank Lorna Woods for her story that inspired "Men's Stories." I extend my appreciation to the T'akdeintaan (Tlingit), my family's clan and my adopted clan, and to Aan gux, Wooshkeetaan, for allowing me to reference his clan and name. I especially acknowledge the Shtax'heen Kwaan, the people of Wrangell Alaska, Kaachxaana.áak'w. In addition, I am indebted to John R. Swanton's *Tlingit Myths and Texts*, for the inspiration for this book.

I am very grateful to Peggy Shumaker and everyone at Boreal Books and Red Hen Press for the opportunity to share these stories. Likewise I'd like to thank my editor, Andromeda Romano-Lax, whose expertise helped shape these stories into a better manuscript and Joeth Zucco for her copyediting work.

I also want to acknowledge the members of two Sitka writers groups— Blue Canoe Writers and the Wednesday Writers Group, fellow writers who have encouraged me along the way. Above all I want to thank my husband, Howie Martindale, and my children for their support and encouragement. Without them this book would not be possible.

"The Woman Who Kicked over a Frog" is a modern retelling of the Stikine Kiks.adi story "The Man Who Kicked over a Frog," recorded in *Tlingit Myths and Texts*. "The Boy Who Shot the Star" is a retelling of a story of the same name. The song "Tsu Héidei Shugaxtutaan" ("We will open again this container of wisdom") was inspired by the words of George Davis, Kich-náalx—Lk'aanaaw, and written by Harold Jacobs for public domain.

"The Woman Who Married a Bear" is a Sámi story recorded in Finland. It is also found among the Kolta Sámi. In the original story, the woman does not transform into a bear but remains fully human. Several versions of this story are known among the Inland and Coastal Tlingit, the Athabaskan, and the First Peoples of Canada.

There are real events in *The Dead Go to Seattle*: Lituya Bay's first contact, John Muir's bonfire, Wrangell's fire (1952), my great-grandfather's boat named *Coffin*, the Presbyterian Church fire, the landslide and flooding of Wrangell's cemetery, and Deadmans Island lore. In addition, the Stikine River, Petroglyph Beach, Institute Beach, Sitka, and most of the islands and landmarks are actual places.

The community of Wrangell on Wrangell Island in Southeast Alaska is a real place and is where I was born and raised; however, all the characters in *The Dead Go to Seattle* are figments of my imagination and other than the aforementioned, any relation to people living or dead is purely coincidental.

These stories are dedicated to my children—Vivian, Mitch, Breanne, and Nikka—and to my wonderful multicultural family representing many nations: Norwegian, Finnish, Sámi, Tlingit, Hawaiian, Irish, German, Aleut, Dutch, English, Chinese, Filipino, Potawatomi, Chippewa, and Russian.

CONTENTS

We are all given one thing by which our lives are measured . . .
Mine are the stories which can change or not change the world.
It doesn't matter as long as I continue to tell the stories.

—Thomas Builds-the-Fire

LETTER OF TRANSMITTAL

Smithsonian Institution
Bureau of American Ethnology
Washington, DC

Sir: I have the honor to submit herewith for your consideration the manuscript of *Wrangell Myths and Texts* by Dr. John R. Swanton, assisted by Tooch Waterson, with the recommendation that it be published in this Bureau's series of Bulletins.

Yours respectfully,

S. D. Harstead, Chief
The Secretary of the Smithsonian Institution
Washington, DC

Recorded by
John R. Swanton
Bureau of American Ethnology Bulletin 39.2

Introduction

The following myths and texts were collected at Wrangell, Alaska, beginning in 1908 and ending thereabouts in the late 2010s CE. John R.
Swanton was assisted with the translation by Interior Tlingit Tooch
Waterson, although the Interior Tlingit dialect is slightly different
from Coastal and Wrangell dialect. Mr. Waterson was eager to assist.
Swanton claims the Wrangell Island folk were reluctant to tell their
stories to an outsider, and they rejected the common term "informant."
Tooch Waterson introduced Swanton to a few of Wrangell's storytellers—Nillan Hetta, Charlie Edwin, and Isak Laukonen—who proved
to be capable informants. Nillan and Isak are not Tlingit but from a
migratory population of unusual people from Scandinavia who have
intermarried among the Tlingit. At this time Swanton does not cat-
egorize them, except to say they are "indigenous," but certainly not
from Alaska, let alone Wrangell. They call themselves "Sámi." There
were also a few younger informants who participated in the interviews:
Mina Agard, the daughter of Isak Laukonen, and Mina's daughter,
Tova Agard. It is important to note Swanton discovered a subject re-
peatedly skirted during the interviews. It is also curious that the Sámi
shared with the Tlingit a similar belief in a maleficent entity, Stallo,

but were less reluctant to name it. Therefore, so as not to upset the locals and those who still hold the superstitions, Swanton does not mention the name *Lutra canadensi–Homo sapien* in the text. But he does, however, use the English word, which is not considered taboo by the Wrangell folk.

Thereabouts the stories are not organized according to a linear timeline, but instead as Mr. Tooch Waterson suggested, to make sense of life "on an island flying to the riverflats." Note that the date recorded and when the story actually occurred may vary.

Although Swanton collected many stories throughout his time in Wrangell, this collection is the only one to have been received and documented by the Bureau of American Ethnology. Due to unknown circumstances, a majority of the stories did not make it to our office. Though it is not a complete collection, the collection is nonetheless exceptional, providing an examination of life on an isolated island in the Alexander Archipelago of Southeast Alaska.

MYTHS RECORDED IN
ENGLISH AT WRANGELL

Date: 2000s
Recorded by John Swanton
Assisted by Tooch Waterson

The Girl with Pink Hair

Tova's coming-out party was not a celebration—she flew four feet through the air and slunk down against the wall. Her father, Karl, came at her again, and she raised her arm over her head to shield his next blow. As his hand came down, she jumped up and moved sideways and headed to the front door. Her father leaped to the door and blocked it with his large body. She turned and ran across the living room carpet and down the hall to the side door, slamming it open and running across the yard toward the woods.

Her dad ran after her. She turned slightly, saw him fall in the soggy grass onto his hands and knees. "Fuck!" he yelled. She turned back and her spirits followed her into the woods, crashing through the alder behind the houses. Soon she found the old deer trail leading to the roaring stream beside the Wrangell Institute, the old abandoned boarding school. There she sat on a rock in a large culvert beneath the road that had been her favorite place to play while growing up. Here she was a troll screeching at the occasional car speeding along the highway. She was a sprite, a stallo, and a Landotter-Woman—all the taboo creatures from her mixed heritages. No one talked openly about those creatures. They whispered their stories around town like they whispered hers.

Tova sensed she was part creature, or something she couldn't name. Her Grandma Liv assured her she was two-spirited, had been since she was born and that was nothing to be ashamed of. By that count, she would have three spirits. Berta, her other grandmother, said she was "that way" because her daughter-in-law, Mina, didn't dress Tova in enough pink, nor enough dresses, when she was growing up. She remembered her mom defending herself, claiming Southeast Alaska was no place for dresses.

They said her two spirits were the Old-Woman-Who-Lives-Underneath, who lives along the Fairweather fault line, which extends along the Alaskan coastline. The other was Káa Litu.aa, a man and sometimes a monster, who lives at the entrance of Lituya Bay. His slaves shapeshift into bears. They shake the water like a blanket, causing large tidal waves.

Several times the spirit shook the ground and the Fairweather fault split and cracked and the mountain came down. In the fifties, the Man-of-Lituya shook his blanket and her great-uncle rode the tidal wave, the largest on record, and survived to tell about it. This was also the place where her ancestors encountered the first white man in Alaska.

Two spirits? Female and Male. If she were an old man, and at the same time, an old woman, then what about her own spirit? Maybe that's why she was a bit unsteady on her feet. Grandma Liv said everywhere she went the ground shook slightly. It must be true because when she flew across the room, the hairs on her arms stood up, and when she landed, the ground beneath her body formed a fissure and the waves on the water in front of town rippled.

It had all happened so fast, Tova thought, dipping her hand into the cold stream and scooping up a drink. She was twenty years old and living on her own for a couple years. She was working her way through college—long shifts all summer at the canneries. She'd been staying at her parents' house. Her mother had handed her a letter she'd intended on mailing to her girlfriend, inviting her to come up and work in the cannery for the summer. It wasn't really a love letter. She'd written something about remembering the way her friend's skin tasted, like new spruce tips in the spring. Her mother had shown the letter to her father and that's when all hell broke loose.

"Queer, lesbian, gay, dyke," they'd questioned, but all she could do was shake her head no. She was no more than what they called her. Now, she took off her shoes and set them on a nearby rock. She stood, her head brushing against the top of the culvert. If she were going to live in the woods, she'd have to have food. Her father, when he wasn't commercial fishing, worked at the waste water treatment plant and he'd be gone all day. Her mother worked at the deli. Perfect time for a raid.

Tova snuck back into the house through the same door through which she'd fled. She rummaged through the refrigerator, taking anything edible, even her father's wasabi and his Frank's Red Hot. She was the Grinch, stuffing her backpack full with several tomatoes, a can or two of green beans, a can opener, a small pot, some tea, wilted lettuce, and a banana. She left a banana for her mother. It was one of her favorites. She took a package of bologna, the half loaf of bread, the mustard, the leftover meatloaf, and a pack of presliced Velveeta. Her dad would call the cops once he figured out she'd been in the house.

Later that night, she slept under a brown plastic tarp in a sleeping bag she'd also stolen from the shed behind the house. In the morning, she left the tarp tied to a tree and traces of her campfire. She squirted the wasabi out on a flat rock nearby: "Fuck You," it said. That was the last thing she did before she packed up her backpack, hitched a ride to town, and headed off on the ferry to anywhere.

❁

Tova set up her sleeping bag on the white plastic lawn chair. The heaters in the solarium roof warmed her despite the chill on the back deck of the ferry. The *Taku* ferry ran the southern route because the *Columbia* sat in dry dock again. She lay down on the sleeping bag as the boat ran across the straits, making its way past Bushy and Shrubby Islands. It would sail around Etolin Island, heading to Ketchikan and then on to Bellingham, Washington, where it would stop for a half day, load up, and then turn around and head back to Southeast Alaska.

Tova stared out at the waves when a man said to her, "Looks like you might need some coffee." She hadn't noticed him there. He sat on the plastic chair near her holding up a silver thermos in one hand, a stack of paper cups in another. She nodded. He doubled up the cups, poured a cup of coffee, and handed it to her.

"Thanks," she said.

"Sorry, no cream or sugar."

"That's okay."

"Do I know you?" the man asked.

Tova shrugged, "I don't know. Maybe. Everyone knows someone on the ferry."

"I think I saw you in Wrangell."

He didn't look like law enforcement, although she hadn't done anything wrong. Hidden in a tree, she'd watched two cops look over her camp back in Wrangell. They were talking about dykes and how one said he could make her change. Just give her some of this, he'd said, grabbing his crotch. She'd almost thrown pinecones at him, the creep.

"I'm an ethnographer," the man said, interrupting her thoughts. "My name is John Swanton. I've been in Wrangell collecting stories for the Bureau of American Ethnology at the Smithsonian."

"Sounds interesting," she said, adjusting herself in the chair.

"It is. But it's also challenging. Sometimes people don't want to talk."

She shrugged. "Maybe they have their reasons."

"Yes, but it's important to record the stories before they're all forgotten." Swanton took a sip of his coffee.

Tova stared out at the silver water in silence. Sometimes there wasn't anything to say. Her elders taught her that. Her silence was full of sound.

Swanton scooted his chair closer and held out his thermos. "Refill?"

She held her cup up and he poured it full again.

"So where are you headed?" he asked.

"Seattle."

"Seattle? But the boat docks in Bellingham."

"Yeah, I know," she said, "but I'm hitching from Bellingham to Seattle, and then I'm going to get a job. Something."

"Sounds like a plan."

She sighed. "It's better than sitting around Wrangell, working the slime line or in the egg room."

"Ah, the cannery. Lots of interesting folks work there."

"You mean Indians . . . Natives."

"Yes. I recorded a story about a man who—" Swanton paused, and then said, "Can I ask you something?"

Uh-oh. Here it comes. The same stupid questions. It didn't matter: tourists or scholars, all those from the wannabe tribe. "Sure," she said.

"Are you Tlingit?"

Tova smiled. Well at least that version of the question was better than *What kind of Indian are you?* Or *A Kling what?* Or *Where are your reservations and igloos?* That kind of crap.

"Yes, I'm Tlingit," she said, annunciating the wet letters.

"I thought so."

"Gee, what gave it away, my headdress, my Chilkat blanket, or my braids?"

Swanton frowned. "I don't mean to offend, but I've learned if you don't ask, you can be mistaken."

"I know how that feels," Tova mumbled.

Swanton patted a brown attaché case beside him. "I've got a lot of stories to transcribe here, but I can always use one more."

"What kind of stories did you *take* from us?"

"Take?" Swanton said, raising his eyebrow.

"Yeah, what kind? The kind that kicks your ass when your grandma tells it to you. Or the kind your uncle tells when he's drunk and sticking halibut gear with your dad. Or the kind your auntie and mom tell when they're having coffee and smoking cigarettes."

"Oh, I recorded some traditional stories, some historical ones. And, you know, the most interesting subject kept coming up . . . the stories of the stallo and the koosh—"

She held her hand up, palm splayed. "No, don't say it. I know what you mean."

"The land ott—"

"Shshh," she said sharply. "Not here." She nodded toward the water. She wasn't going to chance it, being on a boat in the middle of the ocean. No way.

"Oh, sorry. I figured a girl your age would be accustomed to talking about them. Wouldn't worry about the superstition—"

"It's not a superstition and, even if I didn't believe, why would I want to take chances?"

"Good point."

"Yes, I will."

"Will what?" Swanton asked.

"Tell you a story . . . I'll tell you a story."

"A traditional one, a myth, or historical?" Swanton asked.

"True, a true one. I'll tell you a true one. You decide the category. I hate categories."

Swanton took out a recorder from his satchel. He turned it around in his hands, looking at it, as if studying it.

"No, no recorder," Tova said, pointing to the electronic device. "Take notes the old-fashioned way. You'll listen better. If you record it, you'll only be half listening. You anthropologists, you always get everything wrong."

He set it down and then pulled out a notebook and pencil. "Well, I'm an *ethnologist*, and I try not to get things wrong." Swanton tapped his pencil on the page. "Ready?"

Tova leaned back in her chair and rubbed her neck. "Well, we first met you folks up in Lituya Bay. That's where my uncle rode a tidal wave over an island. We thought you were White Raven and, boy, were we wrong."

Swanton had stopped taking notes.

"What's the matter?" Tova asked. "Have you heard this story before?"

"A version, yes."

"But you haven't heard mine."

"No," he said. "Go ahead." He began to scratch on the paper with the pencil.

It didn't look like words. Maybe he wasn't taking notes. Just being polite. She didn't care, though. There were stories in her head, always swirling around like the tide rips in front of Petroglyph Beach. She told him about snails and puffins and bear spirits. And people traveling down beneath and over the ice, following frozen rivers to the sea. She told how her clan broke from another and how some had lived in Glacier Bay and how they'd been run out by ice and later by the government. She told him how her great-grandparents were punished for speaking the Lingít language. And how her great-grandma was raped by a military man, how her white relatives came from Norway and Finland, and how they once had their own clans and spirits.

After a while, she paused. Swanton had stopped writing. He stared out at the water. She'd seen that hypnotized look before: moving water pulling the spirit from its shell.

Tova stuck her hand down into her backpack and pulled out two diet Cokes. "Here, want one?"

He took it and held it in his hand, looking as if he'd never seen one before.

"What? It's Diet Coke." she said.

"Well . . ."

"You from Canada?" She frowned.

He didn't reply. Instead, he set the Coke down beside him on the deck. "Go on."

She led Swanton through ten generations, through a cycle of ice and seashore, and when it came to her own generation, there wasn't a break in the cycle. It was like the Raven stories. The stories kept coming, wave after wave. Her words caught up in the ferry's wake, pulling and dragging like a huge anchor. There was a shifting. The boat groaned as if time had aged it. It had.

❁

She continued, "And so I hitchhiked to Seattle and got a job at a head trauma rehab center where the patients threw shit at you, when they weren't playing in it. Then I enrolled at UW and got my bachelor's degree. Before that, I spent a semester at the University of Alaska in Juneau. Now, I'm going back home to see my family. Back to Wrangell."

Swanton stopped writing. "We're going south. Not back to Wrangell."

Tova cocked her head. Swanton looked confused. His eyes glazed over, like he'd popped a tranquilizer. What was he talking about? "No, this is a *northbound* boat," she said, pointing to the houses coming into view. "And there's the Elephants Nose. We're coming around Woronofski now. We've come around the back side."

Swanton stood up, setting his notebook on the chair. He walked to the railing, leaned over, and turned his head to the right, and then left. He turned back to her. "It's happening again."

Tova shrugged. Again? Was he referring to the tides? Whatever. She had something to attend to. She got up from the deck chair and rummaged through her backpack. She pulled out a small pair of scissors and held them at her side. "Excuse me," she said to Swanton, "I have to conduct a ceremony before we get to the dock."

She walked to the starboard side of the stern, near the far railing. She lifted her long, dark hair from her shoulders, dividing it in sections. She held it in her fist and started to cut. Each section fell off into the ocean.

Afterward, she brushed her shoulders with her hand. Her hair now hung below her ears. She turned to head back to her chair. Swanton took notes. Oh, great. What will he say about this?

Tova grabbed her backpack. "See you—" The announcer interrupted her: "*Thirty minutes to Wrangell. Thirty minutes to Wrangell.*" She lugged her backpack into the back corner of the solarium, to a small bathroom with a couple of toilets and shower stalls, and headed over to the small two-basin sink. She took out her scissors again and trimmed her hair further until it was above her ears. Slipping her shirt over her head and setting it down on the small bench behind, she stood in front of the mirror in her tank top and removed a box of red hair dye from her bag. Tova put on the plastic gloves from inside the package, mixed up the goop, spread it around in her hair, and waited ten minutes. She took off her tank top and pants and set them on the bench then stepped into the shower stall and washed off the dye.

Tova dried herself off with her tank top and dressed. She patted her hair with the roll of rough brown paper towels sitting on the corner of the sink and then frowned at the mirror, running her fingers through her hair. "Fuck." Her hair was pink, not red. Uneven hair stuck out all over her head. She leaned into the mirror, turning her head this way and that and shrugged.

The ferry blew its whistle as it approached the Wrangell dock. Below deck, Swanton stood in the crowd waiting for the ramp to lower. Tova approached him. He smiled at her. With a quick flick of her hand she flung her nonexistent hair. The ramp clanked to the deck and the crew motioned the crowd forward. Swanton lugged an old brown suitcase, and Tova adjusted the straps to her backpack. At the top of the ramp, the crowd dispersed. Tova turned to Swanton and nodded, "It was nice meeting you."

"Yes, nice to meet you too," Swanton said. He held out his used passage ticket in his hand, turning it over. "Looks like I have to get another ticket."

"Don't worry. In a week, the ferry's going south again."

"I already tried," he said, scratching his head.

"Maybe your story's not finished yet."

"My what?"

"Your . . . story," she said, as if talking to a child. "Sometimes our stories take more than our lifetime to tell, you know. They cycle around like the Raven stories, over and over, winter and summer, and they keep on adding to one another, like towing a log caught on a patch of seaweed, how it gathers up some old rope and a plastic thingy, and then pretty soon you have a big story to tow home with you. You can tell where you've been and who you are and who you've become by the story you take with you."

Swanton smiled and nodded. "Sure. But I'm tired. I'll check into the B&B again." He pointed to the big yellow house on the corner. Without looking back, Swanton headed across the parking lot, waving his hand in the air.

Tova trudged to her mother's waiting car where her mother stood, leaning against the open car door.

She reached her and leaned in for a hug, her backpack wobbling on her back. "Hi, Mom."

"Oh, it's so good to have you home," Mina said.

Tova breathed in her mother's scent. She could tell that her mother, the same height as her, did the same. She released her and then peered into the car. "What, no Pops?" she asked.

"You know your father . . ."

"No, actually I don't."

"Tova," Mina said, helping her off with her backpack. "You have to stay with Auntie Suvi."

"What?" She heaved her pack into the trunk of the car. She got into the passenger side, as her mother sat down in the driver's seat.

"It's your Dad, Tova. I can't go against him."

"It's been years, Ma."

"I know, kiddo, but he'll ask."

"Like he asks every time I've tried to talk to him . . . 'Are you still a *homo*sexual?' It ends the conversation."

Mina clasped her seatbelt and put the car in reverse, looking behind her. "Why don't you lie to him? Tell him what he wants to hear."

"No way. He has to accept me the way I am."

"With pink hair, Tova? You push all his buttons, don't you?"

She rolled her eyes. She didn't want to cause problems for her mom; for her dad, another matter. "Okay, I'll stay with Auntie Suvi."

"Good, I'll drop you off there, and when your father's at work, you can come by the house."

❀

Later, Tova tried to call her father so they could talk. Maybe if she talked to him, she figured. Didn't bring up lesbians or sex, he wouldn't freak out. But as always, the conversation trail led to: "Don't let me catch you at the house."

The next day, Tova found herself in front of her parents' house. Her dad's truck was gone. Her mother's old Ford Taurus sat in the driveway. She knocked. Her mother answered, looking around with her eyes. "What, am I gonna get spanked?"

Her mother laughed. "No, I . . . come in."

Once inside, Tova walked through the house she grew up in, touching a wall here and there, fingering an old sealskin doll, a deerskin drum hanging on the wall, tracing the base of her grandmother's butterfly lamp.

"Don't worry," her mother said, following her. "You're still here."

"Doesn't look like I ever lived here," Tova said, noting her old bedroom was now an office and a guest bedroom. Photos of her brother hung on the wall in the living room: Jorma learning to ride a bike. Jorma sitting in his first snow in a blue snowsuit. Jorma's graduation from high school three years after her own. None were of Tova playing basketball for the Wrangell Lady Wolves or commercial fishing with her father. Nothing. Not even a smiling baby picture.

Suddenly, the ache in the walls swelled inward, forcing her backward like she was being spit out of the house. "I gotta go, Mom," she said, rushing out the door.

"Tova! Tova!" her mother called after her.

❀

Tova lugged her backpack down to the cement dock in front of town and sat down. At 1:00 a.m., the sky faded to blue dark, but it wouldn't be dim for long. She reached into her backpack and took out two sets of ankle and wrist weights she borrowed from Aunt Suvi. She strapped them on and put up her sweatshirt hood. She scooted over to the edge of the dock at the space between the bull rail sections.

She sat for a long time in the cloud-covered night, inhaling the ocean. A strong breeze blew out of the south. She turned her face toward it. An orange wind sock fluttering on the end of the dock made her think of the Corpse Eater, the Wind Giant. After all, it took the shape of an eagle, and eagles were always sitting on the pole that held the wind sock.

Then the wind changed and from out of a short gust came her mother's voice calling her name. "Tova . . . Tova . . ."

She quickly tucked the wrist weights beneath her sweatshirt sleeves and made sure her pant legs were pulled down over her ankles.

Her mother sat down beside her and didn't say anything for a minute. The wind breathed against them and for them. "Nice night, isn't it?" her mother finally said.

Tova didn't answer. It wasn't nice. That was a pleasantry that wasn't pleasant: a dumb thing to say.

Her mom spoke softly, "Did I ever tell you about the day you were born?"

"Yes, I've heard my birth story." Tova didn't want to hear a story now. She wanted this ache in her gut to stop. She woke up with it, ate with it, and had studied the last five years in college with it. It was her companion. Always. She wanted it to stop. She was tired. Like that guy she met on the ferry, Swanton. He'd said it. He was tired. Sometimes don't people get tired when it's time to go?

"Well, let me tell you," her mother said, "it was one party, when you came out. You were blue, you know."

Tova shuddered. The wind cooled her skin. She'd heard the story before, yes. But a "party" version. This was a new one.

"The doctor and nurses scrambled," Mina said, "but I yelled at you to wake up. 'Wake up, Tova!' I don't know why I said that because you weren't sleeping, and you weren't dead or anything. You went from water to air and forgot how to be human. Grandma Liv says it's because you were still underneath the tectonic plates looking up through a hole in the earth. Boy, you sure shook them when you were trying to come out.

"So when I yelled 'Wake up!' you coughed and turned pink."

Mina reached to touch Tova's hair. "And when I brought you into my room, there were grandparents and friends and friends of friends and balloons and gifts. Your baby book bulges with all the cards. I think someone brought some beer too, said it would help my milk come in.

Tova chuckled. Oh, great. Drunk at a few hours old. That figures.

"I was only sixteen years old, Tova, and I thought all births were like that."

Like what, Tova wondered, like pink balloons and sparkly cards or earthquakes ripping open the muskeg. Maybe all of that. "Ma," she sighed, leaning toward her mother.

"You, Tova, are a celebration . . . Your dad, he's at Waters Inn. I piled his clothes on the floor and told him to pack them himself."

"What?" She wasn't sure she'd heard what her mom said. It took a second to process it. She pictured her dad, flipping through the hotel's TV channels, a twelve-pack of beer on the bed beside him.

"It's time to go home." Her mom stood up and held out her hand. Tova took it, and it was cold from the night air. Her mother pulled her up, weights and all. As she rose, Tova's weight shifted to her mother, like the landscape around them, rising and moving in all directions.

Date: mid 2000s
Recorded by John Swanton
Assisted by Tooch Waterson
Speaker: Charlie Edwin

His Spirits Kept Turning Back

"I'm going to be respectful here. I'm going to offer them tobacco when I'm done. I don't want anyone to forget the stories I learned when I was young.

"A long time ago, we had shamans and they were very powerful. Lots of folks had them. My friend Isak, he said his people, the Sámi, they had them. We don't have them anymore. Well, I should say we don't point out the people who have the talents. They would go into trances, and whatever they saw was supposed to happen did. One time, there was a powerful shaman. Once, he said something was going to happen to a big town by a lake.

"Many people were afraid of the landotters. But some weren't. They said the landotter people stutter and can't talk like regular people. The people were making fun of the noise landotters make. Landotters can really make a mumbling sound like they are talking.

"Well, one day, two men from the village went hunting near where there were supposed to be landotters. They went to the top of a mountain, and, when they looked down, they saw a great flood come down between the mountains and destroy their town. The lake filled up with silt and dirt and forced the water out and the village flooded. The landotters caused this because people made fun of them for stuttering.

"We had that happen here. The old graveyard flooded because of the landslide out by the new cemetery. The land came down there. Not good.

"There are many things to know about the landotters, like when a woman is having her period, her monthly. If the shaman is around her, it can make him weak and take away his power. You see, women are very powerful. My Jesse is a very good person. If a woman had the landotter's spirit in her and she had her period, sometimes the shaman couldn't get the bad spirit out of her because his spirits kept turning back.

"There is also a story about Raven who created the animals. He told Landotter he'll be able to live on both the land and water. Raven and Landotter became good friends. One day, they went out to catch some halibut. They both loved halibut. Raven wasn't very good at catching halibut, but Landotter was. Because Landotter helped Raven, Raven made him a really big house that's located on a point of land. Even today, that's where you'll find their houses. The landotters like breezes. On a point, the breeze blows both ways. You have to be careful of places like that, it's like time goes back and forth, going both ways.

"Well, Raven instructed him whenever a boat or a canoe passed by the point and capsized, he was supposed to save them and make the people his friends. Landotter had to save people from drowning. Landotter people are called 'Point People.'

"There are other landotter stories, but I don't have permission to tell them to you. You can go ask Mrs. Daniels. She's Kiks.ádi. She'll tell you. If you want the troll stories, the ones my friend Isak knows, you have to ask him. But he doesn't tell them. Some things I can tell you and some things I can't. It doesn't feel right. I have to be careful.

"Landotters can trick us. Raven tricks us. Trolls. So can the weather, the ocean, the government. I read a lot about tricksters, you know. That's how I know. And I listen to people. There are lots of tricksters in the world. I think there is one here, in Wrangell, right now. I think he's been here for a while. I see him sometimes. I'm not crazy.

"You know that dog bones can make landotters die. And landotters eat raw meat and fish. You know, they opened that Japanese sushi restaurant downtown—Tokyo Oki. Sounds like they came from Oklahoma (laughs).

"I wouldn't be seen in there. No, I hear people say don't go there. But, still people do.

"That's all I know, all I can tell you, anyway (laughs). Now, I have to look for some cigarettes. Tobacco. I don't smoke anymore (laughs). *Hooch áwé.*"

Date: mid-late 1960s
Recorded by John Swanton

The Drowning Ceremony

Karl's seven-year-old body sank to the bottom of the harbor. His bare foot set down on the top of a large barnacled rock. He looked up through the floating kelp wands, up through the brown silty water of the Bitter Water People, up to his father's face. His father, Ole Agard, had tossed him into the harbor.

❀

Karl sat on the bull rail, slivered wood against his legs. His dad stood on the rickety dock beside him, smoking a cigarette, his black hair still thick on his head. His jeans rolled up tight on his short legs and his white T-shirt pressed against his broad chest by the misting rain. Today, Karl's dad was going to throw him and his sister Astri into the harbor without their life jackets—a familiar ceremony for the Agard family. A few years back, his dad had done the same thing to his brother Rodney. Now, it was their turn.

Karl sat on the dock shivering, awaiting his turn. His big brother, Rodney, was still up at the house, a short walk from the dock. That morning, when his dad had finished his coffee, he'd announced Astri and Karl were going with him down to the *Sea Wolf* to stick halibut gear. There was that strange sound in his dad's voice, like pilings scraping the dock in a storm. The same way his dad sounded when he explained to his mother that the sore on Karl's head was from smacking it on the bunks in the boat. He had turned to Rodney and pleaded silently. He didn't like to be on the boat with his dad. His dad ruled there.

❀

On the dock, his dad had made him and Astri strip down to their underwear. Karl had not watched Astri's flight into the ocean. He'd stared at his bony knees. Astri screamed and thrashed in the water. She was five years old, and the rule was by the time you were seven you could go on the boat fishing with Dad, but you had to learn to swim. Grandpa Agard always said knowing how to swim could save your life around these islands. More likely, you would respect the water if you knew the shock of having the air forced out of your lungs and felt the cold seeping through your pores.

Astri flailed her arms at strange arches, her hands clawing the green-gray water, trying to reach out for the creosote bull rail. She reached her hand up and Ole grabbed her and flung her backward. "Go away. Not yet," he laughed.

Astri swam farther away from the dock, barely treading water. "Dog paddle. Dog paddle," Ole yelled. Astri arched her arms and paddled with her head and chin up out of the water, her eyes wide, heading for the dock again. This time, she smiled. She reached the dock and her father's muscular arms pulled her from the water up over the bull rail. He flopped her like a halibut onto the dock, where she lay still, flat on her back, smiling. And then, the shivers came.

It was Karl's turn next. He wanted to leave his body, to take his spirit and run down the dock, jump over the electrical cords, the old blue tarp, and the small bucket filled with rotten bait and rainwater. But what good would it do. He'd be yanked back into his body by his hair anyway. Instead, he got up and walked to the rail, chattering in his underwear. The force of his father's arm flung him through the air. It sounded like breaking glass as he crashed through the surface of the water. His small body sank. His feet touched the hard crusty rock. He tried to push himself up, and then tried to walk, but his legs were like heavy rubber. He didn't know what to do, so he did nothing. He stood there tiptoeing on the rock, looking up.

Above him, the red cherry from his father's cigarette dropped and sizzled on the water. Then, as his father leaped, Karl imagined a sea lion, a large blubbery creature with its fat flippers heaving itself through the water after a fish. He'd seen that sight a hundred times in the few years he'd been alive. Though maybe he'd been alive longer than five years. Everything around him seemed familiar. He understood all the mechanisms on his dad's boat: the beam trawl they used for dragging for shrimp, the davit they pulled crab pots with, the girdies they hauled in salmon with. And, strangely, he knew how the current moved in front of his house, the way the brown water from the Stikine brought the salmon to Back Channel, or to the black can, how the river water and ocean swirled around Deadmans Island.

Karl's head tugged painfully sideways. Maybe the bull kelp had wrapped around him. He turned. His father swam beside him and he was being pulled to the surface. When they broke the surface, he relaxed and his dad heaved him onto the dock. Karl's legs scraped the dock and he rolled over onto his back and closed his eyes. Rodney stood above him.

This time Karl was sure he was running down the dock, the other direction this time, away from the house, over and around the orange electrical cords, the piles of dog shit, the harbor cart. The only thing at the other end of that dock was the ocean again. He didn't want to go back in. He didn't want to breathe stingy, salty water. He heard a boat engine whine, maybe a puller starting up, or a boat's radio crackling. His chest was heavy, like he'd sucked in the sound. He opened his eyes. He lay on the dock, his sister, Astri, and his brother, Rodney, cried beside him. His dad rolled him onto his side. He felt a big smack on his back, then another one. He opened his mouth and puked up water from his mouth and nose, and his stomach heaved. He took several deep breaths and held his stomach, whimpering.

After a few minutes, his dad jerked him by the arm and sat him upright, slapping him hard on the back. "You scared the shit out of me. Why didn't you swim like hell?"

"I don't know," Karl said softly.

Rodney took off his jean jacket and wrapped it around Karl. "I take it you didn't learn to swim?" Karl leaned into his brother. His jacket was hardly warm, but it was dry at least.

"Astri did," his dad said, nodding to Astri. "She's little, but she swam good. But I had to jump in to get Karl. I guess he wanted to go live with the landotter people, right Karl?" His dad laughed and then reached into his jacket, which was lying on the dock, and pulled out his pack of cigarettes. His hands shook as he took a cigarette from the pack. He lit it and inhaled deeply. He frowned at Rodney. "Don't tell your mother. She doesn't need to know."

Karl nodded. Astri did too. They knew how to slip hints to their mother. Rodney could turn an arm just right to show a blue bruise peeking through. Astri might complain of a headache or a scalp problem. Rodney and their older cousins hinted a lot after returning home from a two-month summer fishing trip with their dad, as if months of setting halibut skates in Glacier Bay didn't scar them enough: hooks stabbing their thumbs, rope burns, sliced open chins from falling on the boat deck. And there were the usual skinned knees from gathering seagull eggs from the cliffs, and the blisters, the calloused hands. They were his dad's deckhands because no one else in town could tolerate him. Experienced deckhands would be hired and then quit after a short time.

❁

Back at the house, Karl climbed into the bottom bunk and pulled the granny-square quilt up to his chin. His warm pajamas soothed his skin. Rodney slept in the top bunk. The quilt let in the cool night air, which is how he liked to sleep. He fell asleep listening to his dad and uncle

Bernie playing cribbage in the kitchen: "ten," "fifteen for two," "twenty-two," "twenty-eight for three."

In his dreams he walked alone on the beach, the woods calling to him. He'd been told not to go into the woods alone, but it was still daylight. The spruce and hemlock surrounding him wept with old-man's-beard moss. Stumps resembled trolls resting in the shadows. He sat down beside a huge mossy stump. The rest of the tree had long since fallen and now thrived as a nurse log for smaller seedlings. Nearby, a large hole waited like a gaping mouth where the roots had rotted away. He got down on his knees and looked into the dark hole. He needed something. But he couldn't remember what. He stuck his arm down into the hole, touching a long hairy tail like the tail of his dog, Gus. Why would a dog be hiding in a stump? A story prowled in the back of his head. He thought of his grandfather's cigarette smoke, his uncle's laughter woven into story, a cadence of words and numbers: ten—fifteen for two—twenty-two—twenty-eight for three—drowning, human, landotter, don't. Don't.

A hand curled around his forearm and yanked him into the stump, his mouth filled with moss. There it was, the thing he'd forgotten: the warning, the warning. It was a story. He'd forgotten it: creatures, otters, and trolls, who took people into the forest or into the sea to live with them. Wake. Up. Now. He grabbed his blanket, strung his fingers through his grandmother's granny-square quilt. He could feel it, like a rope he had to hang on to climb up. He stuck his bare toes into the quilt and started to climb up from the hole. He awoke suddenly and sat up. He leaned over in his lower bunk and puked a belly full of salt water onto the floor.

Recorded date: 1908
Recorded by John Swanton
Recounted by Old Town Jim

The Man Who Married a Tree
1879

I made short excursions to the nearby forests . . . causing wondering speculation among the Wrangell folk.—**John Muir,** *Travels in Alaska*

John Muir kneeled in the grass near the Presbyterian Church counting tree rings. Missionary Young had recently cut down the large spruce to make way for the new manse. In his notebook Muir recorded dendromemory, layers of wood cells. The old tree had chronicled rain, temperature, and wind velocity for over a hundred years.

Soon Muir became aware of Wrangell folk peeking out their doors at him. By midday locals gathered to watch the strange man talk to himself. From behind him someone said, "There's an even bigger *live* tree up the hill." Muir turned. A local Tlingit, Old Town Jim, stood pointing his wide hand beyond the steeple. "I'd guess he'd be over two hundred years old," Jim said.

Muir found the large tree near the edge of a clearing. He circled the tree, running his hand along its bark, noting the dragon-like scales. Suddenly, he had an urge to hug the tree. "May I?" he asked, reaching his lanky arms around, leaning in, his cheek pressing its scratchy hide—*rough like whiskers*, he thought. He closed his eyes, inhaling its wet scent. He stepped back and poked his finger into the pitch globbing from beneath the bark. He sniffed it, then stuck his finger in his mouth sucking the sticky substance.

For two more weeks Muir visited this tree, discovering its inner stratum. He learned to strip a small tree root and brewed nettle tea. He even climbed to a top branch, straddled its knobby arm to look out over Zimovia Strait to snowcapped Woronofski Island.

One night Muir settled beneath a bark shed, covering himself with his blanket. The tree sheltered him as he dreamed of his youth: skinny-dipping with his friend Scott in Blossom Lake. Afterward, they'd lie naked, drying on the rocks. But one day, Scott brought the girl who lived on the neighboring farm to swim—after that, Muir never went swimming at the lake again.

Now, Muir slept late and awoke beneath the great spruce, its erect pendant cones dangling, its female cones swelling purple. He felt the pith at his center, the xylem, his cambium layer. He got up and ate hardtack crackers, listening to the tree moan its stories. The tree told of first contact with whites, Russian rule, explorers, and gold seekers. Near nightfall, the winds gusted and branches snapped. "Storm coming," Muir said. Since he'd first stepped off the boat in Alaska and discovered the spruce and hemlock forests, he sensed a change—a celebration was needed. "A marriage, yes," he said to the tree.

Muir dragged dead branches and dry grass to the center of the clearing and built a small fire. He added more tree limbs until the fire roared. The large spruce dropped pine cones at his feet, and he tossed them into the fire. The sky darkened and it started to pour. Around him, the forest creaked. Sparks danced like crazed fireflies. He wiped tree pitch on his face, his lips, and then stomped around the fire, arms twirling. He kept heaping branches on the fire until his skin flushed with heat.

⚜

Below the storm-dance, Missionary Young awakened to the rap of frightened Tlingits at his door. The hill glowed behind the church— St. Elmo's Fire? A madman perhaps? Then Young remembered the strange Mr. Muir, wandering around town mumbling to himself. Such actions, he figured, likely meant Muir was smitten with a local girl. Yes, he chuckled, looking up at the sky-fire, lances of gold aurora streaking upward—a madman indeed.

Date: nd (no date)
Recorded by John Swanton
Assisted by Tooch Waterson

First Contact in Lituya Bay Revisited

Tlél tsú dleit ḵáa yá Alasgi awuskú. . . . Aadéi yóo at kaawaniyi yé shukát wé shgóona shudultee nóok.

No white man knew of Alaska. . . . That's the way things happened in the beginning when they awaited the schooner.—J. White, *Jeenik*, "Raven Boat" (1786)

Surrounded by spruce trees, Tova stood on the hill dressed in knee-worn Carhartts, a blue bandana wrapping her shaved head, stinking of salmon roe and slime. Her girlfriend, Lynn, nuzzled her neck. Lynn grabbed Tova's hand. "You smell like money," she laughed.

Tova let go of Lynn's hand. She lifted the pair of binoculars tied to a string around her neck. "I have to see."

"See what?" Lynn asked.

"See if they make it over the rocks, through this god-awful tide." Out on the horizon, the People-From-Under-the-Clouds sailed into the bay. Tova waited for the legend, for the Monster-Who-Lives-Underneath, to shake the Fairweather fault and create a huge wave that would smash La Pérouse's ship against the rocks. Already, she'd heard he'd lost two longboats with twenty-one men on board, trying to get across the entrance to Lituya Bay. This time, no such luck: the schooner stayed beyond the island at the mouth of the bay.

"Damn," Tova said, as the ship readied to drop anchor. She let go of the binoculars. They pressed heavy against her chest. She walked to a narrow opening in the stand of spruce trees, where an old deer trail led down the steep hillside to the beach. She headed down the trail, brushing past devil's club and Indian celery. Lynn stumbled behind her, trying to keep up. At the bottom, Tova stepped out onto the sand, where several elders and two young men waited.

"Hey," one of the young men said, nodding to her.

"Hey," Tova said, nodding back. One of the elders stood next to a canoe as if ready to paddle out and greet the schooner. Tova walked up to the elder, the one she knew to be her ancestor. "Hey, Grandfather," she said.

"Grandchild," he said, beaming.

The elder put his hand on her shoulder and pulled her close. She caught the scent of freshly tanned deer hide.

"What are you doing here?" he asked.

"I'm, ah . . . me and my friend, we're taking a smoke break. Been working in the cannery and saw the ship coming. I thought I could help."

The grandfather said nothing. He stared at her for a minute as if studying her. "You *know* these people who come from under the clouds?"

"Yeah, unfortunately, I do." She thought about the People-From-Under-the-Clouds, how their blood ran through her veins. The Bureau of Indian Affairs had given her a laminated card, a historical legacy, proof of this very day.

She wondered how she could explain it to the elders, how she really *did* know: she knew what was going to happen. The old men and the young ones were going to paddle their canoes out to La Pérouse's ship. The sailors were going to give her people rice and laugh because the elders were going to think they were eating maggots.

After that, the explorer and his men will give them sugar, which the Tlingits will assume is white sand. But the "white sand" will turn into another type of death. In future generations, they'll hobble on severed legs and their bellies will sting with insulin shots. And worse, the sailors will give the young men a bottle of brandy, and the men will spin in circles, laughing on the deck, spinning through her family for a long time to come.

And La Pérouse will inquire as to the locations of all the villages and ask if there are riches: sea otter pelts, copper, and gold. After this first contact, the Tlingits will head back to shore with their gifts, and the sailors will claim in their diaries they were the first to greet the savages.

Tova shook her head. She said to her grandfather, "Yeah, I speak their language. How about I go in your place?"

"You speak their language?" The elder questioned.

"Ah, yeah, I can speak their language—fluently. I can say, 'You better speak English only, you savages, because you're lucky you get to believe in our god and go to our schools, but if you carve totem poles and eat seal grease, you can't go to our schools, and when you finally challenge us to go to our schools, our kids will beat up your kids for generations right into the twenty-first century where kids will spray paint around town "Kill All Natives," reminding you of the good American life: two halibut a day, free health care, a new HUD house, shares-or-no-shares in corporations not tribes, a laminated card, a degree for driving tour buses, and working at the cold storage and canneries, where we will process your salmon up in cans, ship them out to our storehouses, and then, out of the goodness of our hearts, ship the salmon back to you when you receive our commodities.'"

"Ah," said the grandfather. "You *are* fluent, granddaughter. Maybe you should go out to meet them first, ask them what they want."

The two young men helped Tova into the canoe. Lynn kissed her on the cheek before she shoved off. "Hey, be careful," Lynn said.

Tova smiled, shoving the canoe backward with the oar. She turned the canoe around parallel to the beach. She reached her hand into the pocket of her hoodie, pulling a sleek metal blade from its hiding place. She raised it slightly. Lynn nodded. The grandfather raised his walking stick up in the air. The young men on the beach nodded, raising their own knives. "*I gu.aa yáx xwán*—be strong—be brave," they cried in unison.

Tova turned and paddled out toward the schooner, its white sails let down. *Oh, I speak their language, all right.* She had been speaking with the slice of steel every summer at the cannery for the past ten years, ever since she was fifteen years old: cut-slice-scrape, cut-slice-scrape. She knew how it felt to stick her knife in the anus, move it up through the salmon belly, how to spread open the abdomen, rip out the entrails, scrape the backbone, and hack off its head.

Date: 1910
Recorded by John Swanton

A Boat Named *Coffin*

William Binkley pressed his foot on Game Warden McKephin's chest, sinking him deep into Yellowstone's Heart Lake. Blood spurted from the hole in McKephin's belly. Binkley didn't hear the curse rising up in the last bubble from the man's lungs, but he would always remember the smell of geyser sulfur—*For you and your children, the sea is your enemy. The curses of the perishing are upon you.*

❀

Binkley slammed his fist on the counter of Diehl's Dry Goods. "Goddamn, Diehl," he said, flipping back his jacket to show his holstered Savage .45, "when the cows arrive on the barge, I'll pay for 'em then."

The *Los Angeles Examiner* lay beneath the counter with Binkley's wanted poster on page seven. Mr. Diehl thought of bringing it to the *Wrangell Sentinel*, but no one had messed with William Binkley since he'd sauntered off the steamship with Eva and four kids. They'd bought a place on Shustak Point and talked about farming up the Stikine River.

Binkley's son, nine-year-old Albert, warmed his hands by the woodstove in the corner. Binkley tugged the kid up. "Get your ass out there and load up the *Coffin*." When Wrangell old-timers heard what the

Binkley kids named their skiff, they shook their heads. It was young Al's idea. It came to him in a dream smelling of blood and sulfur.

Now they loaded up the cart, rolling it down the boardwalk to the beach where the *Coffin* bobbed against the rocks. Binkley sat in the skiff while the kid rowed toward the point. "Faster," Binkley bellowed, "the tide's catching us."

Binkley stuck a pinch of tobacco in his mouth. Wrangell was the perfect hideout. After all, Soapy Smith used to hole up here. In fact, Binkley chuckled to himself, Wrangell was so rough 'n' tumble that a few years back, Wyatt Earp left town because the place was wilder than Tombstone.

The wind and rain picked up as they rowed the *Coffin* from the harbor. The boat pitched and a wave rolled inside, wetting their feet. "Steer into the waves," Binkley yelled.

"But, Pa," Al said, "the waves are coming from everywhere."

Binkley spit out his tobacco. He tasted blood. *Sonofabitch. Must have bit the inside of my cheek*, he thought. The swells slapped the boat. The smell of sulfur mixed with salt spray. "Damn this tub," he grumbled.

Behind him, an arm reached up from the water and pulled down the stern. The sea poured into the *Coffin*.

Date: 2000s
Recorded by John R. Swanton
Assisted by Tooch Waterson

NOTES: I prefer traditional stories rather than nostalgias, but these two coffee partners are worth recording. It appears bear stories are a favorite of these two men. Mr. Nillan Hetta is sixty-nine, and Isak Laukonen is seventy years old.

Mr. Nillan Hetta is part Sámi with other ancestry from Scandinavia, possibly Norwegian. He is retired from the US Forest Service.

Mr. Isak Laukonen is Finnish with some Sámi heritage. Mr. Laukonen was a full-time fisherman on his boat, the *Miss Janet*, plus worked occasionally at log salvaging. He now fishes only occasionally with his son, Veiko.

Old Men Who Speak of Bears

SPEAKER: Nillan Hetta
"When my grandpa Matti was young he used to spend a lot of time up on the Stikine River. He'd spend seven months out of the year trapping on the Canadian side. He said one time he was camped out in the middle of a lake on the ice and woke up one morning and stepped outside his tent. It was real cold and crispy outside. He was in his long wool underwear. He stepped out, raised his arms, stretched and yawned, and when he looked down, he saw big brown bear prints in the snow. He looked across the lake and saw the bear had traveled all the way across

the lake. The bear's paw prints walked all the way around his tent and then walked off in the other direction. All the while he was asleep. He didn't know he had been checked out by a large brown bear."

SPEAKER: Isak Laukonen
"When my dad was courting my mother in the early days, they were up on the flats walking around. I'm not sure what river, if it was the Stikine or Aaron's crick or Bradfield. Well, they were walking across the grass flats, and my dad spotted a big brown bear out there digging roots. So he told my mom to get on this big stump, a snag. She got up on the stump and my dad snuck down along the slough to where that bear was digging roots. He snuck up on the bear through the grass and kicked him right in the ass. And that bear reared up on its hind legs, whirled around, and my dad stuck the gun right in its mouth and pulled the trigger. Killed him instantly, of course. Shot him right up through the brain. He thought that was great, showing off for my mother. He got back to where my mother was, and he didn't expect her to be mad at him. She was not impressed. She chewed him up one side and down the other. 'You son of a bitch,' she said. 'What would happen if that bear had gotten you, and I'm left sitting up here on that snag. That would mean I'd be next.'"

SPEAKER: Nillan Hetta
"Yeah, Isak, women and bears. We take our chances, don't we? I once went hunting with a girl when I was younger. I was gonna marry her, but after I didn't ask her. The gal was packing a gun. I was in the lead. We started up on this rise, and here come this black bear on the rise in front of us. I told her to hold it and told her to back down a ways. I kept my eyes on the bear all the time. And the bear had a cub with her. The bear was beside a tree alongside the trail, where she'd shooed the cub up the tree. The bear, she stood right there on the trail. I reached back without taking my eyes off the bear and told the gal to give me the gun. And I expected the gal to slap the gun in my hand. No response, no

gun. So I turned around and I looked and the gal still had the gun on her shoulder and was staring ahead. I said, 'Give me that gun.'

"You ain't got much time to react if the bear is charging. So I grabbed the gun away from her and chambered a round, and said, 'Let's back down the trail.' And we backed down enough so we could see over the rise. The bear, she watched us for a while, and, when she thought it was safe, the bear made a noise, *woof woof*, and called her cub out of the tree. The cub came scampering down out of the tree and the bear and her cub took off and ran up the trail and disappeared. I didn't marry the gal. I would rather have married the bear. She had more sense. That's the story of that."

SPEAKER: Isak Laukonen
"We were young. So was she. When we're young we don't have sense at all. Well, my grandpa told me when he was young he had two brown bear cubs. They had a big family, eight kids in the family. They were raising these two brown bear cubs, and they would be wrestling with them all the time. And he said the cubs of course were growing like weeds and they finally got pretty big. They wrestled with them out in the yard. Eventually, the bears would haul off and bat them, and they'd bat the bears too, and the bears would bat them back. The bears got so strong they didn't know their own strength. They'd bat the kids clear across the yard. Finally, my grandfather said that's enough. They are getting too dangerous. They caged them up and sent them on the steamboat to the Seattle Zoo. I don't know if they sold them. But they probably sold them. That's what happened to the brown bear cubs. They were good pets, but they got too strong, and they didn't know their own strength."

SPEAKER: Nillan Hetta
"Lots of bears Back Channel."

SPEAKER: Isak Laukonen
"Sure are. I remember when we stayed at Old Bradfield Jack's place."

SPEAKER: Nillan Hetta

"Yep, how could I forget? Scared me good, that one."

SPEAKER: Isak Laukonen

"Yeah, we were in the living room area, remember, and we had a big fire going in the fireplace. We were pretty comfy, you know. All of a sudden, we heard some racket in the kitchen. There was a bear in the kitchen. It's all brown bear country there. And man, we barricaded that door between the kitchen and the living room area and sat there fully awake with our guns ready in case that sucker came through that door. But he didn't. He milled around, tore things up in the kitchen, and left again. He had been in the kitchen before. Apparently, he came back to check it out once in a while and smelled us too. We didn't get much sleep that night."

SPEAKER: Nillan Hetta

"No, we sure didn't. We didn't. Scared the crap out of me, that one did. And I was scared a lot when I worked for the Forest Service. We ran into bears all the time. Anyway, when I worked for the Forest Service, I was coming down the trail from Conch Lake one day, me and my crew, Anders, Gary, and Martin. I had them up close. I always told them if there's a bear around you can smell them, which you can. Anyway, my friend Anders was right in front of me and he had the rifle. And then there was me and the other guys behind us and we were pretty close together. And pretty soon Anders said, 'You smell that, Nillan?'

"I said, 'Yeah there's a bear close around somewhere. He's gotta be somewhere close because I can smell him pretty strong.'

"We no more got the words out of our mouths, and Gary yelled, 'Bear!' There was these bushes right alongside the trail. And he whirled the gun around and looked and the bear's head was sticking out of the bush and the tip of the barrel was about six inches from his nose. And the bear's eyes got big and wide and we got big and wide-eyed. Martin jumped off the trail over the cliff area. I jumped and grabbed the little tree next to us and Anders stood there. Gary had his gun on the bear and the bear pulled his head back in the bushes and took off up the trail.

NOTES: Tooch is trying out a newfangled digital recorder. I told him to take notes too because I don't trust that thing. After quite a story-telling session, I had Tooch stop the recording and we bought Isak and Nillan some blueberry pie before we left. I asked them about the taboo about talking about bears and saying the name "bear." Isak said the restaurant wasn't the woods so they were okay. They had to do "respectful talk." I asked them if they thought their stories were "respectful." Isak thought for a moment then said softly, "Yeah, I guess." Then Nillan looked around as if looking for something and said, "Please forgive us Grandfather and Grandmother. We were just telling stories. You know how a couple of old farts are."

I probably won't include these stories in my submission to the Smithsonian since they are not traditional stories, just old men talking about bears.

Date: Distant Time
Recorded by John Swanton
Speaker: Mina Agard

The Woman Who Married a Bear

The forest calls to her. She packs some food, water, and a blanket and sneaks off into the woods. After several miles, the woods darken and she sits down near a tree. She pulls out a piece of bread from her satchel, tears a piece off, and eats it. So far, her three brothers haven't followed her. They would never guess she's gone by way of the woods, figuring she would've walked the small road to another village. They are wrong. She chews her hard-crusted bread, recalling her brothers' cruelty: the way they made her wait on them hand and foot, the way they made her sleep on a thin pile of straw on the hard floor, the way she had to wake up at all hours to stoke the fire while they slept comfortably in their beds.

Her brothers have been raising her since she was five years old, after their parents died from the illness that swept through the village. Over the years, the mistreatment worsened. They resented having to care for her, that is, except for the youngest brother. Her youngest brother, although influenced by the older ones, was the kindest to her. He often slipped her extra bread. It was he who stood at the window, saying nothing, as she sneaked out while they were eating breakfast. Her other brothers assumed she was outside stacking wood in the woodshed.

Now she makes her way over stumps, through marshes, wandering on forest paths. After a while, she slows down, feeling the comfort of the woods. She sits down on a large tree root, and it starts to rain and blow.

The branches above her sway and creak in the wind. She's getting cold and wet and night is falling. She should find a place to rest. She gets up from her resting place and walks up over a knoll and discovers a bear den.

Carefully, she enters the den. As her eyes adjust to the dusk, she sees a bear slumbering in the corner. She speaks softly, "I'm not here to hurt you. I just need a place to rest for awhile." She walks over to a mossy bed and collapses with exhaustion. At night, she dreams of her horrible brothers and wakes up crying. She can't stop thinking about how she's been treated all her life—she cries herself to sleep again. In the morning, the bear is sitting up looking at her. Cautiously, she gathers her things while the bear watches her. Before she heads out the door, she turns to the bear and says, "Thank you. You've been kind to allow me to sleep here. I shall be going now."

The bear moves toward her. She presses herself against the cave walls. The bear says, "Tell me, young woman, why were you crying?" Startled, she is speechless, but, in the bear's eyes, she sees he's kind. She tells him about her mean brothers, how her eldest brothers are very cruel, and her youngest brother tries to be kind, but he's bullied by his older brothers. Often, he tried to stop the older brothers from hurting her but was unable.

The bear tells her she can join him in his den for the winter, until she feels safe enough to go back home. During the winter, they pass the time telling stories. They share meals and listen to the heavy snow cracking tree branches outside. In order to survive the coldest months, she curls up next to the bear for warmth. In the cave, her body thickens, her hair grows long and shaggy. Claws protrude from her hands, her jaw lengthens, her teeth sharpen—she becomes a bear.

Eventually, the bear and the young woman become husband and wife. The Bear-Husband is kind to his Bear-Wife. He provides her with the best food: meat, berries, fish, and roots. They live happily together throughout the seasons as she makes the forest her home. Outside the den, she can become a human and meander through the forest. Often, she wanders close to her old house, checking on her youngest brother—they never see her.

One winter, the Bear-Wife gives birth to a son. When the boy is in the bear's domain, he looks like a bear. When he's out with his mother picking berries, he looks human. Over the years, the son grows to be a fine young man—he's half bear and half human. According to custom, the Bear-Wife decides to send her Bear-Son to be instructed by his uncles who still live in the same house. She feels her son has had plenty of time to learn how to be a bear. Now, she wants him to learn how to be a human.

She's reluctant but wants to follow traditions. Her human brothers, despite their cruelness, were excellent hunters and fisherman. Early one morning she secretly leaves her boy at his uncles' house. The uncles recognize he might be related so they take him in. For several years the boy stays with his uncles, learning how to hunt and fish. In the forest, though, the Bear-Wife is lonely for her son.

One day, the Bear-Husband tells her it's time for him to die because he's old and, like all creatures, he must die. The fall air is crisp and the leaves have fallen off the trees. He says hunting season will begin soon, and although all of her brothers are hunters, he will only allow the youngest brother to have the honor of killing him, since it was the youngest brother who was kind to her.

The Bear-Wife is upset at the thought of losing her Bear-Husband and tries, unsuccessfully, to talk him out of it. Eventually, he convinces her to help him with the rituals necessary for his death. She says to him, "Remember our own son will be among the hunters. He's been taught well by his uncles."

The Bear-Husband considers this and, in preparation for the hunt, he instructs her to attach a piece of brass to the hair on his forehead. This ornament will let their Bear-Son recognize his father. Finally, the Bear-Husband instructs her about how his body should be treated after his death.

One day, the Bear-Wife goes outside and sees a red mark on the rocks above the opening to their den. This tells her that soon her brothers will come hunting for her husband. After the first snowfall, the hunter-brothers, along with the Bear-Son, arrive in the woods and make their way to the den. The Bear-Husband greets them outside. He stands up on his hind legs, roars, and snaps his jaws. He does not allow the older brothers to kill him. Instead, he fights back the older brothers and bites them, wounding them so they can't spear him. Then he turns to face the younger brother, allowing the younger brother the honor of killing him. The younger brother thrusts the spear into the bear and the Bear-Husband dies.

The Bear-Wife lumbers of the den. Outside, she stands up. Her coarse hair silkens along her back, her jaw flattens, and her teeth shorten. She clenches her paws as her claws form to fingers. The brothers are amazed at their sister's transformation. She says to them, "You have killed my Bear-Husband and now we have to honor him." The Bear-Wife's brothers do not challenge her. Her Bear-Son is sad, though. He has participated in the hunt that unknowingly killed his own father. She explains to him and the other hunters if they do as she instructs, the Great-Bear will be reborn again and again, giving them the honor of the hunt for many generations. She instructs them in the proper way to dispose of his body and the ritual feast that accompanies the kill.

After the feast in the village, the Bear-Wife remains with her human family. Her brothers try to make it up to her and give her the finest bed in the house and offer her the best food at the table. She accepts their apology, but, once in a while, when the leaves on the birch turn gold and the air stings her lungs, she reaches out for the husband who isn't there.

And one night, some years later, she finds herself waking to the crunch of snowy earth beneath her bare feet. The pull of winter shortens and thickens her legs. She shakes her head rapidly as her jaw snaps into its proper place, long and wide. She huffs the crisp air, her breath circling a new form, and she lumbers toward her old den without ever looking back.

Date: 1980s

Recorded by Tooch Waterson

The Girl Who Paid Attention

She wanted to pull a birdskin over her head and fly away. Instead, she raised the .243 like her dad, Karl, had shown her. They had practiced at least twice. The rifle was still too big for her nine-year-old hands. Her father stood beside her, and her mother, Mina, sat on a log nearby. Her mother didn't seem bothered by hunting so she shouldn't be bothered either, right? But why did she want to slip down into the moss and become a shrew, or open her mouth and growl at her father like a bear. She couldn't escape this lesson: she was learning to hunt.

She pulled the trigger. The shot rang out, deafening her. The deer, only fifty yards in front of her, dropped dead. She followed her dad and mom over a large log and through knee-high alder to the place where the deer once stood. The deer lay dead on the ground. Her dad offered her the knife, but she shook her head.

"Tova, what's the matter," he said.

The deer lay at her feet. It had offered itself to her. At least that's what her mom claimed. She tried not to puke. What *was* the matter? The eyes. It was the eyes. She didn't want to see into them. She turned her head. Breathe. Breathe. She inhaled a small shallow breath, and then let it out slowly. She breathed for the animal lying on the ground. She breathed for the little alder trees surrounding her, trying to grow up in the logged forest. She breathed for the old rotten log beside her, nursing small trees along its spine. She wanted to reach for the deer's warm hide, stroke the hair on its side. But, no, it was meat. They were going to eat it.

Her mom placed her hand on her shoulder. "You can do it."

Tova shook her head. No she couldn't. She wasn't ready.

Her dad stood, knife in his hand, waiting. "Whatever," he finally said. He knelt down.

She turned her head as her father started to gut it, eventually making it into a pack. Her father put the pack on his back and started walking. Tova followed behind him and her mom walked behind her. She slipped, and her mother caught her. They lagged behind, but her dad didn't stop. He kept on hiking. She hated it when he did that. Her dad always walked in front of her and her brother, Jorma, leaving her to hold her little brother's hand. Now, out in front, packing the deer on his back, blood dripping down onto his raincoat, her dad appeared like some kind of creature. Maybe the kind they whispered about, like a troll. Maybe something Raven had created but didn't tell anyone about. She shook her head. This wasn't the time to make up stories or to imagine what was lurking behind the trees. She had to focus. Pay attention. She jerked. The sting of her father's handslap against her head still stung—"If you don't pay attention, you can die."

Tova's boot sunk into the muskeg. She pulled it out, and then searched for a stump root. She stepped on the root, getting her footing again. She took a deep breath. This wasn't so bad. Getting deer for food was harvesting, not killing. That's what Mom always said. "You're an elder in the making." She was supposed to be a hunter like her mother and father and her grandparents before her. She was supposed to learn to provide for herself and her family. But some of her parents' friends claimed hunting was men's work. They didn't make their kids shoot deer. They didn't make their kids go fishing or berry picking for food either. Mom said her ancestors had both men and women hunters. After all, Mom went hunting with her girlfriends. They came back with deer every fall. She'd seen her mom in the shed, skinning the deer. Her mom made jewelry out of the antlers. They used the hides for drums. Once, her mother had shown her a photo of an old rock carving: Woman-with-a-bow. And Tova had once traced her fingers on the photo of a Sámi drum, outlining the woman hunter. Hunting was expected.

While heading back to town in their skiff, her mom sat in the bow, where she always liked to ride, wind in her face. Today, though, it was unusually warm out. Her dad tried to make small talk in the noisy, open skiff, but Tova pretended not to hear him. She would rather listen to the motor's whine. Once they were at the dock, her dad tied the boat up and she helped him put the deer into a harbor cart and pull the cart up to their truck. On the ride home she sat in the middle. Her mom leaned against the passenger door. As they drove, the truck filled with the scent of warm blood.

Her dad gripped the steering wheel, his hands covered in dried blood. "Pretty good shot," he said to her.

"Yes," she said. A good shot. She'd killed it. At least she'd done that. She'd heard the stories about bad kills. That was a strange phrase, but it meant Cousin Cory had to have his father make the kill shot after Cory had missed, wounding the deer in the butt. But Cory wasn't good at much, anyway. He wasn't even good at being good. He'd told her killing deer was easy. At first she didn't believe it could be true. But she knew better now. It was easy and awful. She'd killed her first deer.

Her dad parked the truck in the narrow driveway. She ran ahead and flung open the door. Auntie Rikka had been watching her little brother while they went hunting. "Jorma! Auntie Rikka, I got a deer! I got a deer!" She stopped suddenly, her voice echoing in her head. Grandma Berta told her never to brag, but she'd sounded happy. Why was she happy? The deer looked more like a pet than a wild animal.

Auntie Rikka rushed into the entry hall from the kitchen. "You did? You got a deer? That's great."

Tova stood in her brown rubber boots, her oversized coat hanging below her knees. "It's a buck."

Auntie Rikka pointed to her. "Great. Well, you'd better get out there and help."

"But . . ."

"Go on," her aunt urged. "We'll have heart and liver tonight. You like that."

"Yes," Tova said. Eating the heart and liver after her dad or mom returned with a deer was tradition. She liked the taste of it. She was used to seeing beating salmon hearts fresh out of a fileted fish. And she'd even helped her mom fry fish hearts and deer hearts before.

Behind her, the door opened. Her mom stepped inside the entryway. "Your dad wants you."

Tova turned and headed back out to the shed. It was almost dark outside now and her dad had turned on the light. The shed, like a carport, opened on three sides and was tall enough to pull a truck inside, but not much taller. The deer hung from its legs from the rafter above. Her dad had said it was too warm out so they'd have to skin it right away. Now, her dad stood beside the deer, a knife hanging at his side. Seeing her, he handed her the knife.

Tova reached out for it then stopped. "I have to pee."

"Jeez. Well go. Hurry up."

She ran back into the house. Now that she was inside, she didn't really have to pee. She leaned against the door and took a deep breath. She turned her hand in front of her. Dried blood. Deer hair. Her mom walked into the entryway and seeing her there, said nothing, and cocked her head as if to say, Well, what are you waiting for? Tova knew that look.

Her mom finally spoke, "The deer expects you to do this."

Expect? How can a dead deer expect anything? She'd seen its eyes. Dead. But a lot of people in her life talked about animals having spirits and even trees and stuff too. They said sometimes the spirits linger around even after something dies. If the deer expected her to skin it then it might feel it, right? That didn't sound good. She slowly turned around, opened the door and went outside.

In the shed, her father had already started skinning the deer. As she approached the deer, the rocks from the gravel beneath her boots rolled. The scent of animal and old tools filled the air.

Her dad handed her the knife. "We'll take some steaks to Grandpa Ole. He loves deer steak for breakfast." He pointed to the place where he had stopped pulling the skin from the meat. She grabbed the hide with her left hand, like he showed her. In her right hand she held the knife. She put the knife blade between the skin and flesh and started to slice, tugging at the skin. The more she cut, the more the deer didn't look like a deer anymore. It was shapeshifting, becoming something else. She thought about the shapeshifting stories she'd heard. Humans pulling birdskin and feathers over their heads and flying away. Women who became bears. Women who became salmon. Many times she'd imagined being someone or something else. And most definitely someplace else. If she pulled this warm skin over her head, could she run through the alder thicket behind her house? Could she run up the ancient deer trails to the alpine, to the place where she could look down the mountainside? There, she would graze on the blueberries, leaves and all. There, she would bed down and watch the humans who would be little dots in the town below.

Date: early-mid 1980s
Recorded by: John Swanton

Wrangell Town Fire Story

Speaker: Nillan Hetta

1962. March, I think it was, anyway. It was me and Bernie Dietrich and Warren Frederick. We had been out fishing for spring halibut. We were up at Warren's house drinking. The house was a little tiny shack. We'd spend the night. We had a little kerosene heater in there. We heard the fire siren go off and a bell clanging at the police department. They had a big curfew bell there. Anyway, we looked out and sure enough, there was a big fire downtown. We said, Man let's go see what's going on, you know. And sure enough, that was when Wrangell had the big fire.

We went down there and looked, and Captain's Hardware and Dry Goods store, Captain Jinks' place, was completely ablaze: It was going big time and it was pretty windy too. Anyway, they were trying to control it but couldn't control it. There was ammunition going off and everything. The fire was jumping over to the other buildings. It completely wiped out the beach side. It was all beach side in those days. It completely wiped out that side of town. It burnt several buildings on the other side pretty bad, and it burned the drug store building that's still there now. And it burned the Wheeler building, which is where Far North Gift Shop is now. It burned Dammen's, too. It burned Dammen's first store, which is where the T-shirt shop is now. It burned

Harbor Market, where their store is rebuilt now. It didn't burn them down, but it scorched them. They were on fire, too.

It burned all night long and the next day, and it was about out but there was still smoldering ruins, you know. So, Bernie, Warren, and I, we wondered what we could find down there in the smoldering ruins. I knew they had called the Coast Guard to come from Ketchikan, but they hadn't arrived. We went down there that night digging through the rubble, through the burnt area and the thing was still smoking. In fact, there were some money safes that were still hot, so we couldn't crack the safes. We thought, well, what are we going to scavenge out of here?

We were going through one of the liquor stores and there were all these beer bottles. Cases and cases of Pabst Blue Ribbon lying there. The place was all burnt down. Everything fell down on the beach. And a lot of them weren't broken. We had big gunny sacks so we started throwing in all the Pabst Blue Ribbon. We were going to take them.

We were going through there and it was darker than hell. And nobody was watching the place or anything. And we heard something in the dark ahead of us. I said, "Hello there."

A man's voice said, *Hello.*

It was Mauri Sarell and he's down there with a big gunny sack and he's throwing whiskey bottles, full whiskey bottles, into his sack. Of course, we stopped and talked to him. Mauri was the mayor back then.

He said, "Ah, guys, don't say anything about this. I'll give you a ride home."

He had an old Dodge pickup truck. He had that damn thing full of whiskey. Anyway, we threw our sack of beer into his truck, and he drove us home. The next day, we cleaned up all the beer bottles. And we had a whole bunch of Pabst Blue Ribbon to drink. The next day after that, the Coast Guard showed up and they posted guards all along there because of all the safes. There were lots of businesses along there. Every safe was down on the beach and hadn't been opened yet so they had all that money in those safes and records too. Whatever didn't get destroyed was still in the safes. Some of the safes got so hot it even cooked the stuff inside.

Anyway, that was our experience with the town fire. It was pretty traumatic. We actually got some movie film of it my dad took from the house. Quite traumatic. Big fire. There were lots of businesses burned: a big hardware store, a cold storage. There was a bakery, a big theater. There was another bar, a big gift shop, and a curio gift shop, Walters, a big outfit. And, there was a big hotel. There was another clothing store, another liquor store. It was several blocks long there. The buildings were one right next to another. And, the whore house. Anyway, they all burned down right down to the beach. Nothing left but a few smoldering pilings and a lot of debris.

They said it was started by a furnace in Captain's. They had a furnace in the store, and they said something malfunctioned and the furnace started it. There was always the suspicion, though, that some young boy started it. His name is Dewie Lee. He grew up to be a fireman. His younger brother is a fireman now too. Anyway, I don't know if that's true or not but that's what the rumor was. You know how rumors in small towns go. But, the official story was it was the furnace. So, that's the end of that story.

Date: 1962
Recorded by: John Swanton

Ceremony after the Wrangell Fire

The night after the town burned down, Main Street smoked while kids plundered through the remains of planked and false-fronted buildings. The rain and spray from the water hoses soaked their clothing. Berta, twenty-five years old, rummaged through old Mary Bjelland's Alaska Curios store and discovered her great-grandmother's basket in a broken safe. Mary had refused to sell the basket back to the family, saying it was worth more than the fifty dollars Berta's mother had once offered for it.

Now, Berta left ten dollars and took the basket home and dried it near the woodstove. After it dried, she held it in her hands, running her fingers over the half-salmonberry and the splash-of-raindrops pattern woven on its sides.

All summer she went berry-picking, filling the basket with red huckleberries, salmonberries, and blueberries. Berries bulged the sides of the basket. Leaves and worms made their way into woven raindrops. Berta's fingertips whorled with purple juice, the juice oozing between spruce fibers.

At the end of summer, the weight of ancient memory became too great and the bottom fell out of the basket. Berta dug a hole and buried what remained of her great-grandmother's basket in a shallow grave beneath the berry patch without ceremony, that is, until she spread the jam she and her mother made on a piece of toast, taking her great-grandmother inside.

Date: 1962

Recorded by: John Swanton

The Boy Who Loved Sparks

Dewie Nicholas Lee's ancestral heritage included the invention of gunpowder and fireworks. His five-year-old hands ripped open the package of sparklers his dad, Ken Lee, had bought him for the Chinese Spring celebration.

Great-Grandfather Captain Jinks claimed it was an omen that the Southeast Alaskan town where he'd immigrated in order to work in the canneries had a mountain named Dewey. In Chinese, the name Dewei means "highly noble." So, when Captain Jinks lived to hear his great-grandson screaming his first cry in the back room of the store, he said the baby boy should be named Dewie. Plus, the family having converted to Catholicism in the second generation, Dewie was given the middle name Nicholas after St. Nicholas, who is lesser known as a saint with a special power over flames.

Dewie's father told him he was born in the year of the Fire Rooster. He didn't much like roosters, but he liked the way the small sticks burned beside the house when he piled them up and lit them on fire. He had a great name. He especially liked his name because everyone who met him said, "Oh, Dewey, like the mountain?" Yes, Dewie like the mountain: the *fire* mountain.

His parents told the story of an average man, a cook, who mixed common kitchen ingredients to invent the first fireworks. And everyone in town knew the story of his mountain, Mount Dewey, up behind his church, St. Rose of Lima. There, a famous explorer built a huge fire on the hill. Also, Dewie had books filled with drawings of dragons. He loved Shenlong, the dragon that controlled the wind and rain. He was Shenlong playing down on the beach below the buildings. He was Shenlong running around the town, huffing air from his lungs. It worked: it was always raining in Wrangell.

❀

The thin strip of metal rod dipped in charcoal, aluminum, potassium nitrate, and sulfur ignited fast. The sparks burned Dewey's fingertips, and he threw the sparkler down on the floor. The embers flew out and hit his bedspread. Flames licked his pillow and, in seconds, engulfed his bed. The orange paper lantern hanging by his window exploded like a small firework.

❀

Dewie ran out of his room, leaving the door open. He scampered down the narrow wooden set of stairs into his parents' store. Pa and Ma, and sister Nancy were stocking shelves. Dewie ran past them and into the small kitchen in the back where he stood on his toes and pumped the old faucet, running ice-old water over the small burn on his finger.

From the store area, Nancy yelled, "Fire!"

Pa said something in a combination of Chinese and Tlingit, and Ma ran into the kitchen and scooped Dewie by the hand and led him out the kitchen door. The front doorbell dinged at the same time the bell on the police station rang out alerting townsfolk to the fire. Nancy followed a few seconds later and joined them on the street in front of the store. Outside, the wind blew like a mad dragon.

Soon, Pa ran out. Fire and smoke billowed behind him. In his hand, he carried a small metal bucket. Above him, fire leapt out of the bedroom window and onto the roof of the building next door, eventually spreading from building to building. Ma, very pregnant, moved them to the other side of the street. Dewie peered out from behind her skirt. Pa banged hard on the side door of Hammer's Hardware, awakening Mr. and Mrs. Hammer, who clambered out on the sidewalk in their robes, red-faced.

The police station's bell dinged, and the sirens wailed along with the strong wind whistling through the old false-fronted buildings. Ma led Dewie and his sister up the alley to St. Rose of Lima. Father Rapetti rushed past with two buckets in his hands. He told Ma to take the children up to the church and stay there. He didn't know when he would be back.

Inside the church doorway, Dewie stood in his damp and smoky pajamas as the false-fronted buildings along the beach side burned like huge lanterns.

Later, after two cookies from Father Rapetti's cookie jar, which the priest kept full for the children after Mass, Dewie started to nod off. In Father Rapetti's apartment, he slouched down into the small sofa sitting below the large picture window. He dreamed of a red chrysanthemum firework blasting the night sky. It grew into a dragon and chased him down the boardwalk. He hid in the alley, crouched down by a silver garbage can. He removed the lid from the can and held it in front of him, like he'd seen the comic books warriors do. The dragon blew onto the buildings, crumbling their wood flesh into ash, and one by one the pilings buckled, tumbling their skeletal remains into the sea.

Date: 1990s
Recorded by John Swanton
Assisted by Tooch Waterson
Speaker: Unidentified woman in the Zimovia Bar

In a Light Fantastic

Come, and trip it as ye go,
On the light fantastic toe.
And in thy right hand lead with thee
The Mountain Nymph, sweet Liberty
—Milton, "L'Allegro"

It was 1968. He ran down a shaft of light as if it were a staircase leading him to the ground. Around him, the soft rime of his breath sugared frost onto spruce branches. And as soon as his toes felt the snow-crusted earth, his feet spun and he ran across the mountaintops and slid down snowbanks. He beat feet through the bushes, downhill along the deer trails to the highway, bookin' through the cobalt night down the middle of the yellow line toward town.

In town, he didn't bother to stop for walls, garages, or kitchen windows, either. He was haulin' right through the townfolks' pads, where they assumed the power bumped as electricity shot sapphire sparks from the outlets—lightbulbs blew, toasters tazed, and *Bewitched* fizzled on the Magnavox. He jumped over backyard fences, doghouses, and a snowman with small stones curved up to form a smile. And when he approached one pad, he heard a baby wailing like an ache in its momma's arms—it wasn't expected to live much longer with its small wrinkled brain and all.

As he rushed inside through the patio door, the baby's bawl caught him up and sucked him inside that baby's mouth. At once, the baby's eyes lit up and its skin darkened to the blackest blue. The momma, Jesse Edwin, gasped when she held the baby close to comfort him, nearly dropping him because his skin seared. At first, she thought the baby might be heading toward Jesus right then, but then the baby gurgled at her. It seemed he'd filled out his skin a bit and stopped arching his head back at that peculiar angle. Jesse and her husband were jazzed their baby was still alive and his head shaped itself back to normal—it didn't matter that his skin was navy blue.

Jesse and Charlie renamed the baby Ray, and he grew up here on this island, the only blue boy—although Ray appeared more black than blue, depending on the cloud cover. Freaky thing about Ray, though, he grew up real fast, faster than normal, and he was always fruggin' around the neighborhood as if he had somewhere else to go. And whenever his daddy and momma packed him up for church or a local picnic, he couldn't just walk to the car—the boy had to run. And Ray couldn't sit still and watch television, either. He had to be leapin' off the back of the couch yelling *cowabunga, waahoo,* and *shabang* like Aristotle's jumpin' goats. The school specialists thought Ray was some kind of spaz and wanted to put him on a daily pill, but his momma said, *Hell no, Ray's a gift from God.*

Within a year he was almost grown and girls would show up at his house and ask if Ray could come out and hully gully. He'd hold their hands and skedaddle his way down the mucky streets, poppin' corn over mud puddles like James Brown. The young girls didn't find him square at all. In fact, they thought Ray was groovy, so he always had a lot of girls skennin' near him.

And after another year, when Ray got to be a young man, he was quite righteous. Both men and women thought he was far-out, the way he shot his magnetosphere through their bodies, arching east to west with his dynamo action—their eyes rolled back and their hair stood on end. Ray was quite the disturbance, townsfolk said, buzzing around the atmosphere of bouffant housewives and young folks in their miniskirts and culottes, polyester pantsuits and sideburns. And Ray, that cat sure loved to shang-a-lang at every dance at the community hall, stompin' the Mashed Potato and doin' the Hanky Panky to the Kinks' "You Really Got Me." Everyone called him Ray Magic.

But one week, during the winter of 1972, the weatherman was broadcasting the news about a solar superstorm, and Ray got a bit nervous when he was in the deli buying his regular ham and cheese on wheat. He started jitterin' and a hoppin' on his toes as he listened to the broadcast on the radio talking about how 93 million miles away the sun was twistin' a flash of solar flares. And right at that moment, the solar wind sailed past the Earth with all those charged particles being deflected by the Earth's magnetic field.

That night, Ray went to the center of Shakes Island near the big totem pole. In the middle of the island he started side-kickin' his "Freddy" and flapping wings to Jackie Lee's "Duck," while trampin' the frozen grass. Around him, the cottonwoods were crackin' with ice. And that's when the plasma squeezed toward Earth with rapid spasms of magnetotail and took Ray by the hand, trying to bag him. It yanked him hard up, trippin' the light back up those stairs. But, you see, Ray had adapted to our tunes. He was always hummin' to "Light My Fire" and whistlin' "Dock of the Bay," so he yanked himself back down again.

And when the fuzz found him the next morning, on the grassy field at Shakes Island, Ray was blue naked, talking thick and pointing to the sky. The fuzz said he was mumblin' something strange over and over again. They assumed he was pixed. So they wrapped him in one of them scratchy wool blankets and took him to the Salvation Army where Major Hallelujah gave him a couple sets of clothes and a pair of work boots. But all Ray could do was mumble, and he couldn't even remember his name, although everyone in town knew he was just Ray.

And after Ray tripped, he couldn't dig the daylight anymore. His eyes had turned ice-blue and though he could still see, he put on a pair of shades and sat out on a rusty metal folding chair in front of Sally Ann's, the Salvation Army's thrift store. And that's when I saw him there, that blue man. I'd come from the coffee shop and heard the skinny on Ray's down-and-out story, so I fumbled in my purse for spare scratch. I walked up to Ray and he looked up at me and started to mutter. I held out the money and he grabbed my wrist. I looked down and where he clutched my wrist, my hand had melted off, wetting our feet in a big puddle.

I said, "What-say, Ray, take off them shades and look at me."

He did. His eyes shown turquoise. Bands of light snapped in his irises. This time he said clearly, "Ma'am, I'm not blitzed. I am the Northern Lights."

And I said to him, "I know, Ray, I know. Remember me?" I leaned in and blew a soft rime chillin' against his cheek. "We've panked in the crystal blue persuasion before: I am Snow."

I let my robe fall open and he stepped in next to my cirque. At once I compressed under the weight of us, like crystals near their melting point, semiliquid and slick. We filled in the spaces where they touch and stick, jerkin' the breath from between us, rockin' up to bubbles. Suddenly, Ray freefell toward the treetops with me, and I laughed at the reflection of him arcing, a blue-beat swing above me. He stepped with his feet apart, hands at his sides, swinging his weight left foot to right foot, both knees bending, and with a small kick, Ray shifted his light to the blue-beat flyaway.

Date: early 1990s
Recorded by John Swanton
Assisted by Tooch Waterson

A Blanket on the Sea

Tova felt herself drowning as she fell into the bedcovers beside her best friend, Fern. Fern leaned over and kissed her. They explored each other's mouths with their tongues. Thirteen-year-old Tova closed her eyes, afraid if she opened them, the blanket separating the world beneath the ocean and the people on land, would be broken. It was like in the story her elders told about the creation of the killer whales where the young man, Naatsilanéi, lifted a blanket on the sea and went down to the land of the Sea Lion people. There, the Sea Lion tribe gave Naatsilanéi instructions on how to carve a monster from yellow cedar in order to kill his own brothers who'd left him for dead.

Tova had always been fascinated with the old stories, especially the creation stories. What did the yellow cedar log feel like being transformed? It must have thought it would live out its life as a tree, then possibly a log. The yellow cedar log had no idea it would change. Its long shaggy bark and pungent, oily wood was going to be carved with teeth and a blowhole.

She pressed her eyes tightly together until Fern said, "Open your eyes and look at me, okay?"

Her heart thumped. Was this what it felt like to be in love? The adults she knew didn't talk about love. Fern and the other girls from school gossiped about sweaty junior high boys. No one talked about if they loved girls. Well, they did, sort of. They drew glyphs on one another's backs in the dark during slumber parties, whispering against one another's cheeks. She had felt it first when Fern had touched her back with her fingertip, making the spiral petroglyph on her back, swirling it round and round, until the tide came over her like it did on the rocks on Petroglyph Beach.

Now, Tova opened her eyes. She pulled her head back from Fern's and took a breath. The heat between them was thick and hot, and the mattress beneath her sunk with her weight. She was drowning and could no longer stop water from flowing into her lungs.

She was familiar with the feeling of drowning. She'd drowned once. She was nine years old, when her dad, Karl, tossed her into the harbor. She remembers how the cold water ached on her knees. They still ached once in a while.

❁

"You'll thank me later," Karl said, as he tossed Tova into the harbor. "My dad did it to me." Tova knew better than to argue with her dad. She knew better than to cry, or fuss, or scream, or even frown. Sometimes, she knew better than to be human.

Her mother, Mina, shopped at the grocery store with her little brother. Tova had gone down to the boat to help her dad stick fishing gear for the spring halibut opening. He'd taught her how to use a fid and tie a ganion when she was five years old. She'd gotten really good at it. Her dad often showed off her skills to his drinking buddies, making her stick a skate of gear while they watched.

After she'd been thrown in the harbor, she thrashed around. Man, it's cold. Think. Think. She could float in the bathtub when the water reached as high as the overflow drain and she sucked in air. She turned over on her back and floated, then turned on her front again and started to dog paddle toward the dock. As she reached the dock, she raised her hand up to her dad.

Karl ignored her and unclenched her hand from the decking and flung her backward. "No, get used to it. Swim around a bit."

Tova turned over on her back and fluttered her arms, imagining herself making snow angels. Southeast Alaska water was nearly as cold as the snow, and she shivered, her lips turning blue. The water tickled her ears and she heard her dad holler something. What did he say? She didn't care. She ignored him, floating farther and farther from the dock. Her dad hollered again. She took a deep breath and inhaled something she could not name, something keeping her buoyant, her chest high.

Her dad screamed at her again. She turned her head slightly. He stood on the dock, hands on his hips, his face turning red. She kept going, swimming on her back toward the boat ramp on the other side of the harbor, watching the clouds shapeshift above her into a large killer whale swallowing the last of the afternoon blue sky.

Date: 1989, June 4
Recorded by Tooch Waterson

Deadmans Island

She opens her eyes and remembers that she is an island. Latitude 56°29'37.35"N. Longitude 132°22'13.56"W.

❀

"What to do with a dead Chinaman," the white folks considered. *I and all sentient beings . . .* Cannery worker, far from your homeland, your head was severed, and your arms and legs free floated in the barrel. I embraced your disembodied life. I washed the salty brine from your body, washed you with rain. It was 1890. The government will come for you, you said. *May no one ever be separated from their happiness.*

> My prayers for you lasted one hundred days. According to your religious beliefs, I prayed every ten days. *The path begins with strong reliance.*

❀

It is not horror to consider you, barrel after barrel, no—person after person, held in my lap, embraced in my arms. We told each other we were islands. We brought each other to life. We were each other's bodies, mouths open, our words circled like a current.

I performed your rituals. I cleaned you with a damp cloth dusted with powder. *My body, like a water bubble, decays and dies so very quickly.*

❁

I am but a small island, at the mouth of a bitter river, only big enough for a few houses. But who would live here anyway with such a current and icy winter winds? Instead, together we imagined my house covered in red paper, mirrors taken down, a white cloth over my doorway, a gong at the entrance.

I dressed you in your best mourning clothes: white, black, blue, or brown. Never red. I only had a small piece of fabric, an old linen apron that had washed up last year. *Just like myself all my kind mothers are drowning in samsara's ocean.*

❁

The old stones and a patch of dirt was our geomancy. The "lucky day and hour" was chosen. The April wind was cool, clouds soft, a pale blue sky. The snow geese returned that day to the river flats.

I placed the coffin on the rocks, your head facing the inside of my belly, which would be the "house." I offered you duck, Hudson Bay tea, and Tlingit rice. I had no portrait of you; instead, hemlocks scratched your image into air. *Just like the shadow of a body.*

❁

There was no sister, brother, or cousin to guard the funeral hall, to observe mourning. Only me. Me. And who would believe an island could mourn, could hold secrets like ancient glacial boulders broken down into grains of sand, could hold your blood in the crevasse of seashells.

I wore a hemlock bough in my hair, dressed in black, as I grieved the most. I've washed blood from broken boards, barrels cracked open. *When I become a pure container through common paths, bless me to enter . . .*

❁

One hundred days of ceremony. We listened to the tiderush circling us, the rhythm of words, like wind through hemlock. You may have heard it like mourners' cries.

No gold paper for your tradition, no ghost money, but I burned paper scraps that'd floated up from the sea. I burned lichen from timeworn stones. I burned old-man's-beard moss. I burned the spruce bark, the rounds shaped like dragon scales. *The essence practice of good fortune . . .*

❁

I told you stories, memories of old people coming downriver, then ice breaking, cracking, warming, more canoes, then more. People have turned to stone around me. Hunters, fishermen, wives, sons, even children, have lain at my feet, tumbled from overturned skiffs. These were the best prayers I knew.

At the foot of your coffin, I lit a candle and burned incense, though it was only smokewood and dried moss. *My sacred vows and my commitments.*

❁

While you waited the fleeting of your soul, I wanted to tell you stories of dragons, though I'd never seen one before. But I knew a killer whale story would do. Killer whales round me every spring, hunting, hunting. Each story has given an offering.

There was no trumpet, nor flute, nor gong to recite my prayers to. I relied upon the river current, clack of rocks, wind through the trees. *And take delight in the holy . . .*

Ravens hopped along the beach, bowing, bowing, bowing. He left a clamshell on the log.

May I always find perfect teachers.

❁

Planes and birds have circled and dipped, tipped their wings to me. Go. You are winged now. Fly among the black swifts, the pipit, the ring-billed, the mew, and kittiwake. *Accomplish all grounds and paths swiftly.*

One hundred days I prayed. One hundred days I kept vigil. One hundred days of stories—a bird steals the sun, a log becomes a killer whale, Grandfather Heron convinces a woman to swallow a rock. *Through the blessings of the holy beings, and through the force of our heartfelt prayers . . .*

❁

I've never told anyone this, but seven days into your burial ceremony; I understood your soul was supposed to go home. That would've been China, yes? I imagined there was a small field behind your house. Your grandmother and sister were still there, still waiting for your return. And here, I was supposed to dust powder by the door in order to tell if your spirit returned for a visit. That day, the snow fell unusually late in the year. Your footprints were pressed into fresh snow.

May all our prayers be fulfilled.

Date: 2000s
Recorded by John Swanton
Assisted by Tooch Waterson

The Terrible Wild Children

MINA: Liv said when she came to babysit us after Momma had run off, we were like wild animals. She said I rocked back and forth in the corner pulling out my hair. She had to teach us manners.

SUVI: I caught momma in bed with that guy, Bob, and told Daddy. Momma hated me after.

RIKKA: When I was young, I didn't remember Momma at all— it was weird. I don't remember the cult—just images like I was being smothered by a man or someone on top of me.

VEIKO: I don't remember her, either, because I was a baby when she ran off.

MINA: More like she got run out of town by Daddy and his friends.

RIKKA: Suvi remembers a lot. She doesn't like to talk about it do you, Suv?

(Suvi says nothing.)

(Mina laughs.)

❁

SUVI: I remember being kidnapped, when Momma tried to steal us from Daddy. I remember what the bushes smelled like. I remember my feet hurt in my boots. I remember the van Bob and Momma shoved us in and how scared I was.

MINA: I remember that van too. The smell. I still can't stand the smell of rusty tools.

RIKKA: I can't stand small dark places. Reminds me of the van.

SUVI: It's a good thing the airline agent was a friend of Daddy's and didn't sell Momma the plane tickets.

MINA: What do you think would have happened if we'd gone with her?

RIKKA: We'd be begging in the airports.

SUVI: We'd be dead like the Hale-Bopp cult.

MINA: Heaven's Gate?

SUVI: Yeah. They all killed themselves.

MINA: They thought they were aliens from outer space just like Momma and her friends.

RIKKA: Yeah, do you think we would have done that?

SUVI: Well, Momma's spaceship never came to save them from this planet, did it?

RIKKA: No.

SUVI: So how were they going to get to their planet then?

RIKKA: True.

VEIKO: I don't remember it anyway. And I don't want to think about it.

MINA: Well, I stopped some little girls my age from playing with your penis. Momma said it was okay and I got mad. You were a baby. She said they were curious. I stopped them. I was only about five years old then, but I knew enough not to trust her or Delia's kids either.

SUVI: I think Momma left because she was in love with Delia, her best friend. I don't think it was about the men in the group at all.

RIKKA: (Shrugs.) Could be.

MINA: When I was little, I thought Momma was a devil worshiper, then, when I was a bit older, I thought she was following Charles Manson. Don't you remember, if the subject ever came up, which was hardly ever, we used the word "cult." But no one, not even Daddy or Liv, explained what one was. I figured out what a cult was when I was a teen and read *Helter Skelter*. I thought Momma had crazy eyes like

Charles Manson. I didn't have a photograph of her; instead I had the book cover of Manson on *Helter Skelter*.

RIKKA: Yeah, I was afraid of everything under my bed, in the closet. Everything.

MINA: I remember there was a children's book about a little bird that fell out of a nest and kept looking for his mother. I remember there was a monster, but I think it was big heavy equipment or something picked up the bird. Maybe a front-end loader. I couldn't read that damn book without getting upset. One time, I think when I was a teenager, I read that book again and I actually cried. I hate that book.

Date: nd (no date)
Recorded by John Swanton
Assisted by Tooch Waterson
Recounted by Tova Agard

Men's Stories
1951, Winter

Helene stood on a stool at the kitchen sink, her hands in soapy water. She cocked her ear toward men telling tales in the living room. She tuned out the women's talk at the table behind her. Beyond the kitchen window, Elephants Nose silhouetted against the moonlit sky. The moon cast a path from the strait to the harbor, and the brightest star was the Christmas star high above the island—her dad told her it was the planet Venus.

Helene, nine years old, sneaked from kitchen-talk—a recipe for deer stew, cousin's pregnancy, a breech baby—to the living room near the Sparks oil heater where the men sat: fishermen scrubbed after a week in slime and scales from fishing the salmon grounds, dressed in black jeans and wool shirts, and rolling Prince Albert tobacco into cigarettes. She inhaled their smoky tales: UFOs—the one Jim saw, cigar-shaped—while trolling near the beach at Elephants Nose. Or the story about ball lightning zipping through the rigging, blue fire chasing Uncle Chet round his boat deck. Or talk of the landotter man jumping from the bow of her grandfather's boat—no splash, no sound. She hated, though, the stories of drowning, and all that talk of a drowning curse in her family. Maybe she could live far from the ocean.

Sitting on a small padded ottoman near the big picture window, she turned and stared at the planet. The frost on the window formed an alien landscape of tall spires and deep valleys. She'd read about aliens in the *Spaceway* magazine. Her aunt said there might be aliens on other planets, but she wasn't sure. What would it be like to go to another planet? Would her skin turn green like the aliens? Would there be machines to help cook dinner, or magic unicorns? Maybe there she could be the princess of all the aliens. She'd have long silver hair, which they would brush for her every day. It would be perfect. Perfect.

Helene inhaled the cigarette smoke. She loved this visiting time—the time before television came to the island, before outboard motors, before she was bedridden with scarlet fever, before marrying young, before she learned to gather data while doing laundry, reading *Worlds of Tomorrow, Thrilling Science Fiction,* and *Spaceway,* before Father gave her psychic research, years before she starred in her own myth, before she ran off to follow the saucer people.

Date: nd (no date)
Recorded by John Swanton
Assisted by Tooch Waterson
Recounted by Tova Agard

The Woman in the Final Frontier
1968, Summer

Helene followed her oldest child, Suvi, and her middle daughter, Mina, up the trail to the top of Mount Dewey. Suvi and Mina each carried a Folgers coffee can on a string around their necks.

"Over here, over here. This is the best spot, Momma," Suvi said, skipping to a big patch of salmonberries.

Helene had left her toddler, Rikka, and the baby, Veiko, home with Grandma back at the house on the hill. Now, farther up the hill, the town below came into view. She helped her girls pick their salmonberries, filling up one can nearly halfway, although Mina's was nearly empty because Mina couldn't stop eating the berries.

She spread out her wool halibut jacket on the ground for the girls and herself to sit on. All around them, the old spruce trees were draped with old-man's-beard moss. A raven chortled in the branches. She took out two peanut butter and jam sandwiches from her pocket and gave each girl a half and ate one of her own.

She pointed to the island directly in front of town. "There's Elephants Nose."

"Yeah," Suvi said. "It does look like an elephant."

"Yes, hon, and did you know that's where the spaceships are, too. You know, like the one Captain Kirk flies."

"I like Captain Kirk," Suvi said.

Mina flung a pinecone off the coat. "Do you think he can take us for a ride on one?" She asked.

Helene closed her eyes. The forest smelled old. She wandered the same small road by their house, driving the same few miles on the island. "I don't know. They say space is the final frontier." She recalled her last channeling from Albert Einstein. He explained to her how flying saucers were propelled. She had written it all down. "Yes, people are going there, way out there, away from here."

"How come you want to leave us?" Mina asked.

"Leave? No honey, I don't want to leave you. I want . . ." Helene said, her voice trailing off.

She thought about the voice in her head repeating: Delia and your destiny are together. Delia and your destiny are together. No, not a voice, but something in her gut, deep down, spreading warmth. It ached in her chest, too. Delia was so smart, different from any friend she'd known. Delia claimed one of her children had lived another life on a planet made of metal. Imagine that: metal. What would the planet sound like?

There were other men and women who hung out with Delia. Sometimes she felt jealous, but she wouldn't admit that to anyone. Every morning was new and exciting. She'd practically leap out of bed in the morning to get the kids ready after Isak went to work. With the kids, she'd head over to Delia's, leaving the laundry and dishes. At home all day with Suvi and Mina and Rikka and Veiko, things were stressful. She shook her head. How awful her fingers had felt around Mina's little neck. How Mina looked at her with those big trusting blue eyes. "I'd like to kill you," she'd scream.

Helene sighed. "Yes, I want to leave," she said to the girls. She reached into the coffee can setting beside her and took a handful of salmonberries. She enjoyed spending time with her two oldest girls. She loved reading them stories, like "Snow White and Rose Red."

When Helene was a teen, her friends liked to hang out with her because she'd tell them her imaginary stories. Then, later, she'd read the ones she'd written in her notebook. Now, the town of Wrangell lay below. She was on the edge like that *Star Trek* episode, "The City on the Edge of Forever." The ancient ring in the television show was like the one Father used to communicate with her and Delia. There it was again, that temporal disturbance she'd been feeling lately. Isak told her she had to stop staring off into space. "Spacing out," he called it. But that space she went to . . . lovely and silver and shiny with the dishes stacked neatly in the dish rack without her getting her hands soapy. And the diapers were all folded and the children's toys put away. How could she, after knowing all this, and seeing all this, allow time to resume its shape and leave all as it was before.

Date. nd (no date)
Recorded by John Swanton
Recounted by Tova Agard

Escape from Planet Alaska
1971, May

In the dusk, Helene climbed out of an orange van and trudged up the trail to her former house on the hill to kidnap her children. Last night, their spaceship, *Starlighter*, failed to arrive. The Family of Caeli Lumen figured they must have misinterpreted the data they had channeled from their god, Father. Now, new data revealed the *Starlighter* was going to land in Oregon.

As usual, Wrangell Island folks left their doors unlocked. Helene roused her four children while her ex-husband slept. The Family told Helene her children were spiritually asleep. It was her job to wake them, to raise them in the Family. She carried her toddler son across the yard toward the salmonberry bushes. Her three young girls, Suvi, Mina, and Rikka, followed behind.

Suvi's feet slipped inside her rubber boots. She stopped. "Momma, where are we going?" she asked.

"We're going to Oregon," Helene said, grabbing Suvi's hand.

"Why?" Suvi asked.

"Well, we get to ride on a spaceship," Helene explained.

"Is Daddy coming?"

"No, hon, Daddy's asleep, and he won't wake up."

"Why?" Suvi asked again. Her final why went unanswered.

Halfway back down the trail, Helene looked out toward Woronofski Island's silhouette, wondering about the lights often seen zipping over the treetops. These sightings were common in Wrangell lore. Local fishermen often saw them, her grandfather had seen them, she'd seen them. She convinced herself the lights proved the existence of alien spaceships, and the *Starlighter* would soon rescue the Family—displaced gods and goddesses—and transport them back to their planet. She imagined her planet like the utopias in *Worlds of Tomorrow* magazine.

Inside the van, her new lover, Bob, smoked a joint, listening to the radio blare Count Five's "Psychotic Reaction." The children climbed into the back of the windowless van. They held hands and sat among oil and black mold. Rusty tools clanked at their feet.

They drove to the airplane pullout. Soon, the Grumman Goose would be landing on Zimovia Strait and crawling up the ramp. The Goose was the only way off the island—other than hitching a ride on a troller—to Ketchikan in order to take another plane to Oregon. But Alaska's gravity was already folding in on her—sensing a kidnapping attempt, the airline agent refused to sell her the tickets.

Near the event horizon, Helene stood outside the small airline shack with her four children, not realizing the lights flickering above the island would never reach her. The flash of insight would eventually come, but light cannot escape a black hole and neither could she—for the next twenty years—the alien goddess from the universe called Home.

Date: nd (no date)
Recorded by John Swanton
Recounted by Tova Agard

The Girl with Demons All Around
1971, August

Jesse sat with little Rikka on her lap. Rikka's red hair stuck up in all directions and snot dried on her cheeks. A few minutes before, Jesse had tried to rinse the child's face with a wash rag but Rikka had started to cry. Now, Rikka rubbed her eyes.

Jesse held Rikka's pale fingers in her own brown ones and touched the monster on the book cover. "See, it can't hurt you. This is a funny book. He has people feet and big horns. And see that boat there? The monster is going to meet a wild little boy very soon."

Rikka's sisters, Suvi and Mina, played outside Jesse's house on the swing set. Jesse and Charlie's son, Ray, had outgrown it.

Jesse scooted her rocking chair over to the large picture window so she could watch the kids play. The girls had come down Mount Dewey through the trail ending across the street from her place. Typically, they'd run around all day at Petroglyph Beach beside their house. Now Rikka, the littlest girl, had tuckered out. Rain or shine, she always played outside in her boots, clomping around behind her big sisters, making them carry her whenever she tired. Jesse loved this about Rikka.

Jesse draped a small granny-square quilt she'd made across her lap, covering Rikka's skinned knees. The little girl leaned in against her, nuzzling Jesse's chest.

Jesse opened the book and started to read.

Rikka fussed and turned her head. "What's wrong, honey?" Jesse asked.

"Did momma leave because I'm ugly?"

"God, baby. Ugly? Who told you that?"

"They did, sort of," a child's voice said from behind.

Jesse turned. Suvi and Mina stood there. Suvi had helped herself to a glass of Kool-Aid, like she'd done a half-dozen times at Jesse's house. Suvi walked over, glass in hand, a red mustache above her lip. She said, "Bob, Momma's boyfriend, he told Rikka to sit on the couch all day and not to move. She minded him. We were at school, Mina and me. He told Rikka she had demons in her, and the demons were all around, and they were going to get her if she got off the couch."

Jesse frowned. "Did you tell your momma?"

"Momma knew," Mina said. "She said we all have bad things in us. That's why she left us. We have bad things."

Jesse's mother told her about the missionaries who punished kids for speaking Tlingit, saying it was the language of the Devil. Jesse gritted her teeth. Kids taunted her in school as being an "Indian." When she was five, she once tried to scrub the pigment off her hands.

Jesse said, "No, you girls don't have bad things in you. You're made in God's image, and you are all beautiful—every one of you."

Mina and Suvi smiled at Jesse, and then the girls turned and skipped out the door back to the swing set. Jesse leaned back into the chair with Rikka. She moved her moccasined toes up and down, rocking the chair back and forth. She inhaled the pale, red-haired child's scent. She remembered her own baby, limp in her arms one night from a fever she knew he'd never wake up from.

Rikka flipped through the book's pages. She stopped and struggled to read the words:

"And . . . the . . . w-wild things . . . roared . . ."

Date: 1970s

Recorded by John Swanton

Girls with the Sun in Their Eyes

The cold water jabbed Suvi's skin like a thousand sea urchin pricks. There was only a couple of degrees difference between winter and summer water temperatures in Southeast Alaska. But now, she could hardly feel it. She hung onto the dock, and then plunged her head into Wrangell's green harbor water. When she raised her head, she spit water up onto her sister Mina.

"Cut that out," Mina cried, wiping water from her skin. Mina sat on the bull rail, her bright orange life jacket pillowed under her chin. Beside her, Rikka, the youngest sister, sat without a life jacket in cutoff Levi's and a blue Hawaiian-print halter top.

Rikka hung her legs over, the waterline licking her calves. "I'm not sure this is a good idea. It's only May." Rikka's red hair tied up in a ponytail, but it was still too long. The ends of her hair brushed the dock like a deck broom.

Suvi nodded, her old orange life jacket rising to her ears. She wiped her wet hair from her eyes. "Jump in. It's only cold for a second and after you're numb."

"I'm busy," Mina said, nodding toward the large white troller moored across on the next finger.

Suvi sighed. One would never know Mina was boy crazy, but she was. She didn't talk about it much because she didn't like to be teased. Mina was the quiet one, Momma had always said. Mina was the "mousey" one, Momma said, too. Momma called Mina's hair "mousey." Mina yanked her mousey hair out whenever she was stressed. Momma called her girls "kaleidoscope girls": one red, one blonde, and one brunette. And they were close together in age. She was the oldest, sixteen; Mina, fourteen; and Rikka, twelve. But Momma wasn't giving advice anymore. They'd forgotten how Momma looked and what she even sounded like since she'd run off with the cult weirdoes. They'd spent half their life without her already.

Suvi moved her arms back and forth, trying to keep warm. She knew what a cult was. She'd read about them in the book she snuck from the library: *Helter Skelter*. They weren't supposed to talk about it. No one, not even Daddy, had explained it. She used to think Momma might be worshiping the Devil because Rikka had overheard someone saying that at school. Maybe that was true. Now, they all slept with cross necklaces on and stuffed animals around their bed. Something was going to protect them.

Suvi turned around, bobbing in the water. She eyed the newly painted *Sea Wolf* and the young man on deck sticking halibut gear. "Oh, him."

"He is cute," Rikka said.

"Shhh," Mina said. "Don't you know sound carries over the water? He'll hear us."

"So what," Suvi said, turning to float on her back. She clasped her hands on the large column pads on the life jacket and started to sing, "Mina likes the cute guy. Mina likes the cute guy." She turned her head to the side. Mina frowned at her.

Suvi continued with her song "Mina wants a baby. Mina wants a baby."

Mina jumped up to her feet. "You little . . ." She leaned forward and in a split second she jumped into the harbor, her life jacket popping her fast up to the surface. She flapped her arms toward Suvi. Suvi twirled and swam toward the *Sea Wolf*.

"Ah, come on," Rikka yelled from the dock. Then, without a life jacket on, she sat up straight and arched her back and shoved her body out.

She slunk down into the water, like a seal sliding off the dock. As she entered the water, she gasped "God, that's cold."

With a few long strokes of her lanky limbs, Rikka swam next to Mina. Mina still dog-paddled toward Suvi, who floated near the boat already.

Suvi reached the side of the *Sea Wolf*. The young man looked over the gunwales at her. "Hi," she said.

"Hi," he said, smiling.

"Water's fine," Suvi said, tucking the life jacket strap below her chin. "Really?"

"Really. Really. It only stings for a second."

The young man laughed.

Grease dotted his white T-shirt. His dark brown hair was cut with sideburns like Elton John's. Even his hair was receding a bit and he was stalky like most of the men in their father's side of the family, and, like Elton. It was then the song came rising from her toes. She had to sing. She couldn't control the urge. She started to sing the one song she knew all the way through by heart.

The young man took a cigarette out of his T-shirt pocket and lit it with his Zippo. He blew smoke down at Suvi. "I get that all the time. You know that's a Beatles remake?"

"I do. But I like Elton's version better. And I think Elton is sexier. Seems like guys are trying too much to look like Jesus. Elton's different."

Suvi sunk down into the water. Bubbles floated up to the surface. She popped up, wiping water down her face. She opened her eyes and sang.

The young man smiled down at her. "Well, I don't sing. Not at all. Well, except when I'm out fishing and there's no one to hear me."

Suvi laughed and flopped around to her back, kicking the water. She smiled at him. She liked the way he looked at her.

Mina paddled up beside her, almost out of breath. "*What* are you doing?"

"I'm visiting. And this here is . . . is . . ." Suvi said, pointing up.

"Hank," the young man said, blowing out smoke from his cigarette. He sat on the rail now. He flung the remainder of his cigarette out into the water.

Rikka joined them treading water. Her hair, undone now, spread around the three of them like a bed of kelp.

Suvi liked the way her sister's hair felt like wet feathers. She brushed it away and asked Hank, "Why don't you join us?"

Hank grinned and then turned to look at the pilothouse. "Sure, why not."

Hank hopped off the rail, standing up on the deck. He undid his belt, letting his Levi's fall to his knees. Rikka turned her head. But Suvi and Mina stared at Hank's white underwear. He pulled his T-shirt over his head and let it fall on the deck on top of his pants. He stepped up on the rail and leaped into the water beside them.

Water splashed over them. "Ohhh," Mina screeched.

Hank exploded through the surface of the water, shaking his head like a dog. He inhaled. "It's c-c-c-cold," he chattered.

"Naw," Suvi said, splashing water at him.

Hank splashed her back and then turned to splash Mina.

Rikka dove beneath Hank, jerking at his legs. Hank went down, and Suvi and Mina laughed. As Rikka released him, Hank bobbed back up and swam to the surface and splashed Mina again.

Mina giggled, blushing despite the cold.

Suvi splashed Hank. "Oh, Hank. Hank," she blinked her eyes with exaggeration.

Hank laughed and then coughed.

"Shouldn't smoke so much," Mina said.

"Yeah, it's bad for you," Rikka added.

Hank half-coughed and half-laughed, sounding like a barking sea lion.

Rikka moved toward him, her long red hair caressing his bare chest. He smiled at her, looking into her steel blue eyes, and, for an instant, her eyes flashed.

"Ah, Rikka, do you have to?" Mina asked.

Suvi shrugged. "Hey, Mina, sing with me."

"How does it go?" Mina asked. "Oh . . . I remember. She started to sing but it didn't really sound like words but more like the sound of a ball of herring rising to the surface. Suvi started to sing, too.

Then Rikka, so close to Hank that her breath nearly met Hank's breath, joined them. The three girls sang together, Hank closed his eyes.

Suvi swam to Hank's side and Mina dog-paddled up to his back. They joined hands with Rikka. Round and round they went like they used to play washing machine when they were little girls, when they used to play every day down on the dock, when their hands and feet were still webbed with familial syndactyly, before Doc Heggan had convinced their daddy and stepmom, Liv, to clip their delicate skin. "You don't want to raise ducks," the doctor had said.

Suvi started to hum. The current pulled around her, spinning them. In the swirl, Rikka's long hair wrapped around them like a momma otter keeping her pup safe in a patch of bull kelp. Suvi loved the weightlessness, the current keeping her up. She sensed Hank liked it too. Hank kept his eyes closed. The girls sang some more, the notes flooding together into a single note, sounding like a ship's bell clanking in the rigging.

Suvi unclasped her life jacket and it floated away from their circle. Mina undid her life jacket too. This released something in them. Suvi felt it. The sea flowed through her fingers, where her skin once was. A memory lurked there, a power she couldn't control. Kind of like when she first started her period. There was a change, a difference.

The life jackets floated nearby. Beside her, Hank sank below the surface. Mina and Rikka sank too. Suvi tucked her head and submerged quite easily. Several feet beneath the surface, herring swam through Rikka's hair that was splayed out like seaweed. Mina and Rikka's mouths opened. They sang, the song moving through the water. Hank's eyes opened wide, his mouth remained closed, his cheeks puffed out. Then he opened his mouth, trying to sing along. Cold harbor water rushed into his lungs. He sank beneath them. Suvi reached for her sisters' hands and held them tight, spinning around and around, tumbling through green water sliced with gold sunlight, a splay of her sister's red hair, and silver fish. Flashes from the herring netted the sunlight, reflecting iridescence in the girls' eyes, now tumbling with colors.

Date: early 1980s
Recorded by John Swanton

The Boy Who Shot the Star

Veiko stepped over the log, sinking his foot into a muck hole. He jerked his foot up. His rifle sloughed off his shoulder and banged the log. "Crap," he said. He was warned about hunting on Woronofski Island. No, it wasn't the steep terrain people warned him about. It was the lights. Could be an alien landing strip, joked his cousin, Jason. Could be the landotter village, his friend had whispered. Even the stallo could be lurking here.

Sure, he knew the stories. But everyone in Alaska told strange stories. He ignored them. Besides, he'd been hunting with his father, Isak. Now he was on his first hunting trip alone with a small pack and his rifle. He would get a big buck and pack it out himself. The airplane had dropped him off at Sunrise Lake early that morning. He planned to hike out in the evening and meet his dad on Sandy Beach below.

But after falling for the sixth time and twisting his ankle, he was going to spend the night on top of this mountain. He didn't want to sleep in the cold and dark. His father would probably wait at the beach, maybe look around a bit, then head back home and wait for daylight. It was stupid to go into the forest at night. Veiko leaned two large branches together, laid down some moss, and then spread his small green tarp over the branches.

He'd been hunting with friends since he was nine and now he was fifteen. They'd shot nearly everything in the woods behind his house.

But, his stepmother, Liv, didn't approve. She'd told him the next time he shot something he'd have to eat it. It had been three years and he hadn't forgiven her for making him skin, cook, and eat squirrel. This time, though, when he got a deer, he'd give most of it to his cousin's family. After all, he could do anything he wanted with it. It would be his deer.

A large moon rose above the peak. The man on the moon appeared more like his stepmother's face. She looked mad and hilariously scary like she did when she saw the dead squirrel. "Kinda looks like you, Liv." Liv had given him her typical disapproving look as she set the squirrel onto the kitchen cutting board. She nagged at him: Careful what you do and say. There are consequences.

He lifted his rifle, aiming at the moon. "Bang," he said without pulling the trigger. At once, a bright star came into view beside the moon. Veiko stared at the star. The star seemed to move. He watched it for a while until he closed his eyes.

The wind fluttered his tarp, waking him. He stepped out from his shelter and rubbed his eyes. Bright moonlight surrounded him. The moon remained in its place in the sky, but the huge star pulsed above the island. What the heck? An airplane? Around him, the wind began to hum. The star pulsed blue and spit a wand of light to the side. He crouched down as the light swept the lakeshore like a searchlight. Suddenly the light sucked up a shape he knew well. "Holy crap," he said, stepping back, "the thing is sucking up deer."

The light swept across the alpine, heading toward his shelter, toward him. Veiko raised his gun to the bright light. As soon as the bullet left the barrel, the light pulled him up, his mind spun like the inside of a washing machine. The sound hummed louder and louder in his head, then *wham*, he was on the beach.

Veiko's back smacked against the sand when he fell. He took shallow breaths. Slowly, he sat up. Across the strait, Wrangell's small-town lights twinkled like a miniature village. Around him mosquitoes hummed louder and louder, sounding like a huge swarm, like something winding up. Then, the light swathed him as if he were a convict escaping from prison. Above him glowed the belly of a huge disc. In the light, something dark tumbled in slow motion toward him. He moved backward, crawling like a crab. The dark object twirled and then thudded to the ground as the search light switched off. Darkness enveloped him like a thick sleeping bag. He coughed. Beyond him, toward the water, the form appeared like a boulder in the sand. He got up, wobbly at first, and walked over to it. A huge buck splayed out, dead, in front of him. "What the hell?"

He reached for the buck, its skin still warm. He rubbed it like a good luck charm. It was a big buck. He stumbled around to where he'd been lying, searching for his rifle he figured wasn't going to be there anyway. He shivered. He had to get warm. He hobbled along searching for firewood. The moon glowed, though he could see it would be daylight soon.

He built a small fire with the beach wood and sat beside it. He poked the fire with a stick for a long time, occasionally glancing up at the stars. How many people would that deer feed? His father always gave the deer's heart and liver to their elderly neighbor. He thought about Liv's face, bright as the moon, grinning as he gave her the hindquarter. For the rest of the night, mosquitoes hummed in his ear, and he jumped at the sound of every snap and crack and moan and cry drifting from woods and shore. When the night faded to blue, then to gray as the clouds moved in, his father's small boat came into view, heading toward the campfire.

Date: mid-late 2000s
Recorded by John R. Swanton
Assisted by Tooch Waterson
Speaker: Charlie Edwin

Charlie Edwin's Trapping Stories

"We'll start this off as the trapping stories. My dad taught me how to trap. When I was real young, I would go out trapping—get excused from school once in a while. The trapping season was every other year. We'd go out occasionally and do trapping. Our trapline was down at Madden Bay. He taught me how to make all kinds of sets and traps. That's how I learned to trap.

"I used to trap in the harbor when I was a kid. We'd set traps for otter and mink on the ends of the floats. The floats were made of logs in those days. They'd have a place to set traps on the ends of the floats, down underneath the outhouse. We got quite a few furs that way. Then, I'd trap along the beach toward the ferry terminal, toward Point Highfield. I'd set along there. I got a few mink and a couple of cats.

"One day, I was down there at Point Highfield, and somebody had been into my traps. I thought, *What the hell*, you know. I had some otter-slide traps there. I could tell someone had been messing with them. I happened to be up in the woods and I heard a skiff, coming along the beach, slow down and stop. I was sitting on a stump up in the woods. And I thought, *Well, someone's coming back to the scene of the crime.* And, sure enough, up through the woods came my cousin Lowell. He came up there and he starts checking the traps—my traps. I was sitting on the stump and I had a gun. I was holding a gun on him.

"I said, 'Lowell!' and he about shit his pants. I said, 'You know better than that, I've got it posted. These are my traps. This is my little trapline. You stay the hell off of it—cousin or not,' I said. 'Go back in your skiff and leave this area.'

"He did, and he knew I was pissed. And, I had a gun too. My own cousin. I was sitting out on a stump and I was perfectly still and I was wearing brown clothes. If you sit like that, it's hard for anyone to see you, unless you make a movement. It's hard for anybody to pick you out. I was sitting on this stump above him and he was fooling around with my traps. After I scared him, I never had any more trouble with him after.

"Then, one year, I don't know how old I was—late teens, early twenties—it was wintertime, and I wasn't doing much for working then or anything. Conrad Gunderman had been chopping wood and cut his foot open with an ax, and he still wanted to go trapping. He couldn't go trapping, and he heard I wasn't doing anything, so he called me up and asked if I would go trapping with him and be his legs. I said sure, so I went down there and talked to him. He made out a grocery list. I got groceries. It was the month of December.

"We took off and went trapping for a whole month. His trapline was down at Anan—down on the mainland shore south and then on the Wrangell shore from Hamm Island down to Fools Inlet. My uncle Frank Edwin, he had his trapline in Fools Inlet. Anyway, I went out with Conrad, and jeez we got along good. He'd run the skiff, and I'd run up and get the furs and rebait the traps and set the traps. And in the evening time, we'd skin out and stretch out everything—all the mink and otter. We got along good. We had a great time.

"One night, in the middle of the night, a storm come up and ripped the skiff loose from the boat. We had the big boat, the *Lorelei Sea*, Conrad's big trolling boat. The storm ripped the skiff loose and put it up on the beach. The breakers came in and filled it full of sand. The next morning the tide was out. Conrad eased the big boat over to the beach, and I jumped off with a bucket and a shovel and got to the skiff. It was full of beach sand from the storm. I shoveled all the sand out of the skiff again before the tide came in. The motor was still good—still worked. I got all the sand out of the skiff, and we got it back to the big boat and we didn't lose it. It was a nice, flat sandy beach there. It was pretty spooky for a while.

"We didn't know what was happening. We wondered about it. Who did that? What did that? I decided I didn't want to trap with Conrad anymore. On account of his luck. I didn't want to drown. I'm done. I don't want to tell any more stories. I'm sorry. This is enough. Thank you."

Date: 1980s
Recorded by Tooch Waterson

Salmon Woman

Aino sits weeping on a rock of many colors. The rock sinks under the weight of her lamenting. In her grief, she cannot move. The water engulfs her. She slips into the sea, shapeshifting into a salmon.

❀

From her float-house above the tideline, sixteen-year-old Mina walks through a thimbleberry patch to the beach. The bushes scratch her arms as she holds her two-month-old baby daughter closer. On the beach, she sits on a log. No one hears Mina's lament. The baby looks into her mother-child's eyes and fusses. From beneath the blanket, a pink bottle tumbles onto the sand. Mina picks it up and wipes the nipple off on her jeans and then puts the bottle in her baby's mouth.

The breeze pitches the waves to whitecaps. Mina imagines her mother-in-law in the house on the hill above her, at the window, conjuring yet another storm. Behind, her young husband yells her name from the open windows of their float-house.

She rises with a familiar ache in her arms and walks to the water's edge. She pauses, sensing her baby's breath ebbing with hers. She looks out to Zimovia Strait: a troller chugs toward the fishing grounds. She turns, hearing her husband cursing again. He searches the bushes beside the house, his anger crashing closer. Water soaks into Mina's shoes, swirling cold tongues at her ankles. The circling gulls join her whimper as she walks farther out until the water is at her knees. Her thoughts stir the sea, and time cools the air, allowing a moment of reflection—Ahtolaiset, her people-of-the-seas, live in the ocean, rivers, and lakes. She thinks about her oral tradition, of Aino fleeing from her husband. She tells herself she'll migrate to Ahtola and swim around the salmon rocks, live with the Host-of-Waves.

It is then she recalls her own life cycle is like the ocean—she's not only herself, she's her baby too. She whispers her ancestors' incantation: *Woman-Beneath-the-Billows, rise on the foam. Gather the foam together; direct the current and the whitecaps.* But this change of tide is unable to drown out her husband's threatening voice—he yells for Mina and their daughter. Mina opens her mouth, but says nothing. Her baby fusses again and Mina looks down. The baby sees her shift from scaled creature to human face.

Mina slogs back through the water, her feet cramping against the cold. She returns to sit on the log. If she remains here, perhaps Raven will hop by and command, "I turn you to stone." She will become a rock formation, appearing to cradle her babe in arms. Then, hundreds of years from now, someone will tell a story about her, the Salmon Woman.

The waves quiet down, but she still feels the lure of the sea. She wants to run toward it, to embrace its depths. Instead, with her baby held close, she turns toward the brush, toward the sound of her husband's voice. She turns away from the ocean. She turns away from her ancestors. She turns away from her own shapeshifting.

Date: 1980s
Recorded by John Swanton

The Man Who Saves the Dead

Karl sat soaking in the hot tubs in Shakes Slough. His legs lifted up from the cedar bench, and he swirled the water with his feet. He took a sip of beer and leaned his head back. The water pressed against his chest, making it hard to breathe. Maybe this is what it feels like to drown. He shuddered. When he was a kid, his father had tossed him off the dock. He wasn't really scared, at least he didn't think so. Now, he lifted himself out of the water and sat on the tub's circular rim. Shit, he couldn't drown. He saved the drowned. At least that's what people called him behind his back, anyway: The man who saves the dead.

Karl didn't want to be known for saving the dead. It just happened that way. Sometimes, in fact most times, that's the way things were in Wrangell. They just happened. How can you save the dead? Weren't the dead unsavable by their deadness? But, then again, being rescued and saved, or taken, are divided by a narrow crack between the human world and the animal world, a line he couldn't quite see. There were stories about those creatures, the ones he couldn't mention. The creatures "saved" people from drowning, but they took the drowned to live with them. That's how the old-timers told the stories. They said the landotters "saved" people who drowned. But what did that make him? Part of a weird myth? Maybe he *was* saving folks, like they said. If he found their drowned body, they wouldn't be living in that world they couldn't see, the invisible place. He knew that world existed. It was there all right, and it was gray as gray can be—like alder bark in winter, like his dad's old wool halibut jacket. Life was a gray cloud, sucking the life from gray water surrounded by gray islands, gray trees, and gray moss.

The first time he saved a dead man he didn't intend it to happen. It was one of those gray days when he was eighteen years old and working down on his dad's boat, the *Sea Wolf*. The VHF radio blared out a call that One-Eyed Tom, an old-timer, had fallen in the water. Karl got in his skiff, which was tied next to his dad's boat, and sped across the harbor. He asked the bystanders what had happened, but no one knew. The body, they pointed, might be stuck under the dock somewhere. They'd heard the old guy yell for help.

Karl made note of the tideline, nearly all the way up onto the grid, and noted a seagull floating by, heading toward the harbor entrance. The leaves on the big old cottonwood standing near the tribal house on Shakes Island fluttered in the breeze.

Karl took off running down the dock in the opposite direction. "Over here!" he yelled back. Fifty yards down the dock he stopped and knelt down, searching on his hands and knees, looking through the planks into the water. Sure enough, a blue sweatshirt bulged with air beneath the slats. He yelled for a crowbar. "Shit!" Time slipped away like the ripples from the dock. He yanked down the top of his rubber boots. They made a sucking sound when they came off. He discarded his jacket beside his boots and jumped in. Once he was in the water, he tucked his head and shoulders down and fought to get under the dock. Having previously been more of a sinker than a swimmer, he was surprised to discover he could sink if he let the air out of his lungs. He went down, then back up again. He took a breath and squinched himself under the dock. He grabbed at the only thing he saw, a dark shape, and jerked on it, and the body floated out from under the dock with him.

Karl popped his head up. His friend Cooper, an EMT, and several other guys and their rescue equipment stood on the dock. He heaved the old man upward, and Cooper and another guy reached out and rolled the old man over the rail and onto the dock. It was like working with a huge halibut on the back deck of his father's boat, and for a second the image stayed with him: the slicing and hacking and gutting. He turned away.

The EMTs worked on the man, but Karl had already sensed his deadness. The gray day had gotten him. "His name's One-Eyed Tom," said another fisherman, who stood smoking a pipe nearby, watching the attempted rescue. "One-Eyed, on account of him having one eye. He had the *Lady Jaye* down on the third finger, tied next to the *Minnie Sue*." The man took one long suck from his pipe and turned to walk away.

Karl didn't want to watch them load the man up on the stretcher. He didn't want a pat on the back or a stupid sad look making him sick to his stomach. He walked back to his skiff and motored across the harbor back to the *Sea Wolf*.

❊

Karl's friend Cooper sat across from him on the edge of the wood hot tub. Steam rose up from their skin. "You look like you're gonna have a heart attack," Cooper said, slurring his words.

Karl put his hand to his face. It burned with heat. He inhaled the cool May air and flicked off a mosquito. He was tired, that's all. It had been a hell of a halibut opening, a seventy-two-hour grab from the seafloor. He and Cooper had been up the whole time, and, after they'd unloaded their fish, Cooper suggested they head upriver to soak in the tubs. Sounded good to him. The fishing had been good and it was time for a reward.

Karl came from a family of fisherman. He was part Tlingit and part Norwegian on both his parents' sides. His mother, Berta, had told him the Norwegians and the Tlingits had always gotten along because they all liked to tell stories and eat fish. In Wrangell, his great-grandfather met and married a Tlingit girl because when he told her stories, she didn't laugh about dark elves living underground or about the Nidhogg, a dragon that eats the roots of the world tree. She had said she believed in those things too.

Those were the kinds of stories Karl secretly liked, the ones that told of dragons and elves and spiny, slimy, yellow-eyed creatures. Growing up, he and Cooper had that in common. They traded adventure comic books. Cooper used to tell him dragon stories. Cooper was part Chinese, his family history going back to Wrangell's salmon cannery days. They still shared stories. They had skiff adventures, hot tub adventures, trolling adventures, salmon and killer whale adventures. And, of course, women adventures, family stories, work stories, and beer stories. Lots of beer stories. Heck, he was a story. His life made a good story. Especially all the people he saved or, rather, dragged up from the sea.

The second time he saved a body was a bit disturbing. Even he had to admit that. Someone had seen a guy inside the boat, a young deckhand. But after the fire died out, the deckhand's body wasn't there. He'd found him thirty feet beneath the boat, almost sitting up on a rock staring ahead, like he'd done when he was a kid, waiting to be rescued. But the deckhand was dead. He hadn't known until he reached out toward him. It was the way the guy swayed, the way his mouth opened slightly.

He shook his head then sipped his beer. He shouldn't think about that; time to celebrate their catch. After they sold their fish, Karl and Cooper had grabbed a couple cases of Rainier and headed off in his river scow. Several of their friends were supposed to meet them at the tubs, but the high tide that carried them upriver was already going out. If their friends weren't here already, they probably weren't coming up until the next tide.

Karl tipped his beer back and guzzled what remained. He tossed the beer can down into the soggy beer container sitting next to the tub and reached for another. The beer slipped from his hand and bobbed in the tub. He grabbed it. He held it up to his face, cooling his skin. He hadn't even said good-bye to Mina. Sure, she knew he was unloading fish, and that they'd done well, but he'd forgotten to check in. Shit, how could he have forgotten to tell her he was going upriver? By now she already knew. She'd be off work from the deli and she'd see his rifle wasn't propped up next to the bed and that his XtraTuf boots and coat were gone, as well as the checkbook.

Karl slunk back down, until only his eyes and the top of his head were above water. Cooper remained sitting on the edge of the hot tub, sipping his beer. "Did you feel that 300-pounder tug the line when we pulled it in?" He laughed. "Shit, I thought it was a skate, and then I thought, fuck, it must be 400 pounds the way it came up and fought."

"Sometimes the smaller ones fight more," Karl said.

"Yeah, but that one, it's gonna pay the fuel bill."

Yeah, he hated that the most: paying the fuel bill, the grocery bill, the stall rent, the boat repair bills, the new gloves and raingear bill, the bait bill. He finished off another beer and tossed it out of the tub. It rolled onto a small patch of grass.

If they'd only pay him for hauling up the dead people, he might be able to pay off a few things. He should charge them. A lot. Just because finding them seemed to come easy didn't mean it was easy.

The third time he saved the dead, it was a white guy, an out-of-towner, who went canoeing between a small island and the shore outside of Pat's Crick. Considering the current there, the man was an idiot. Karl figured with the incoming tide, the body would be pushed up the shoreline. For hours, the search-and-rescue and EMTs looked in the wrong area. Eventually, Cooper came and got Karl. "We need you for retrieval," Cooper said. *Retrieval* was Cooper's new lingo after all his training. God, that sounded like he was going out in his skiff to pull a log off the beach for firewood or turning his skiff around to grab a crab pot buoy. But that's what they called it now.

Karl found the dead man face down pressed under a submerged tree near the north end of the small island. Took him about ten minutes, searching the area where he'd guessed the body might have been, and, sure enough, it was. After that, the rescue squad was impressed, so much so, they decided he should have his own dive suit, which was really a wet suit, a scuba tank, and a mask and regulator. But he'd always jumped in with his jeans and T-shirt on. He didn't know the first thing about scuba diving. He'd spent most of his life on the water, avoiding going down into the water. Besides, his mother would freak out. She warned him about the water and drowning. It was her worst fear—to have a relative disappear and never find the body. She'd seen it happen to other people: fathers, mothers, uncles, aunts, brothers, sisters, cousins, cousins-twice-removed, friends, strangers.

❁

The sun finally peeked through the clouds. Daylight lasted longer these days, nearing 10:00 p.m. The sun felt warm and had already reddened his skin. Whenever he tanned, his skin shaded like the inside bark of an alder tree. Sometimes his wife, Mina, called him beautiful. She was New Agey. She embarrassed him. She said it wasn't New Age, that she was Sámi. That it was how she saw the world, like a circle. Mina said he blended in with the island—green eyes and brown skin. Every generation, a child or two was born into the Agard family with sea-green eyes. Great-grandfather had had them, a great-aunt, and then his own father. He had them. Green-eyed Indian. Kids used to tease him. His five-year-old daughter, Tova, had those same eyes. He called her his green-eyed Indian. But no one was going to tease her about it. He'd make sure of that. He'd always figured his kids would look like Mina: light skin with blue eyes. When they were first married someone pointed out that his wife was a white Indian, and he thought they were cutting her down. He didn't know she was a Lapp. He had been ready to fight. He'd been fighting his whole young life. He would probably die for Mina, his kids too. He put his hand to his chest. Maybe he was already doing that.

In the grand scheme of things, he couldn't die. Who would replace him? He was the only one who could read the water. He was the only one who cared about remembering where people died, how they died. At first he kept a notebook, writing down the people he saved. Their names, where he found them, what the weather was like. The fourth time he saved a body, he saved it from beneath a giant tour ship tied up at the cement dock downtown. A woman had jumped in to kill herself and she did. He found her still clutching her expensive purse, her hand outstretched, reaching for him.

He was destined to fetch bodies with nearby life jackets floating just out of reach, bodies with hooks and lines wrapped around their ankles, bodies with bulging eyes or no eyes. No one in town wanted anything to do with drowning. In a community of mixed Scandinavian and Tlingit heritages, himself included, he knew why: the landotter people. He couldn't or wouldn't say the name in the Tlingit language out loud. He'd been taught it was taboo. Saying it in English was a different matter, though he didn't do that either. As a kid, he used to laugh about the taboo, but not now. Better safe than sorry. He'd grown up with the stories, knew the taboos, but it was never talked about directly. In the stories, it was sort of mentioned, skirted. Once he'd heard his grandfather mention the old-timers used to check their babies for tails. He'd checked his babies for skin and eye color.

❁

Karl clanked another beer in the box. "Let's head back."

Cooper swigged the last of his beer down and threw it across the tub, hitting the side. The can plopped into the water. "Twin Lakes. Let's go there. We can crash in the cabin."

Karl left his wet T-shirt hanging over the side of the hot tub. He and Cooper dressed and headed back down the trail to the scow, leaving their empties scattered and the cardboard beer container soggy with rain and steam.

The Twin Lakes cabin was a half-hour trip back down the river. They would stay the night there rather than try and make a run through the flats on an outgoing tide. If they went now they'd be stuck for sure. The snowmelt had left Shakes Slough deep and muddy, their wake washing small trees behind them. Cooper drove the scow, getting the boat up on step in order to make it over some of the more treacherous spots in the slough: the sandbars and fallen trees blocking the river were invisible due to the high water. The scow skipped over the submerged logs, occasionally scraping the bottom of the boat. Cooper steered the scow, twisting his body with the sideways maneuvering. Karl sat in the bow, sideways, one leg out over the flat surface of the bow, the other leg down in the scow, braced against a heavy plastic tote of gear.

They rounded the last corner and shot out of the slough onto the main river. The colder air washed over his hair, sticking it to his head.

Cooper reached into the console and grabbed a beer, tossing it to Karl. Karl opened the beer and guzzled it down, then threw the can into the bottom of the scow. Karl shivered. He zipped up his black jacket to his chin and turned his head from the wind.

On the way to Twin Lakes, they passed huge trees floating down river and small ice sheets. As they entered Twin Lakes Slough, they slid sideways. The current ran fast. Karl opened his mouth, but no sound came out. In his mind he yelled "Holy shit!" He glanced toward Cooper. Cooper's eyes widened. The boat skipped to the side again. With a suddenness that surprised Karl, Cooper dove off the side of the boat, leaping toward the riverbank. Karl felt a deep pain on his cheek and then nothing.

When Karl woke up, he lay on the sandy riverbank. A bluejay squawked. His feet faced the slough, almost touching it, and his head faced the treeline. He moved his fingers and wiggled his toes inside his rubber boots. He turned his head to the right. The scow, about thirty to forty feet away, was wedged up in a large spruce tree that had fallen across the river. The motor was silent, the red jet unit a foot or so out of the water. The scow was suspended as if someone had carefully placed it there. No sense of the violence that had shoved it into the trees' branches. Cooper wasn't around. God, hopefully Cooper wasn't twisted along the riverbank where he saw him jump, or worse, floating down the river.

Karl sniffed the air: a strong musky scent. Bear? No. It was stronger, muskier, like the woods and the sea both. He took a deep breath and raised himself up slightly. To his left, a set of oddly placed tracks, like four paws with a longer track in between dragging behind, made their way across the sand. The tracks had come from the woods. Whatever it was circled him and then went back into the woods again, through the weeds and up the bank into the willows.

A cough startled him. Still stuck a few inches in the sand, he turned the top half of his body toward the sound. Behind him, Cooper walked out of the willow brush with a cigarette dangling from his mouth. "You awake?" he asked. "I didn't want to move you in case your neck was busted. You want to be able to use your prick for a lot more years."

"Well thanks for that," Karl said, grimacing as he tried to move. "What happened?"

"I dunno. I was out for a few minutes too. Hit my head, I think," he said rubbing his head. "Motor's shot," he added, pointing to the boat, "got wacked."

Karl raised himself up onto his knees. "I saw you jump from the boat. That's when I knew something was wrong."

"I saw you jump too, after I jumped."

"Jump? I think I was thrown."

"Oh," Cooper said. "Sorry. What a bitch of a ride, huh? I'm sure Sven and Veiko will be coming up on the high tide again. Maybe we should walk the bank and see if we can make it to the cabin."

Karl remained on his hands and knees. "No, I don't think I can go far. Besides, how would they get to us? The tree is in the way," he said, nodding to the spruce spanning the slough. "They'd have to cut their way through."

"Yeah, I guess you're right." Cooper sat down on a log.

Karl wobbled and then finally stood up and stretched his back. "Christ that hurts."

"That sucks. Maybe you cracked something." Cooper flicked his cigarette out into the slough. "I'll gather some wood then." He headed down the riverbank, yanking up sticks from the sand.

Karl rubbed his back, below his belt. Maybe his ass broke. That wouldn't be good. His arms and legs barely moved, but now he had to pee. He walked a few steps up into the grass to face the willows. He started to urinate on a small patch of stunted trees. He sniffed. His pee smelled strong, worse than when he ate asparagus. He lifted his head again and took another sniff. Animal? The thick willows led into the big cottonwood and spruce lining the slough. He scanned them briefly, looking for movement and shape. Nothing. He zipped up his pants and as reached to flatten his hair down, the stench became stronger. He lifted his arm over his head and sniffed his armpit. "Jesus, I stink." He lifted his other armpit, sniffing himself. "Whew."

He shook his head and started to walk down the grass to the riverbank. Each step felt like a sharp knife poking his lower back. "My ass hurts," he grimaced. He sat down on the log.

Cooper walked down the beach with an armload of wood in his hands, puffing on a cigarette. He plopped the armload in the sand a few feet from Karl. Cooper stacked the wood in a teepee shape: smaller sticks on the bottom, the inside filled with grass with larger sticks on top.

Cooper sniffed the air. "You stink, bro. Shit your pants?"

"No, I smell. I think a critter marked me while I was out." That would've been a sight—something peeing on him while he lay unconscious.

Cooper took out his lighter and lit the fire. It smoldered and then burst into a small flame.

Karl wiggled himself on the log trying to get comfortable but couldn't. He stood. He arched his back, trying to relieve the pain. He rubbed his butt down by his tailbone. Something protruded. What the heck? *Is a bone sticking out?* He patted it. It wasn't hurt bad, just sore. He felt the rounded end. He couldn't sit again, so he stepped a few feet away from the fire and lowered himself to the ground. He knelt onto the sand, taking in a deep breath. He leaned over and put his hands down so he was on all fours. It seemed natural. He stretched out his back. That felt better.

"Maybe someone will be here soon," Cooper said.

Karl cocked his head, listening for the sound of an outboard, a rescue coming upriver. No prop whined in the distance. The noise of a distant prop sounded to Karl like a large mosquito. He swatted a mosquito from his face.

"Better get back near the smoke," Cooper said. "The mosquitoes have found us."

"No, this feels good." Karl pressed his feet and hands into the sand. A mosquito buzzed him again. He tried to lean back, put his weight on his legs to stand. Pain shot up through him. No, it would be better to stay put. It felt good on his hands and knees. In fact, it felt really good. No pain. He decided to wait like that for high tide to bring another scow upriver. He listened again for a prop. Instead, the muddy slough water flowed by, lapping against the fallen logs, the rocks, and the riverbank.

Date: 1980s

Recorded by John Swanton

The First Assimilated Sámi in the World

On the back deck of the *Miss Janet*, his commercial troller, Isak peed into the sea. A small white patch on his dick caught his attention. Paper? Lint? He brushed it, but the spot didn't wipe off. What the heck? He finished peeing and zipped up his pants. He closed his eyes and inhaled deeply. Cold salt air filled his lungs. Sometimes, if he let his mind go, if he didn't think about things, he could believe they hadn't happened. Uncle didn't die last week. He didn't find Uncle's boat flipped on its side, floating like a whale sleeping on the sea. He didn't find Uncle drowned, entangled in the troller's rigging.

Isak turned and walked over to the fishhole and looked down inside. Only four bright salmon lay in ice. After three days of fishing it wasn't looking good. The past few years hadn't been good at all. But what could he do? His family had always been fishermen: his grandfather, father, and now he, and maybe his son. Back home, in the old country, his family had once thought he might grow up to be a *noiade*, a shaman. But what kind of job was that? His parents didn't reveal this to the missionaries, of course, They'd only whispered about it.

Now, he shook his hand. It still stung. He still felt the rap of the schoolteacher's ruler. He was supposed to write his punishment a hundred times, but he'd defied that schoolteacher. He'd written it a thousand times, no maybe ten thousand times: Do. Not. Speak. Sámi. He'd written it, once, for each one of his people. The blackboard chalk had filled the room like a smoky campfire. They said maybe he was sick in the head, but he wasn't sick. He couldn't stop writing. Over and over and over and over. And maybe that's when he noticed the first spot on his pointing finger. He'd been very young then. He didn't tell anyone. After a while the spot had disappeared, but maybe he'd become comfortable with seeing it there.

Isak remembered when he'd finished writing on the chalkboard, on the walls, on the floor, on the desks, and on the windows, that he'd stood back and looked at what he'd done. Do Not Speak Sámi. Do Not Speak. From that day on, he didn't. But wait—maybe this was not his story. Hadn't he heard this same story before? Wasn't it his grandfather's story, one that had been passed down from generation to generation, told so many times the story had become his? But wasn't he born in Wrangell, not the old country? His grandfather was the one born in Finland, on the border of Norway. It must be his grandfather's story, or his father's story. Yes, that was it. But why could he still smell the chalk dust? He remembered how the drum sounded when the old shaman pounded it. He remembered how his language felt on his tongue, the way the letters formed words, and tumbled over tundra and lake. How could he know this? He had only recently started speaking his traditional language.

The Sámi language had reappeared to him one day. Maybe because he was far from the parsons and priests, and the missionaries and the government bureaucrats, the looks, and the downcast eyes, he was now able to remember. It had happened a few weeks ago. It was early morning when he'd stepped out onto the front porch of his house. The sun hadn't risen over the mountains yet. It was cold out. At first, it felt like a "senior moment." But he wasn't really old. He was fifty now. But the English word for what he saw wouldn't come. What came instead was *bihci*, then *duollu*, then *ritni*, then . . . nothing. Not even English. The words melted into a small puddle on the porch rail. It had left him with a hollow feeling. He had finally remembered the English word, though, on his way to his truck. There was frost on the truck's windows. Frost on the road to the harbor. *Frost*—that was the word.

Now Isak went back into *Miss Janet*'s cabin and shut the door and then headed across the strait. Back in Wrangell, he unloaded his four salmon at the seafood plant and tied his boat up in the harbor. He got into his small truck and headed to the post office before going home. The post office was an old building left over from Wrangell Fort days. It had been refurbished over and over again. The post office wasn't open, but the lobby was unlocked so folks could check their mail after-hours. Inside the lobby the old brass mailboxes gleamed. One might imagine there were treasures inside: a shiny bar of gold, an old coin, a single ruby. Each box was magic, bringing Stallo. No, here it was Raven the trickster. The trickster left the white envelopes in the boxes: a license to fish halibut, a license to fish for dungies, a renewal notice, a property tax, a business license, a permit. Then again, maybe it *was* Stallo. Stallo was meaner than Raven, scarier. He'd never imagined Raven as scary, but like a brown-skinned man with long black hair, sometimes with a bird's beak. Sometimes Raven appeared in his head as a black bird. But Stallo was different. Stallo was a troll. Stallo was ugly and vicious and stole children and drowned people. Uncle? What the heck was Uncle doing that caused his boat to flip sideways? Sure, Uncle shrimped with a beam trawl so that could happen, but Uncle was experienced. He couldn't think about it.

Isak fumbled for his keys inside his wool jacket. He grabbed the key ring, and as he brought his right hand up to the keyhole, he stopped, his breath caught in his throat. A white patch of skin spread between his forefinger and his middle finger. It looked like he'd dropped Clorox onto his hand. He flicked it, but it didn't come off. He brushed it on his jacket. He hurried and opened the post office box and removed one white envelope, a letter from the Fish and Wildlife office. Probably they wanted him to renew his license to hunt deer, or worse, they wanted him to report he didn't get any deer when he hunted. Who reports nothing? Nothing is nothing. Bullshit paperwork. There was a time when there wasn't paperwork. His family used to hunt for deer whenever they needed to eat. They knew when the deer were fat and when they were thin, when they were rutting, when they had babies.

They knew when the deer would be in the mountains and when the deer would be on the beach. They'd learned this from living on this island for generations, from living among the Tlingit. But this was another world. Now there were tags, and licenses, and permits, and stickers, and even signs. Everything had to be written and documented. He tried to avoid it. They wanted him to pay them money to get a license and tags. He gritted his teeth and opened the envelope. Crap! He took a deep breath. They, the state, the feds, whatever, were denying him a permit to fish halibut. What the heck? It must be a mistake. He walked over to the garbage can sitting beside a tall wood table. He ripped the envelope in half and dropped it into the can. He paused. If it was Stallo, he didn't want to jinx anything. He didn't like to speak bad about it. Them. Even though it was bad. It was the same with the Tlingits: careful what you say out loud. He stuck his arm into the garbage can and retrieved the two halves of the envelope and stuffed them and his mail keys into his coat pocket.

Back in his truck, he placed his hands on the steering wheel. "Fuck," he said out loud. This time, on his left hand another white spot spread across his knuckles. By the time he got home, the spot had grown larger. Inside the house, he hid his hands from his wife, Liv. She didn't need to know yet. But then, what if he gave it to her? Whatever it was? In the bathroom he stood at the toilet afraid to unzip his pants. But he had to pee. He inhaled and unzipped. He made a sound like a kid, and then muffled it. He didn't want Liv to come marching into the bathroom. If he'd closed his eyes it would have felt normal. It would have been normal. But it wasn't. The white spot was much bigger now.

In their small kitchen, he sat down to dinner with his wife. Liv had made a good meal of creamed shrimp on toast. He ate with his right hand, the one with the smaller spot. She didn't seem to notice. He kept his left hand sitting on his lap. Liv didn't ask him about his day. As always, she waited for him to talk. Silence was one of their familiar houseguests. It had always been this way. Halfway through dinner he asked her what she did today. But he didn't really listen. She said something about the phone company where she worked part-time: their new billing system was crappy. She had gone grocery shopping. She worked in the garden. Finally, he nodded to the two ripped pieces of envelope on the table. "I got that in the mail. It's a letter from the state. It's about the halibut moratorium." *Moratorium* was a stupid word. No one he'd known had ever used that word before the government started regulating the halibut fishery.

"I fished," he said. "Me and Luther fished together on his boat that couple of years. My knee hurt. I couldn't fish by myself. He offered to help. He got the permits."

Liv nodded. "I remember. I told you to—"

He held up his right hand to stop her. She stared at his hand, but she didn't say anything.

"I know," he said. "Remember when I didn't fill out the paperwork, and then you made me. I did. I told them all about the halibut I fished for all these years. I told them I was fishing with Luther. I gave them all the receipts I could find. But I didn't get a permit. I didn't get one. This here says it." He waved one half of the envelope. "They say I can't fish without it. They aren't issuing any more."

Liv set her fork down on the plate. Was she going to say "I told you so"? She sometimes did that. She'd warned him that Luther was going to screw him over. But Luther was his friend. Sure, he'd hinted to Luther about how he should write a letter on his behalf to the state about how they'd partnered. He'd always thought of it as a partnership. But Luther died last year. Liver failure. Luther's son or daughter would probably get the permit to fish halibut now. His son was a teacher in Nome, and his daughter worked for the city.

"Can you appeal?" Liv finally said.

Isak picked up the letter and read it, trying to make sense of their language, which blurred on the page: verifiable date on such participation; non-viable amounts of QS; allocation formula. "I think so." But he wasn't sure. Maybe he'd fish anyway? It's not like anyone told on anyone in Wrangell. People were tight-lipped, unless you were sleeping with their wife, or something like that. So what if he fished without a permit? They'd think he was dumb. Stupid Lapp. Dump Lapp. All his life he'd heard the words, "Lapp Family," "Savages," "Trolls," "Midgets," "Card People," "Dirty Folk." His father had said, "We're Finnish." Only Finnish: that's what he was supposed to be. He'd said the word *Finnish* almost as many times as he'd written those other words on the chalk board so long ago. On the first government paper he'd ever filled out, he'd checked the box "Other." It might have been a credit account at the grocery store, or maybe it was a NOAA form. But after a while of filling out paperwork, he finally started to check "Finnish." It was easier. If you checked "Other" there was a space for what "Other" meant. He didn't know how to describe himself.

Now, Isak set the piece of envelope down. Liv took another bite of her dinner. She was usually opinionated, saying what she felt she had to say. Maybe she didn't want a fight. He held up both of his hands above his second helping of creamed shrimp. He twisted them for her to see. "I'm turning white."

She laughed, and then a frown crossed her face. "I'm sorry, I didn't mean to laugh. I . . . I don't know why I laughed. Jeez." She reached over toward his hands, but he pulled them away.

"No, it might be catchy."

"Oh? What is it?"

"I don't know. Can you look it up?" He meant in their encyclopedia set.

Liv got up from the table. "I'll do it now."

He pushed his second helping aside. She hadn't finished her dinner, either. He followed her to the small desk in the corner of the living room. From a nearby bookshelf she pulled out her Home Medical Encyclopedia and set it on the desk. She sat down and thumbed through to the skin section. Isak stood behind her, as she touched a photo of a dark skinned man holding up his blotchy forearm. In another photo, a white spotted hand splayed out with fingers wide.

Now, he stood behind Liv as she typed into the search engine the words: skin turning white. She clicked the word "image." Immediately, photos filled the screen—people with blotchy skin.

"Wow," he said.

Liv clicked on an image: a man leaned toward the camera, his fore-arms white, the rest of him brown. She clicked on another photo of the dead pop star Michael Jackson. They stared at it for a minute or so. And in another photo, a hand splayed out, with a body of water in the background. He splayed his hand out like the one in the photo and turned his white fingers around. Liv twisted around to look up at him. As he rotated his hand, the white spot spread up his arm. He felt it moving up to his elbow. He wanted to tear his shirt off, to rub and wash and wipe. It wouldn't do any good. Tomorrow he'd go see old Doc Heggan. Maybe Doc Heggan would have a pill? Or a shot. Something.

Isak stared at the people and the limbs on the screen: the unsmiling faces, the shoulders and feet exposed. He felt the white spot spreading now to his groin, down his thighs. He wiggled his toes, pigment mov-ing over his whole body like a creation story. He held up his hand again, turning it around, and imagined his body now looked like the nautical charts on his boat, reforming itself at mean low water: 150 fathoms, 121 fathoms, Stikine Strait, Mud Bay, Wrangell Island: a snow goose flying to the river flats.

Date: 1990s
Recorded by John Swanton
Assisted by Tooch Waterson

The Switching Season

This year's switching seasons flared when the cottonwood was especially sweet, when the salmon swam thick at Babbler Point. This year's
season caught Rikka up in it. Every three years or so, the season floats
down the Stikine River along with downy cottonwood seeds, resting
like dust on windowsills and settling on the rims of open beer bottles.
During the season, cousins marry cousins, best friends sleep with best
friends, older women leave husbands for younger men and, on occasion, a man leaves his wife for a man or a wife leaves her husband for
another man's wife.

With her only child in public school all day, Rikka had found work
at Dr. Modon's as his dental secretary. The first spring she'd worked for
Doc, he'd invited her and her husband, Sven, out on his boat. Several
years before, Doc Modon had purchased a forty-foot troller, the *Ocean
Maiden*. The *Ocean Maiden*, built in Seattle in the 1950s, had a steel
hull and was painted white with a fine blue strip licking her stern. A
marine oil stove and a small table warmed the pilothouse, a couple of
bunks snugged down in her bow. She was rigged for salmon trolling
and halibut long-lining. She was beautiful. She was perfect.

Doc had taken them for a ride around Woronofski Island. The
Ocean Maiden handled the small chop well. Like rocking a baby, her
bow went up and down. Near Elephants Nose, the northern point of
the island, Doc let Rikka steer while Sven and Doc tried their hand at

trolling. She steered and sketched the landscape in her drawing book. She sketched sea creatures, the *Ocean Maiden*, life on Wrangell Island.

Rikka had spent most of her life around boats. Her father, Isak Laukonen, was a fisherman. She'd nearly grown up on the *Miss Janet*. He'd told her that boats were like women and you had to treat them right: paint yearly, maintain the engine, and keep the hull clean from barnacles.

Now she sat in the dentist office going over the day's appointments: an amalgam filling, a crown. She opened the window to enjoy the cottonwood scent. The scent reminded her of the day Doc had tilted her backward in his state-of-the-art Sting dental chair and rubbed her shoulders. At first, she thought it was a mistake, but he kept talking of fitting snap-ons to longline gear.

It wouldn't happen again, she'd told herself. So it surprised her, really, when she found herself packing a bag, a note tucked into her jeans from Doc that said, "Meet me after work down at Reliance Harbor." Doc closed the dental office for three months every summer so he could commercial fish. This time, he'd invited Rikka along. He told her he wanted her bad. She wasn't falling for that line, but she couldn't resist the thought of spending the entire summer with salmon scales stuck to her XtraTufs. Her sister promised to watch her kid for the summer, and she figured Sven and the rest of the family would pick up the slack.

As soon as the *Ocean Maiden* slipped out of the harbor, Rikka stripped down to her bra and panties and lay on a blanket on the bow, the Cummins diesel rumbling beneath her. It was the end of May and the whales were bubble-feeding in front of town. She filled a whole sketchbook that summer, but when she returned home from the fishing season, she found Sven had filed for a divorce.

❀

Three years later, Doc set a photo on Rikka's desk. "What's this?" she asked, picking up a photo of a large house on a beach.

"It's your dream home," Doc said.

"You bought this?" She wasn't really asking. How could he have done this without asking her first?

"Done deal," Doc replied, leaning over the counter to kiss her.

Rikka turned her head so his kiss planted on her cheek.

He looked confused. "It's a surprise. I bought a house and property on Orcas Island in the San Juans, Washington State."

"You did?" Of course he did. He was impulsive. But why wouldn't he buy something in Wrangell?

"Yeah, it's your house on the beach."

"Ah . . . ah . . ." She didn't know what to say. Really? She would rather live *on* the water in a float-house, a live-aboard, or a house on pilings. Actually, she'd always thought one day she'd live on the *Ocean Maiden*.

The phone rang. Good, an interruption. She had to figure out what to say to him. She answered the phone. Mrs. Ingram cancelled her appointment. She hung up.

Doc tilted his head sideways. "Is there something the matter?"

"No," she said, standing up. She walked around the counter and stood near the window overlooking the harbor. She rubbed her finger on the soft white fuzz along the windowsill and inhaled the sweet cottonwood scent wafting inside the room.

Doc walked over to her and set his hand on her shoulder. "I'm retiring April 1. I've sold the *Ocean Maiden* to the new postmaster, Willy Lundgren."

She turned. "You did what?"

"I got a good price for the boat and permits. There are two docs coming to town to look at my practice. They're very interested."

She shrugged his hand off and walked back to her desk. "You never talked to me about this." She took a deep breath and sat down. How could he have done this without asking? *I'm not going anywhere. Ever.*

"You told me how you want to live on the water," he said, almost pleading.

"*On* the water and *here* in Wrangell." She shook her head. What was he thinking? She'd told him her dreams. She'd shared her drawings with him. She'd sketched girdies and running lights, and had told him how she felt when she first stepped on board the *Ocean Maiden*, how her body swayed with the sea. "Why would you sell her?"

"Who?"

"*Ocean*, the *Ocean Maiden*."

"I wanted to surprise you. I thought . . . we can retire and be together. You'll have everything."

"Everything?" No, that wasn't true. She would have nothing. Nothing at all. She would have no contour lines, or vanishing points. Her canvas would be blank.

❁

Rikka handed her job application to Colleen at the post office window. It had all happened so quickly: Doc Modon retired, sold his practice, and left town. Now she could see Willy Lundgren stacking boxes on a back shelf. He didn't look so bad. His middle-age paunch didn't seem too big. He still had most of his hair.

"Willy," Colleen called back to him. "Rikka is applying for the job."

Willy came over to the counter. He grinned at her at the same time he adjusted the collar on his postal uniform.

"I need the job," she half smiled at him. She knew how to do this: a shy smile, look directly into his eyes. Then be confident. Make him guess.

"Don't you work for Doc?" he asked.

She sighed. "He sold his business. I don't want to work for the new dentist and I also heard you need a deckhand on the *Ocean Maiden*." She'd heard no one wanted to work for him. He was a greenhorn captain: the worse kind. The kind where the deckhands had to do all the work, especially if they were experienced and wanted to make money.

Willy looked her over. "You have experience with boats?"

"Oh, yes. Lots," she smiled, recalling the tang of diesel-soaked wood and salt spray, salmon scent on her rubber gloves, bright silver salmon slapping at her feet. There was nothing like porpoise free-riding the *Ocean Maiden*'s bow and the rigging-chime clanking her to sleep at night. There was nothing like her in the whole wide world.

Date: early 1990s
Recorded by Tooch Waterson

52-Hertz

Scientists have been unable to identify the species of the 52-Hertz whale, which was discovered by a team of oceanographers in 1989. As of 2004 the whale has been detected every year since. It travels as far north as the Aleutian and Kodiak Islands. Scientists call it "the Loneliest Whale in the world." They speculate it could be malformed or a hybrid of a blue whale and another species.—Wikipedia

Stories are moon jellyfish. Stories are wormwood, old-man's-beard moss, a timeworn gravestone. Tova traced the outline of driftwood in the palm of her hand. This, too, was a story. How far did the driftwood float to get to the beach where she found it? Was it lonely out there on the sea? She turned to her grandfather, Isak, who sat beside her on the porch overlooking the ocean. The fishcamp had been in their family for five generations. Only twelve years old and she knew how to live off the land. At fishcamp, every summer, her mother's family fished, picked berries, and harvested crabs and shrimp. Every fall they put up deer and moose. This was Tlingit land, originally, but for generations this had been Isak's Fishcamp, named after her grandfather and great-grandfather. Did her Tlingit ancestors fish and hunt here? They probably did. But her dad never talked about it. Sometimes he told her he was a "good Indian," but she didn't know what that meant. Did he mean he knew how to fish and hunt? Or did it mean he didn't like the taste of seal meat, that he liked hamburger from the store better?

Grandpa Isak ate seal meat whenever his friends gave him some. Now he sat behind a small card table. A bald eagle feasted on the beach beyond their porch. On the table, several chunks of red cedar formed a small pile and a tackle box filled with tools sat near the table's edge. Grandpa Isak picked up a small block of red cedar. He sliced off a chunk. "Do you want to make pegs?"

"Sure." Tova stood up and put the driftwood she'd been holding on top of the porch railing. She could make herring pegs. She'd seen Grandpa make them before. A lost art, he'd told her. She had seen how he inserted the narrow, pencil-like object in his herring, bending the herring into the right arch. Salmon like the scent of cedar, he'd said. Probably true. A lot of things happened in the ocean she didn't understand but still believed.

Tova sat back down in the lawn chair. She loved hanging out with elders, although Grandpa Isak wouldn't like it if she called him an elder. He'd just laugh. He laughed a lot. Every summer she'd spent as much time as she could at fishcamp. Already, her mom, rather than staying all summer at camp, had taken a job at the deli back in Wrangell, on another island four miles across the strait. Her grandmother, Liv, worked in town and traveled out to camp once in a while. All her aunties had town jobs now, too. And lately, her dad had been talking about how she was old enough for a summer job. By "getting a job" he meant doing something stupid like working in a relative's garden or learning to mow lawns, maybe even babysitting. This should be her job: listening to Grandpa Isak's stories, remembering them. Grandpa Isak's friends had good stories too. Often a troller or two would anchor in the bay out front for the night. The fishermen would get in their skiffs and row to the cabin to join them for coffee and a story: one of the best times of the day.

She'd decided if she could, she'd be a storyteller when she grew up. But was there such a thing? Did people make a living telling stories? She loved stories and it seemed stories loved her too. They were everywhere. Once, she lifted a patch of seaweed on a rock and a story lay beneath it, stuck to the rock like a gumboot. Another time, a bald eagle rose up to glide on the air current with a story entangled beneath its wings. Stories dangled in the blueberry bushes, were heaped in piles at the local garbage dump, and even slept at Cousin Cory's HUD house.

Now, Grandpa Isak handed her a knife and a small piece of red cedar. "Cut a chunk off like this," he said, demonstrating.

Tova hesitated then sliced a thin piece from the cedar. The best stories, though, were discovered while doing camp work. The problem was never about getting Grandpa to talk, it was to getting him to tell a different story, one she hadn't heard before.

"Grandpa, did you ever hear of people who can call whales to shore? Our people, I mean."

"Our people? Which ones, the Irish, Norwegians, Finnish? Lapps?"

"Yes, Lapps." She'd hesitated when she said the word *Lapps*. Mom had told her not to say that word. "Mom says we're Sámi. She is and you are too."

Grandpa didn't respond. He sat there whittling on the cedar. She was used to silence, how her elders paused and thought about things before they spoke. Sometimes she'd ask a question and wouldn't get the answer for a day, maybe more.

"Are we?" she asked again.

"Yes."

"So how come you never told me."

He shrugged. "I didn't think I had to. We just are."

"Oh." She'd heard her mom's stories, the stories had come to her bedroom from down the hall in the early morning hours. Those stories, the ones she wasn't supposed to know, smelled like coffee. Her aunties and mom would tell them, never Grandpa Isak. The stories floated like jellyfish migrating down to her room. She slept with the door open because she liked the sliver of light from the bathroom to be her nightlight. She hated dark bedrooms. Often a word in the story like *spank*, *hit*, and *cry* would jar her from her early morning sleep. Her bones would ache as if the stories had gone down stinging through her pajamas and into her bones.

Sure, she could shut the door so she couldn't hear about a great-grandmother who wasn't allowed to cry in her own language. Or a great-grandfather who was mean to everyone around him. That grandfather, when he was a kid, beat up other kids. And when he grew up, he beat up other men, and even beat up his wife and kids. Then there was an uncle who killed himself, an aunt who drank, another aunt who gave her baby away, or maybe the story was someone took the baby. Maybe the same aunt who drank was the one who gave up her baby? She didn't know. But what she did know was someone had to remember the baby was last seen wrapped in a small yellow blanket. And someone had to remember the baby's name was Heidi. That was all she knew. The name and an image of a yellow blanket was all she would ever have.

Grandpa Isak showed her how to hold the piece of red cedar, slice it thin, and then form it into a peg. He was careful but fast. She took in every detail. Remember. Remember. Remember. Remember how he holds the knife. Remember how slow he moves it on the edge of the wood.

Tova held the cedar chunk in her hand, shaped more like an old barge, the kind tugs towed back and forth among the islands. She held it up to the sky. The light wood could lift up and fly away if she carved it like a bird. But maybe Grandpa would let her carve it like a boat. The cedar would float on the ocean for sure. Her driftwood piece, though, still lying on the railing, she wasn't sure about. Would it float? It had floated in to the beach, hadn't it? Grandpa had taught her how to tell the difference between a spruce, a hemlock, and a cedar in the forest, and recently he'd been teaching her how to tell what tree a piece of driftwood originated from. This driftwood was heavier than the cedar, likely made from spruce. She'd placed the driftwood on the porch rail, balancing it ten feet above the ocean below. She closed one eye. From that perspective the driftwood looked like a whale. She raised herself up in her chair, nearly standing, until the tideline beyond matched up with the porch rail. In her line of sight, the driftwood appeared to float right on the water.

She sat back down in her chair. "Can we call whales to shore?"

Grandpa Isak sighed. "I don't know about the 'we' part. Shamans used to do that kind of thing."

Shaman? She'd heard that word before. Her aunties and her mom had talked about a healer who was burned. What had he done? She couldn't remember. That was probably important. How was she going to be a storyteller if she couldn't remember?

Grandpa Isak suddenly made a crying sound. She jumped. She'd heard that sound a hundred times. It sounded like a whale. She held her own breath, afraid she'd make the same sound if she exhaled too.

"Like that?" he finally said, taking a deep breath in.

Tova nodded and then she laughed. "I guess. Yes . . . like that."

Grandpa laughed too. Grandpa Isak set another finished peg down onto a pile of pegs. "I think the chowder is done. Ready for dinner?"

Inside the cabin, salmon chowder simmered in a pot on the woodstove. She placed two bowls, two small plates, and silverware on the table by the window. Grandpa brought the hot pot over and set it in the middle of the old plywood table. He never used a hot pad to protect the table. Heat rings staining it reminded her of a star chart. The new heat ring, bigger than the other rings, could be the sun.

During dinner, Grandpa Isak told her that while she was out beachcombing, her dad had called on the radio. "He says he found you a job. He's coming to get you next week. Thursday."

What? She didn't want to go yet. She wasn't ready. She'd never be ready. She still had to help put up more fish. Then she wanted to experiment with making low-sugar jam from the blueberries. She loved it here. It was so peaceful and quiet. The tide rolled up to the big logs on the beach near the cabin. The waves sounded like curtains in the wind. A kingfisher chattered from the roof in the mornings. Small boats zipped by, and whales puffed their breath into the air. Back in town, in her noisy neighborhood, five homeschooled kids lived next door. A chainsaw carver lived three houses down. Sometimes it seemed like he carved in her living room. Bears made better neighbors.

After chowder and homemade biscuits she helped Grandpa Isak clean up the kitchen. Afterward, they played a game of rummy. There was no TV out here on this island. Tomorrow, they'd start the smoking fish process and then can it up for the winter. This was the best part of summer, when everything, even her hair, reeked of fish scent and smoke.

When Tova finally crawled into her bed, it wasn't even dark outside, though it was fairly late. She loved that about summer. Her bed sat below the open window and despite the lumps in the mattress, it felt good at the end of the day. The wind rattled the eaves of the old cabin as she started to fall asleep. Suddenly, she sat upright. She'd forgotten the driftwood on the railing. Through her bedroom window, she could see the front porch. The wood wasn't on the railing. It had blown off. Darn. She liked that piece. It would have been a good one to add to her beach collection. At the end of the season, she usually returned home with assorted seashells, driftwood, and chunks of bear bread. She didn't know what she was saving the stuff for. She put it in a wood box beneath her bed. They were stories for later.

That night, breath from the ocean rose high into the sky, mixing with her dream world. At first she couldn't tell if she swam underwater or walked on land. She turned when she heard the big puff of air. A large eye stared at her. She wasn't afraid of the creature. She was curious. She knew it was a whale even though she couldn't see its entire shape. Then she was on the beach again. Her feet stepped on the popweed. It was cold. She put her arms around herself. She could feel things in her dreams: a gray cold day, an empty stomach, a fluffy pillow. And she usually dreamed in color. At first everything in this dream was blue and now it was orange: seaweed, sky, sun. The cold and the color pulled her in, blended her with the land. She lay back, like she was a moon jellyfish floating on the ocean, but in this dream the water and the land were one. Then the dream took her with it, became a story like returning salmon in the current, like the morning sun rising over the islands. She circled the island, flowed along with it, rounding Point Highfield, past Deadmans Island, down Eastern Channel, and down around Southeast Cove and up past Old Town, and back up Zimovia Strait toward home.

❁

Outside, the small piece of driftwood absorbed the sea again, filling it to its seams. The ancient whorls of time the tree had once gathered in its rings now absorbed the knowledge of diatoms and seaweed, salt particles and sand. The driftwood grew and grew until it filled out its shape. The oil from the girl's hands mixed in its skin and memory. And when the driftwood rolled and spun and balanced itself on the sea, the wood realized it had changed into something else. And the current took it back home, toward the old cabin with the porch next to the sea. And there, the whale blew its first breath high into the blue-dark night.

Date: 1990s
Recorded by John Swanton
Assisted by Tooch Waterson

The Woman Who Governs the Tides

Kirsti liked to stand in front of her window naked. The urge to stand in front of any window, in fact, sometimes flooded her, filling her thoughts with silt. She couldn't think clearly unless she was naked in front of the window. Today, though, she sat at a small table by herself at the Wrangell Public Library, a stack of books in front of her, and among them, *Bathymetry Understood* and *Boater's Bowditch*. Books were good distractions from windows, from looking out at the ocean. The big picture window at home framed her in this world where she didn't feel like she fit in, a Scandinavian woman among the Tlingits. Yet, she didn't fit in in Petersburg either, the home of the Petersburg Vikings. Actually, she was Finnish. Grandma had told Mother who told her. The story was never the same when it was repeated. "Your great-grandmother was a prostitute who was working at the cannery in Petersburg. She got pregnant and a Tlingit couple adopted the baby girl and took her to Wrangell. Your grandmother was blonde and fair-skinned and was raised as Tlingit."

Sometimes the story would add a French prostitute, or a Filipino father, but as Kirsti stood in the window tracing her hands over her pale skin, her reflection told the story of dishwater-blonde hair hanging over her shoulders and a long lean body. She was probably Finnish. Based on what she'd read about their women and views on sex, she was most definitely Finnish.

Her apartment sat up on the knoll with a view of the beach and the waves splashing on the rocks the city had piled to build the low road below her house. Every morning, she'd stand in the window, about nine o'clock, after her shower when she was freshest. In front of the window, the moon pulled her; the waves rose and fell, even though the waves couldn't reach across the road, and up the grassy yard and the long driveway, to her apartment over the Troutte family's garage.

A week ago, she'd pulled her blinds for good. At first the waves out front of the harbor were calm, a bit too calm. Then they became violent, like they were rolling under her skin. A week ago, the police department had sent a young officer and she'd answered the door respectfully, in her bathrobe, loosely tied. The officer told her the neighbor, a mother of two teenage boys, complained she stood in the window with no clothes on every morning. What? She wasn't showing off for the neighbors, she was letting the clouds caress her skin, the waxing moon sigh through her cells, the curl of wave rush over her thighs. They had been watching her? Maybe it would be better to live in Sitka, with the wet ocean on your upper lip, always ready to waft into your nostrils. She'd always wanted to live in Sitka. Sitka smelled more like the ocean than Wrangell.

Who was she kidding, though? If she pulled the shades, if she no longer stood in the window, there would be consequences. So why was she sitting at the library next to the big window overlooking the street, and beyond, the ocean, provoking the high water swaying like a slow dancer against the seawall? Could she deal with the consequences of denying herself the pleasure of an open window, of framing herself in syzygy and neap tides? But, of course, people would have to deal with that. She was tired of dealing with things. Maybe she could move to Petersburg, where there were more millionaires per capita than anywhere else in the United States, or so she was told. In Petersburg, fish guts smelled like money. But that idea soon waned like a faded yellow moon: there was a new man in town. She loved the new men who wandered into town and the stories they brought with them of the Outside, Down South, which was what townsfolk called the rest of the United States.

Her grandmother had told her the new guy in town was a marine biologist. He'd already been all over town interviewing elders, attempting to learn the Tlingit words for the critters on the beach and the beach greens. This intrigued her because, since there was no college in Wrangell, she spent a lot of time at the library reading books, devouring books, actually. As for the men, it wasn't their bodies she loved, it was their brains, the way they could tell her about the long bolt engine design on the new Merc outboard or the I-beam structure in the hull of their skiffs.

And, if she was honest with herself, she even liked local men. Dating them was a problem, though. In her experience, men wanted women to let *them* fix things, like the hot water heater whistling when she turned it up too high. She could fix that herself. She'd replaced the element in her oven, wired a new light in the dining area, made a shelf with her new miter saw, and screwed her entertainment center together without reading the directions. She'd been learning to fend for herself since she got a great job at Hammer's Hardware. At Hammer's they sold everything from cigarette lighters to skates of halibut gear. She knew where every nut and bolt, power saw, and fish hook was located. After a year of working there, locals started asking for *her*. They didn't want the young men who worked there, or even the cranky owner— that old Norwegian, Mr. Gunnar Hammer—to help. Pretty soon she had dates. Quite often she'd be asked out in the nuts and bolts section, while she bent over digging through the bins, asking about the best way to screw in the bolts: an electric drill or a cordless? The question frequently ended with a date. Eventually the gentlemen would come over to her house to help her *fix* something.

A man who fixed the light in the refrigerator stayed late and the tide had gone down to a minus 3.3 feet and everyone went clam digging. Someone even brought a bucket of clams for her. She'd made clam fritters for the next gentleman who came to fix the overhead light in her bedroom. She thought it might have been a short in the light switch.

Another time, the high school principal helped her fix her bathtub leak. Later, he'd told her that when he saw her hair, the same shade as bull kelp, floating in the tub around her, it made her look like a mermaid.

Up and down, and up and down, the tides went, moving pretty regularly for several years. She loved this regularity. But then, it seemed she'd begun to run out of loose door hinges and leaky faucets and her dates dwindled. Still, she helped everyone out at the hardware store. She still leaned over the bin of washers just so, and tightened her work apron, the one with the large screwdriver on it. Now she only noticed a scrawny arm or five o'clock shadow. She was bored. Maybe what she needed was not a date but love, real love, the kind rushing up the shore and holding you against a beach log. The kind swirling around your blue mussels and licked your supralittoral zone. After all, it seemed all her high school friends were now on their second husbands. But if she chose from the townsfolk, she'd have to pick a third cousin twice removed or a high school fling whose lovers she also knew. Now that she thought about it, what she needed was someone new in town, which is how she came to find herself at the library reading John R. Swanton's *Tlingit Myths and Texts*. She needed to create her own myth.

Kirsti's story pulled toward her—a young man walked through the door lugging his heavy backpack. She tried to look away, but she noted the way he carried himself, like a hunter in the forest. Had she seen him around town before? She thought she had. He came right toward her and set his backpack on the large round table where she sat. As he settled himself into a chair, she bent her head, trying her best to read the story "The Woman Taken Away by the Frog People" when she felt her cheeks flush. *Flustered* is what her mother called it. "Now don't go getting flustered, Kirsti," she'd say. Flustered, she figured, was a sensation that happened when her body was acted on by the gravity of another body, when the strain on both bodies distorted them.

The young man pulled a stack of books out of his backpack and then went over the librarian's desk. She heard him say something about an interlibrary loan and then she looked down at his books. She ran her fingers across the book spines: *Marine Mammals of Alaska, Life in a Tide Pool*, *Tlingit Language Dictionary*. Her fingers traced a book of Latin terms for Alaska sea creatures. She loved *Eumetopias jubatus*, *Megaptera novaeangliae*, and *Gavia pacifica*. She knew some of them in the Tlingit language: *taan* and *yáay* and *kageet*, sea lion, humpback whale, and loon, terms her grandmother could remember, but the language had been dead in her family for a long time now. An aunt once mentioned something about relatives who were punished for speaking Tlingit, and she'd heard stories about kids being abused at the Wrangell Institute. Now, here was a guy from out of town trying to learn the Tlingit words. Good luck. People around here didn't like to give up their stories. Share them, sure, over a cup of black boat coffee, or sitting side by side at a picnic table at City Park.

The young man walked back over to the table. Kirsti was still flipping through his book. She saw him looking at her. "Oh, sorry." She set the book back on his stack. "It's just that new things interest me."

He sat down and held out his hand. "I'm Tooch. Tooch Waterson."

"Kirsti," she said, feeling that same flush move through her body. "So, you're the marine biologist?"

"News travels around here," Tooch replied.

"We don't call it news. We call it stories. Our stories travel fast and keep on going."

"Yes, that explains it," he said.

"Explains what?" Oh, right, sometimes when she talked in metaphors, people would politely excuse themselves. She fingered her hair, which was draped over a shoulder and hung down in front of her. She was comforted by her hair and often held onto a piece of it, like a baby sea otter clinging to bull kelp.

"Well, so far I've heard I was a gay writer, a gay biologist, a gay photographer—" He paused and reached for his own black hair tied behind his head in a loose ponytail, with a beaded band around it.

She let her hair fall from her hands. Was he trying to relate to her?

"I'm doing research and working for an ethnographer recording First Nation stories."

"First Nation?"

"Oh, sorry, Alaska Natives. I'm from the Interior. Telegraph Creek, up the Stikine. I'm an Interior Tlingit."

"Oh, I thought there were only Tahltans up there."

"No, there are both."

Kirsti fidgeted in her chair, linking her ankles and pressing them hard like a wind blowing steady across the ocean, inducing counter-rotating cells on her surface. Maybe this guy was one of those intellects who thought they could tell what a woman was thinking. She hoped not, because right now he was in her apartment, in her bed lying next to her with the curtains fluttering.

"So, are you from Wrangell?" he asked, interrupting her thoughts.

"Yeah, born and raised."

"Doesn't that get boring?"

"I wouldn't want to live anywhere else. I can't really . . . live . . . anywhere else. I think about moving once in a while, but it'd have to be near water. I love the water, the Stikine, the Inside Passage."

"I know what you mean." He picked up one of his books. He started to thumb through it. "I was raised by the upper rivers. But here, near the ocean, this is lovely. I'm drawn here too."

"Drawn?"

"Well, my work draws me. I've been working in Wrangell off and on over the years. This time I'm studying the local beaches, their flora, and their creatures for the UAF School of Fisheries. I love naming things. Taxonomy, you know."

"I know. I love hearing the words . . ."

"Really? You know, I've been having trouble lately because the tides around here are really weird. It's November and we're supposed to be getting higher tides, which means lower ones, too, but that's not happening." Tooch reached for his bright orange tide book. "See, this dot says it's going to be a minus three-foot tide today, and it wasn't. It hardly went out. Whenever I ask around town, people say it's been like that for a while now but they have nothing to do with that. They tell me to call the government."

Kirsti smiled. "Yes, I suppose it's been frustrating for everyone, especially the clam diggers and the fishermen who troll according to the tides."

"Sounds like you know a lot about the stories here."

"Stories? I suppose." Yeah, maybe she did know too much about everyone, all their countercurrents and undercurrents. "Well," she said, standing, "I'd better go. I have to go home and see what's wrong with my window in the living room. It leaks when it rains."

"Oh," he said.

Of course it really wasn't leaking, but she kept hearing his voice, as he lay on her pillow saying those Tlingit words, over and over again in her ear. She'd heard the language spoken a few times, and now she imagined those delicious sounds scraping the back of his throat. And the Latin, oh the Latin. There would be words she had never heard before, new meanings.

"I don't know what to do," she said. "I live alone and have to fix my own stuff. You know that little tool with bent plastic handles. It looks like scissors."

"Pliers?" Tooch asked, raising his eyebrows.

"Yeah, that thing."

"Um . . . I can help you check the leaky window. I'm handy with tools. Helped my parents build their house."

"Really?"

"Sure," he said. "But how about something for lunch in exchange? I'm tired of restaurant burgers."

She smiled. "Of course, sounds like a deal." Kirsti gathered up her books, shoved them into a big bag, and headed out of the library.

Tooch followed her outside as she headed right toward the ferry terminal. At the terminal, she headed left, back the same direction, but down a small one-way street right next to the ocean. She turned to Tooch. "I like to walk along the seawall whenever I can. So I'm taking the long way home."

"Oh, okay."

She started to walk faster, taking brisk, long steps. This left Tooch a few paces behind. Soon she was about twenty-five yards in front of him, and she turned but only waited a few seconds. She continued to walk, with him following behind her. She'd been told she swayed when she walked. Hopefully, he didn't find it odd. Her hair swung back and forth across her back. They walked along the seawall that had been built and rebuilt over the years. The tide rose higher, almost to the road, and, as she walked, the waves seemed to roll in and follow along behind her as if they wanted to lick her heels. She turned slightly again, checking on Tooch. Behind him, the water was calm. She nodded to him.

She led Tooch through town along Campbell Drive and then down to the low road and on to her house. She reached her apartment before him and stood on the porch above the garage, waiting for Tooch to come up over the slight hill. When she saw him, she waved and he turned and walked up her driveway.

As soon as he was inside her apartment, she noticed him staring at the large wall in the living room. "Clock collector?" he asked, noting that more than a dozen brass round objects on the wall.

"No, those are tide meters. I collect them."

Tooch set his pack by the door, took off his shoes, and wandered over, examining the tide meters. There were brass ones, some with elaborate maps, and some plain, a few others set on a long coffee table nearby. She stood beside him, nearly touching shoulders. "I'm in sync with semidiurnal tides," she said. Tooch reached to touch a brass tide clock.

She leaned in next to him. He smelled like wet hemlock trees. Nice. She leaned back.

Tooch walked over to a large picture window, with blinds pulled across it. "Is this the leaky window?"

"Yeah, but it's really not that bad." No, it wasn't really bad but he didn't need to know that. Yes, it leaked a bit, but what window or roof in Wrangell didn't? It rained a lot and all the time.

Tooch peeked through the blind. "I'll bet you have a great view from here."

"Oh, yes, I do . . ." She didn't move to open the blinds and instead sat down in a rocking chair. She reached for one of her antique tide clocks on the coffee table. "I think this one is broken," she said. "I bought it at a garage sale a few years ago. Never could get it to work."

"How's this one supposed to work?" Tooch picked up a sand glass filled with sand.

"Well, it indicates high tide when you turn it on the green side, and the blue side is low tide. By the time the sand gets to one side, the tide has completed a cycle. Chicken noodle soup. Would you like a bowl? Tuna sandwich?"

She got up and Tooch followed her to the kitchen, where they sat at a small table and ate their lunch. After they finished, Tooch asked, "Do you want me to look at your window now?"

"Sure, I guess. Let me clean off the table." He went into the living area while she put the dishes in the sink. Oh, great, how was she going to get him to stop thinking about fixing the window? She didn't want to open it again, ever. Her neighbors would send the cops again if she stood in front of it.

"Don't pull—" Kirsti said, when she entered the room, but he already had the string in his hand and drew open the large blind across the window. Gray afternoon light streamed in, flooding the room. The brass clocks shone.

"What a great view," he said.

She sighed. There it was: *Her* ocean. She could already feel the effects.

Tooch turned toward her. "So where is the leak?"

"Leak? Oh, right here," she said, going over to the right side of the window. She traced her finger over the water in the rubber along the rim of the window. "Feel here," she said taking Tooch's hand. She leaned her head forward and her hair fell in front of her. With his hand she traced her collarbone and along the back of her neck. Tooch moved in and inhaled the scent of bull kelp on her neck and then kissed her there.

They nestled onto the long green couch below the window. The sky darkened and the clouds thinned. A full moon emerged from hiding, casting the room in shadows. The moon pulled her back and forth, back and forth, and she hardly sensed Tooch above her. She closed her eyes and lifted her legs up: the tide rose higher and higher until it finally crashed against the large boulders holding up the low road below the house. And then, when the moon pulled completely through her, when the next cycle rose completely, she sighed and lowered her legs and the tide finally went out.

⚘

She turned over on the couch and stretched. Tooch stood in front of the window naked. Low tide and pungent orange popweed scent filled the room. She smiled. The sea urchins were happy, busy sweeping with their cilia, and gumboot eggs in their gelatinous strings swayed in the waves.

The next morning, Tooch lay beside her, his head on her pillow. And like she'd imagined it, he whispered strange words to her. And, in turn, she whispered back to him: amphidromic point, harmonic constituent, and tidal node. His voice was familiar. He'd mentioned he'd been in Wrangell before. Had she seen him around? Maybe it was that thing people talk about, how some souls already know each other. Maybe this was like that. Now, the wind fluttered through her bedroom curtains. Tooch leaned up on his elbow and reached for her hair and splayed it out with his fingers on the pillow. Then he leaned in and kissed her, a long kiss rushed her down across the tide pool, over spiny green urchins, and wiggling bullheads, to the mucky dark sand at the water's edge.

⚘

That afternoon, Tooch walked the long driveway from Kirsti's apartment to the road and then crossed the narrow road and over the boulders. Down the beach, families with white buckets and shovels were running after squirting clams. Cars began to line the road, and people piled out to forage the tide line for corks, ropes, and old life jackets—anything they found handy.

Notebook in hand, Tooch crouched, looking at a small bullhead swimming in a tide pool. He wrote down its Tlingit name: *té tayee tlóoxu*. He moved a rock aside and saw a purple sea urchin: *x'waash*, *Strongylocentrotus purpuratus.* As the Earth spun through the shallows, shifting around in space, across the road and up the hill in a small apartment above a garage, Kirsti stood naked in front of her large picture window.

Date: mid-late 2000s
Unedited transcript from *Wrangell Myths and Texts*
Recorded by Tooch Waterson

The Man Who Loved Indians

SWANTON: I'm invited to a naming ceremony tonight at Institute Beach at four mile. You know where that's at?

TOOCH: You're getting a name?

SWANTON: Yes, I want you to record the ceremony. Maybe I'll get a few more stories too.

TOOCH: You're getting a name?

SWANTON: Yes.

TOOCH: But that's an honor reserved for . . . (*Tooch pauses.*)

SWANTON: Yeah, I'll finally be thought of like Strauss, Rosewood, Kaminsky, and Dederick. You know the "big" list.

TOOCH: There are no women's names on your list. What about McDonnell and Pelham?

SWANTON: The women? They intermarried with the Tlingit. That doesn't count. They aren't objective enough. It takes years of humble study and scholarly work among the people. They just wrote about their children and living among the Tlingit. Not real ethnological work, certainly not anthropological.

TOOCH: (*Tooch raises eyebrows.*) Oh, I see. A matrilineal perspective doesn't count.

SWANTON: I . . . I didn't mean it that way.

TOOCH: Well, Institute Beach is out the road by Shoemaker Bay. You're sure you were invited to a naming ceremony?

SWANTON: The young people, Johan, and his sister, Sarah, invited me.

TOOCH: (*Tooch grins slightly.*) Oh, I see. Yes, a naming ceremony. I'll get you there.

❀

Setting: Wrangell Institute Beach

In attendance: JOHAN, SARAH, FERN, and TOVA.

Notes: It's dark and there's a bonfire surrounded by several large logs. Four young people are in attendance: all twentysomething, three females and one male.

(*Swanton stumbles down the rock embankment, sliding and then righting himself with one arm. He stands up. Behind Swanton, Tooch walks down the embankment effortlessly and sits on a log away from the others, away from the fire. He has a headlamp on.*)

TOOCH: I'll sit here out of the way.

(*Tooch takes out a notebook and paper.*)

(*Swanton sits next to the young man named Johan. Tova is by herself on one log and Sarah and Fern sit on another together.*)

JOHAN: Wow, some entrance, Mr. Swanton.

(*Swanton wipes off his pants and sits down next to Johan.*)

JOHAN: (*Johan reaches over and gently brushes the dirt off of Swanton's thigh.*) We were just discussing the ceremony.

(*Fern hands Johan a pipe.*)

JOHAN: (*Johan inhales and then hands Swanton the pipe.*) Here, it's part of the ceremony. You know, smoke a pipe first.

(*Sarah covers her mouth then lets out a small chuckle.*)

(*The fire pops.*)

SWANTON: Build trust and rapport at the entry stage. Remember the researcher-observer is also being observed and evaluated.

(*Tova uses a stick to move the logs around in the fire. Sparks fly up.*)

SWANTON: (*Swanton clears his throat.*) Well, I'm studying the mind, and I'm trying to find out if the "savage" mind has the same structure as the "civilized" mind. I'm testing my theory by studying your stories. I'm also interested in your traditions—whether or not you still participate in the culture.

FERN: (*Fern is staring at the fire.*) Well, I come from a family of weavers. My great-grandmother, my grandmother, and my mother are weavers. I paint. I don't weave.

SWANTON: Oh, why not?

FERN: I don't know. I don't like weaving.

SWANTON: Aren't you worried about carrying on traditions?

JOHAN: I weave.

SWANTON: You?

(*Swanton looks Johan up and down.*)

JOHAN: Yeah, there are a few of us men weavers. (*Johan winks.*)

(*Swanton nods to Tooch to write this down, but he sees Tooch has been taking notes all along and frowns at him.*)

JOHAN: Yeah, we're all fucked up.

SARAH: Speak for yourself, brother.

SWANTON: (*Swanton points to Johan.*) Is he your tribal brother?

SARAH: No . . . no, my brother, as in we have the same mother and father.

SWANTON: Oh.

FERN: (*Fern takes a puff from the pipe has passed to her.*) Yeah, we're all fucked up. Our families.

SWANTON: Naturalism is the goal of social research, which is to capture the character of human behavior in a natural setting. This can only be accomplished by first-hand contact.

TOVA: Speak for yourself. My family is insane.

SWANTON: (*Swanton stares at Tova.*) Have we met?

TOVA: I've been around. I've seen you around town. In Wrangell, everyone knows everyone and everyone's business.

SWANTON: Yes, that's it. Maybe I've seen you around town.

TOVA: Or, we could have met on the ferry. Everyone meets on the ferry at one time or another.

(*Tova looks away, uninterested.*)

SWANTON: (*Swanton turns to Johan and the others.*) Tell me your tribal stories, where your families migrated from.

JOHAN: Our oral traditions?

SWANTON: Yes.

FERN: What are you going to do with them?

SWANTON: Your stories?

(*Tova takes out a carving knife from her backpack and starts to work on a small piece of wood. Shavings fall at her feet near the fire.*)

FERN: Yeah, our stories. What are you going to do with them after you write them down?

SARAH: Make a book?

SWANTON: Well, they'll be recorded forever and kept at the Smithsonian, and you can access them there. Your grandchildren can. So they won't die.

JOHAN: They won't die. We know our stories.

SWANTON: It's a precautionary measure. So, Johan, how long have your people been here?

JOHAN: About six months.

(Swanton's eyebrows rise.)

JOHAN: We moved back from Ketchikan. My parents lived there while my sister, Sarah, and I grew up, then they decided to move back home, so we followed them back to our ancestral homeland.

SWANTON: But, I understand your tribe is from here—this region.

JOHAN: Well, my ancestors came down the Stikine River under the ice. We had the first drag queen party on the river.

SWANTON: A what?

JOHAN: (Johan winks at Swanton then stands up near the fire.) The Haida or maybe it was the Tsimpsians. Yeah, I think it was the Tsimpsians. They were waiting for us when we came down river and killed our scouting party. You know, "fool us twice"? No way. Our warriors dressed as women and went into the woods to "pick berries," and when the Tsimpsians came after us, we ripped off our skirts and *wham!*

(Johan slaps his hands together.)

(Swanton jumps.)

JOHAN: We killed them and then went on our merry way.

(Johan sits back down and sighs.)

SWANTON: (Swanton nods to Tooch.) Tooch, you get that?

FERN: Is that true or did you make that up? I heard a different version.

JOHAN: (Shrugs.) Ah, the universal question: What is truth? It's a story. All stories are true.

FERN: Oh, well, my people came down the Alsek River from the Interior.

SARAH: Mine came down the Stikine, too.

TOVA: (Tova points up.) Mine came from up there.

JOHAN: (Johan looks up.) Up there?

TOVA: My mother's people are aliens.

(Tova points to Elephants Nose with her carving tool.)

SARAH: Was she Finnish or something? The Finns, they came from the sky.

TOVA: Yes, Finnish and a bunch of others.

JOHAN: Aaah. I see.

TOVA: No, you don't. Your mothers are Tlingit, matrilineal. I get a great-great-grandfather who murders a man in Yellowstone, then escapes to Wrangell and his granddaughter, Grandma Helene, starts an alien cult.

SARAH: How come you never told us this? We've known you for six months.

FERN: Yeah, and I've known you since sixth grade.

TOVA: It's not something you tell people: Hey, my family is fucking nuts. Example: Did you know my grandmother blew up Mount Saint Helens? She and some of her friends did an Indian dance and it blew its top. She wrote my mom a letter and told her.

FERN: (*Fern jumps up and dances by the fire.*) Haya, haya, haya. Haya, haya, haya.

JOHAN: (*Johan nods toward his sister and Fern.*) Yeah, that's what John Muir did when he built the bonfire up on Dewey.

TOVA: The pyro.

JOHAN: (*Johan sighs.*) I think Muir was sexy with those wild-man whiskers and woodsy look. Don't you think?

(*Swanton says nothing.*)

(*Fern is still dancing around the fire, chanting softly now.*)

(*Tova pulls on Fern's sleeve and sits her down on the log.*)

SARAH: Yeah, I'd say your family is fucked up more than mine.

142

TOVA: Grandma used to channel Cinderella with her hair, and the guy she ran off South with was Rocky as in Rocky and Bullwinkle. They had a fantasy realm on the other planet, where they came from, and they could access it by channeling.

JOHAN: (*Johan takes another hit of grass.*) No kidding? Like she put foil in her hair and stuck her finger in the light socket singing bibbity-bobbity-boo?

SARAH: Be proud of it. Cool.

TOVA: How am I gonna be proud of ancestral heritage?

SARAH: Well, you guys have great imaginations. You know, I had an uncle once. He died before I was born. But, they say he was born blue, more like blue-black. He was a good dancer. That was before the ANB hall burned down. He disappeared one day. No one ever found his body. Maybe he was one of those aliens.

JOHAN: Could be the you-know-what got him.

FERN: Them? Sure hope not.

TOVA: He's probably in Seattle somewhere. The dead go to Seattle.

FERN: Yeah, there's more dancing there than here.

SWANTON: (*Swanton points to Tova's shirt, which says, "I'm part white but I can't prove it."*) What's this, a statement?

TOVA: My life is a statement.

TOVA: (*Tova pulls her shirt—stretches it in front of her.*) Yeah, I'm also part alien and I *can* prove it. My mom says we should get alien cards. Laminate them and everything.

JOHAN: Maybe you should have your DNA tested. We did. We're part Norwegian on Dad's side.

SARAH: Yeah, I think DNA is a great idea.

FERN: I don't know about that. I have a friend in Juneau who thought she was mostly Tlingit and some Filipino and found out she is Tlingit, Haida, and Tsimpsian. Really messed her up. She wasn't even Filipino.

JOHAN: I believe in DNA. My mother says she's a lesbian and I like men. Might be something to it.

SARAH: Mom's not a lesbian. She's married to Dad.

JOHAN: She was before she met him.

(*Sarah looks confused.*)

JOHAN: Who do you think Aunt Bernadine is? Bernie? She keeps writing Mom. That's her old girlfriend.

SWANTON: Others argue causal relations are to be found in the social world, but that they differ from the "mechanical" causality typical of physical phenomena.

SARAH: (*Sarah, quiet at first, thinking.*) Oh.

SWANTON: Are we going to do the naming ceremony?

(*Everyone ignores him.*)

FERN: So really, I would have understood, Tova.

TOVA: Yeah, well, my grandma thought she was an alien from another planet. Their spaceship crashed here, and the aliens who died, their spirits went into human bodies. And once they almost drank the Kool-Aid like the Hale-Bopp cult. Remember them?

SARAH: Yeah, I remember that cult. Scary.

TOVA: The space people were supposed to come and get my grandma and them and take them back in a spaceship to their planet. Later, after Grandma Helene ran off with the cult, leaving my mom and her sisters and brother, Grandma's group thought they were going to their planet on dragons.

JOHAN: Fuck so? Dragons? Really? Your heritage is like a Raven trickster story for sure.

(Swanton gets up and stokes the fire with several more logs. He sits back down and looks at Tova.)

SWANTON: You do look a bit Tlingit. Your eyes. Who are your people?

TOVA: You mean my slanted eyes, the epicanthic fold? Some people think I'm Chinese or Japanese. Of course, I found out I might be part Chinese too. But that's another story. Well, I am part Tlingit on my dad's side. My mother's people are Sámi.

SWANTON: Sam-me?

SARAH: Never heard of them.

TOVA: You know. "White" indigenous people.

FERN: Yeah, I can see how Indians might look white. I mean look at my sister, Rose. She's pale and blonde, and our mother is dark-skinned with black hair. I look like Mom and Rose looks like Great-Grandpa Joe.

JOHAN: White?

SWANTON: (*Shakes head.*) No such thing.

TOVA: Yes, we invented skis. You know—reindeer herders.

SWANTON: White?

TOVA: (*Tova sighs.*) Yes, I said *white.*

SWANTON: (*Shakes head. Looks blank.*) Sámi. Never heard of them.

TOVA: Goddamn. Happens every time.

FERN: What?

TOVA: I always have to say the N word.

JOHAN: The N word?

TOVA: Yeah, I have to use a dirty word, you know, an "N" word in order to say who I am. Every fucking time, I have to call myself a nigger so you'll know who I am.

JOHAN: Whoa.

FERN: Words have power, Tova.

TOVA: I'm a goddamn Lapp, okay? Heard of me now?

FERN: (*Fern sighs.*) Yeah, I've heard of your people.

SARAH: (*Sarah squishes up her face.*) Oh man, I'm sorry.

TOVA: I'm a Laplander, a Lapp. Lapp. Lapp. Lapp. (*Tova tosses a rock into the fire.*)

(*There is silence. No one says anything for a while.*)

TOVA: The Sámi used to be called Lapps. Same people. A long time ago, here in Wrangell, my family was known as the Lapp family. I didn't even know the word "Sámi."

FERN: Yeah, but I've heard of your people. You ride in sleds pulled by reindeer, wear clothes with bright colors like Santa's elves or something.

TOVA: Yeah, you stole that from us. All you politically correct people, that is. Talk about misappropriation of culture. Well, every damn Christmas season, I deal with it. Santa and his elves and it don't matter if you're American, Japanese, Irish. You all steal my culture and I don't make a fuss.

JOHAN: (*Smiles.*) You are now.

SARAH: I never believed in Santa.

TOVA: You never sat on Santa's lap?

SARAH: Lapp? I get it.

TOVA: You laugh and ring bells and sing about Rudolph the red-nosed reindeer at our expense. It's like carrying a tomahawk around, chopping your opponents at a football game, only it's millions of Americans doing the Santa thing every year and the Americans are spreading it around the world. Could be billions now.

JOHAN: (*Shakes his head.*) Bah humbug.

SWANTON: It is argued that, if one approaches a phenomenon with a set of hypotheses, one may fail to discover the true nature of that phenomenon, being blinded by the assumptions built into the hypotheses.

FERN: (*Frowns.*) You ruined my Christmas.

SARAH: And it's only June.

FERN: Are you sure it's true. Santa and your people?

TOVA: I read it on the Internet.

FERN: Oh, then it's true then. That settles that.

TOVA: Hey, we've lost some of our stories. It's been generations since we lived in our homeland. I have to look up our stories.

FERN: And you make them up?

TOVA: No . . . It makes sense. The Santa thing does.

FERN: (*Shrugs.*) I guess.

SWANTON: You do have some interesting lineage but not really believable. My audience wants Indians. Real Indians.

JOHAN: She is a real Indian. She's Tlingit. She already told you.

SWANTON: I prefer matrilineal heritage.

SARAH: You won't get a lot of that around here.

TOVA: I told you my matrilineal heritage.

SWANTON: From real Indians, not adopted ones.

TOVA: I'm not adopted. You don't need to be "adopted" when you're Tlingit.

JOHAN: Adoption is a white man's concept. My grandma says it's called "taking you by the hand." I don't know the Tlingit word.

SWANTON: Can we get the ceremony started?

JOHAN: Sure. Stand up.

SWANTON: Stand?

JOHAN: Yeah, we can't do this sitting down.

(Fern stands and gets a warm stick from the fire, charcoal on it. She picks it up and blows on it to cool it off a bit.)

(Tova looks confused. Raises her eyebrows.)

FERN: (Fern gives the stick to Tova.) Now, when we say his name three times, you can put a mark on his forehead with this.

TOVA: What?

FERN: (Winks.) It's tradition, Tova.

(Swanton stands firm.)

SARAH: And you have to hold this. (*Pause. Sarah hands him her burnt marshmallow on a stick.*) It's a ceremonial staff. And, we have to feed our ancestors when we do ceremonies.

(*Tova frowns at them.*)

FERN: I know. I know. (*She lowers her voice and speaks to Tova.*) Our ceremonies are sacred. I know. But this guy . . . I'm going to have a ceremony for the ceremony. I promise.

SARAH: Fling the marshmallow in the fire.

(*Swanton looks at the stick and flings the sagging marshmallow off, and it drops into the fire.*)

SARAH: Good shot.

JOHAN: (*Johan clears his throat.*) I hereby give you the name Tóok Chán. Repeat after me. You, too, Mr. Swanton.

SWANTON AND OTHERS: Tóok Chán, Tóok Chán, Tóok Chán.

(*Johan nods to Tova, and Tova steps toward Swanton.*)

(*Tova marks on his forehead a big X.*)

(*Johan leans toward Swanton and kisses him long and hard on the lips.*)

SWANTON: (*Swanton's eyes get big. He wobbles a bit and then sits down.*) What does my name mean?

SARAH: I don't know, but my grandmother used to say it to me. I think it's passed down in our family. It's an honor.

JOHAN: I think it means something like "mighty warrior." Something like that.

(*Swanton rises and gets up and stretches.*)

SWANTON: Well, I'd better get going.

JOHAN: We're not done. This is an all-night thing. Sometimes, these ceremonies last for days. Our stories can last days, months, years, even. You might even get stuck here in our stories. It's not bad. It feels good. Really. Stay.

SWANTON: (*Shakes his head. Looks afraid.*) No, sorry. I have to get stories from Charlie and Jesse Edwin in the morning. Early.

SARAH: They're my auntie and uncle. You'll get good stories from them. Too bad you have to go.

FERN: Yeah, nice to talk to you.

(*Swanton gets up and leaves, clamoring up the embankment. They hear his car start up, and he drives off.*)

TOVA: So, Johan. You're supposed to be a fluent Tlingit speaker, and you don't know what his new name means.

SARAH: No, he doesn't.

(*Fern giggles.*)

(*From the darkness Tooch is still sitting on the log. He raises his head and his headlamp shines brightly at them.*)

TOOCH: Hmmmm.

FERN: (*Jumps slightly in place.*) Jeez, I forgot you were there.

(*Tooch's face contorts in the light of the fire. From where the young people sit, it looks like his hair is standing on end around his ears. The light from the headlamp shows down on his sharp nose, and the shadows make it look like a beak. They stare at him. No one speaks.*)

TOOCH: His new name means Stink Ass.

❁

Swanton goes to Seattle, Washington, en route to Washington, DC, and presents his work among the Indians of Southeast Alaska. He gives a lecture at the Blue Moon Tavern. He fumbles through his Tlingit introduction, mispronouncing every word: saying the a like an English a and forgetting the tones. He scrapes his throat raw on the x's. At the end of his presentation, Swanton proudly stands and tells everyone in Lingít that his Indian name, given to him in a traditional tribal ceremony by elders and youth, is Stink Ass, Tóok Chán (though he doesn't know what he's saying). Swanton says the name means "Mighty Warrior." No Tlingits are present in the audience to laugh at him. No Tlingits are there to accept the research he's presented as truth, or as trickery, for that matter. Back in Wrangell, Raven is still sitting by the fire at Institute Beach writing down stories.

Date: nd (no date)
Recorded by John Swanton
Assisted by Tooch Waterson

The Woman Who Kicked over a Frog

Elaine tossed the poisonous package of red meat into the garbage can. She'd read on the Internet about chemicals in beef. She was never going to get sick again. Ever. She was tired of getting the flu and the cold, and bronchitis, and the shingles. Lately, she spent time surfing the internet while working the night shift as a ward clerk at Wrangell City Hospital. The hospital was built on muskeg, and after thirty years the corners were settling and creaking. She hated all the noise: moaning patients, nurses' squeaky shoes. Especially, the sounds of those damn frogs in the bog. They carry diseases.

Elaine lived from one conspiracy theory to another. Last month it was high fructose corn syrup and gluten. She was, most certainly, NOT going to let those things affect her health. The internet was full of articles and warnings and strange diseases. And the photos, oh the photos of rashes and scabs and sallow skin and strange growths. But then again, the hospital where she worked was icky too. It paid well, but the people who worked there were peculiar. Dr. Reed was strange, always staring at her. And it seemed like the nurses and the nurse aides, even the coder, and the housekeeper, were sick with runny noses and gravelly coughs. Probably their nasty smoking habits. The staff went in and out the back door quite frequently. Especially at night. They got away with all those breaks because they were on the night shift. She'd rather work the day shift, but they won't hire her for any other hospital job, not even dumping the garbage.

Now, she strolled with her cousin Mina down the sidewalk heading for lunch at Tokyo Oki, the new sushi restaurant. Mina questioned her. "Are you sure? No one eats here."

Elaine shrugged. "I've given up red meat. Fish is good for you."

"Yea, but *raw* fish?"

"You can get tempura," Elaine said. She led Mina up a narrow path through a tiny Japanese garden dotted with stone pagodas, a pointy-hatted gnome, and a green ceramic frog.

As they walked through the garden, Elaine's heavy purse fell from her shoulder to the crook of her arm. She stumbled.

Mina bumped her. "Sorry."

Elaine stepped forward, walking slightly off the path. The toe of her foot nudged the ceramic frog. It tumbled off a rock, cracking into pieces.

"Eee," Mina said, staring at the broken frog.

"Damn thing," Elaine grumbled, kicking a shard aside.

Inside the restaurant they took a table near the door. A thin woman set two menus down. Elaine ordered red snapper sushi. Mina ordered tempura crab. After they ate, they split the bill. Mina rustled around in her purse. "I don't have a tip."

Elaine rolled her eyes. "I didn't get the hospital kitchen job." As soon as she had said it, she figured maybe that was good thing. All that saliva on the forks and spoons, the half-eaten toast.

"That's too bad," Mina said.

"Yeah, they all hate me there."

"They don't hate you, El. There aren't jobs these days."

Elaine scowled. "They stare at me. It's like I'm skanky." She'd seen them with their big staring eyes that seemed to roll back with disgust. They didn't even try to hide it from her.

Mina covered her mouth, trying not to laugh. "I'm sure it's not that."

Elaine scooted out from the booth.

"Aren't you going to leave a bigger tip?" Mina asked.

"No. The sushi wasn't fresh and the crab was imitation."

They slipped on their coats and headed out the door. Outside, they passed the waitress crouching, scooping ceramic frog shards into a garbage bag. "Sorry about the frog," Elaine mumbled. The waitress blinked her large green eyes but said nothing.

That night, she sat at her desk behind the glass shield. The frogs out back croaked as loud as usual. The nurse walked down the hall in her squeaky shoes. Tonight, there was only Mr. Severson, a gallbladder surgery patient.

It was already past 2:00 a.m. and she leaned her head on her desk. She bobbed her head back up and yawned. On her computer she opened a news page: outbreak of swine flu. Oh, great. No way. Not me. She got up from her computer station and went into the small employee bathroom behind her desk and scrubbed her hands. No. No. No. Her chest tightened with the thought of mucus and pus. She scrubbed some more until her hands reddened. As she stepped out of the bathroom, frog croaks pulsed through her small cubicle. Down the hall, the back door stood open. She huffed, "No wonder."

Elaine stomped down the hall, following mucky prints on the floor. A damp mossy scent hung in the air. She peered out. No one was on the small porch. She slammed the door and headed back, passing Mr. Severson's room. The nurse was tucking in his blankets. The nurse turned her head. Her large full lips widened into a grin. Her long eyelashes blinked. Was the nurse flirting with her? Elaine shook her head.

She plopped down at her desk and with her sanitizing lotion. She rubbed her hands and then rubbed a sanitizing cloth across her desk. She couldn't seem to get rid of the stench of rotting leaves. Maybe someone opened the door again. "That damn door."

"No, don't close the door," a voice said from behind her. She started to turn at the sound of Dr. Reed's voice, but her head jerked back violently. "What the hell. Dr. Reed?" She tried to pull her head back. She wiggled but Dr. Reed held her hair in a fisted ponytail. The night nurse now stood in front of the cubicle grinning. Suddenly, the nurse flung herself up, legs, body, and all, onto the lip of the desk, splaying her hands flat against the glass. Her knees were bent at an odd angle out to the sides, her crotch facing Elaine.

The doctor jerked her hair again. She screamed but it came out more like a baby wailing in the nursery. He kicked the cubical door open with his foot and she thudded off her chair onto the ground. He pulled her down the hall. "Hey," Elaine cried. The nurse jumped off the counter, landing beside them. Elaine tried to scream again, but instead, the air in her lungs gurgled. They're going to get fired for this. I'll file a report. I'll call the police. Her arms flailed and she tried to grab at their legs. She glanced up. The waitress from Tokyo Oki walked beside her. The waitress leaned down. Snot dripped onto Elaine's face.

❀

The door to Mr. Severson's room was open. Without his glasses, he saw Dr. Reed and a few nurses hauling a bag of laundry toward the back door. At once, the frog chorus began, droning and bellowing, growing louder and louder, throbbing throughout the hospital. All night long the back door remained open, the air reeking with a sweet mossy odor.

Date: 1970s
Recorded by John Swanton
Assisted by Tooch Waterson

The Woman Who Shushed

Berta held her purse close to her body. A man bumped into her. Excuse me. Excuse me. People seemed polite in Seattle. She wasn't really watching where she was going, though. Their faces held little interest to her; she was looking for a pair of small feet in red rubber boots, when it occurred to her she should be looking for red high heels. That gave her hope. Thinking about the alternative, that her sister had disappeared, presumed drowned when she was young, was to consider the taboo.

How do you talk about something that shouldn't be talked about? Something taboo: *jinaháa*, bad mojo, whatever you want to call it. I guess you don't talk about it, you skirt it, you insinuate, you talk around it. She understood the taboo, and so did her sister, Mariela. They learned about it when they were kids sneaking up on their aunties' and uncles' card-playing sessions. They heard stories of people marrying creatures, and creatures drowning people, tipping their skiffs over. And whenever they asked the adults, they would be shushed. Their parents warned them to never say that name in the woods or on the water. Maybe Mariela had accidently said the word that day? She would never know.

They were told never to say the Tlingit word out loud, which is why, now, as Berta was in Anita Bay picking their crab pot, they didn't talk about it, yet they did talk about it. She closed her eyes and imagined Mariela with her. Was it taboo to imagine the dead living? Berta tucked her gray tendrils into her blue bandana. She held the throttle of the outboard with one ungloved hand and the gunwale with the other. The salt spray coated the hand holding the throttle. They were in her husband, Ole's, fourteen-foot Lund, heading into the bay to pull his crab pot. Ole had gone long-lining for halibut and had asked her to go check the crab pot. He'd be gone about ten days, he said, so he figured she'd be able to pull it at least a few times. He wanted her to do this every couple of days, but it had been four days already. And their kids were grown now and had their own fishing skiffs or were raising kids of their own. Besides, Berta loved any excuse to go out on the water. She'd been waiting for a sunny day to take the skiff out. She was a fair-weather skiffer. She didn't like to bounce around in the gray waves. Mariela never minded, though. Mariela was braver. Was.

Berta looked across the length of the skiff toward Mariela. Mariela's long black hair was tied in a ponytail and tucked into the front of her rain jacket. She had on a dark green rain hat tied beneath her chin. Her feet flopped out in front of her in her favorite red rubber boots, her back to the wind. She grinned like a dog hanging its head out the window of a pickup truck.

Today, Anita Bay was glass-calm. Berta slowed the outboard down. She wasn't worried about using the old Evinrude outboard, the one that said *rude* on the side. The rest of the red letters chipped off from years of river sand beating against the cowling. Ole was an expert mechanic. He had to be since he'd spent his whole life running the Stikine River and running his skiffs and his assortment of fishing boats around the bays surrounding Wrangell Island. So, no, she never worried about the motors. Ole taught her how to change the spark plugs, pump the bulb, get water out of the gas—general maintenance stuff. And he always provided a nice kicker, just in case.

Originally, Ole had wanted to put a steering console in the skiff, but she'd resisted. She was taught to run a skiff by steering from the back, not from some sissy steering console. She liked to feel the engine, to listen to it for clicks and ticks, and to check to make sure the water was still streaming out the back like it was supposed to. Now, she twisted the throttle back and the skiff slowed as it entered the bay.

Mariela turned away from inhaling the wind and said, "Why don't we use the electric kicker. I like the quiet."

"Okay, sure." Berta slowed down and killed the engine. At once the sound from the outboard escaped into the thick green mountainsides surrounding them. Her ears still rang. "How's that?"

"Nice," Mariela said, closing her eyes, "real nice."

Berta started the electric kicker and it hummed to life. She turned the motor toward the beach, creating hardly a wake behind them. Midafternoon in August, the sun moved over the hilltop. "You keep your eyes out for the white jug. I'll find the creek," she said, almost too loud, forgetting the larger engine was shut off.

"Isn't this bay where, you know, where some of those stories come from?" Mariela asked.

"Where what?"

"You know," Mariela nodded toward the woods. Then she lowered her voice, "You know."

"Oh *that*, them. Yeah, Grandpa told me a story about this bay once ..." She had no intention of telling this story out loud, but Mariela liked to scare her. It was annoying sometimes. So turnabout was fair, right?

"Shush," Mariela said.

Berta smiled. They were always shushing each other. "I think Gramps was full of it 'cause he didn't actually see anything."

Mariela looked down at her hands, "Somehow you never do. In those stories, no one ever sees anything."

Berta turned the skiff closer to the shoreline and began to run the boat parallel to the beach, her eyes scanning. She liked to run the shore in case she saw something interesting to check out; always an overturned skiff, a buoy, a sea-washed board, or an old life jacket. But whenever she saw a life jacket, she wondered if sometime she might find a body attached to it, caught in the seaweed near the tideline.

The sun finally made its way over the treetops. "When we were kids, people used to see lights on top of this mountain," Berta said. "Some people used to say there was an alien landing strip there. Maybe the government doing some kind of experiment."

Mariela's eyes widened, "Maybe it was, you know, *them* doing something up there. Like their village: the Transparent Village."

"Mariela, why would they need a landing strip, anyway?"

"I didn't say anything about a landing strip. You did."

"Well," Berta said, "maybe the lights weren't a landing strip but something else, something that causes people to investigate." Yeah, right. She would never be brave enough to investigate. Mariela would though. Mariela would always check out the bumps in the night, head out onto their porch with the flashlight. She'd even scared off a bear once.

"The aliens?" Mariela said.

"No, the *them*. Maybe there is something causing people to go and see if it's *them*. You know," Berta said. "But I don't know why anybody would want to go and check that kind of thing out."

Mariela shrugged. "Curiosity, I guess."

"I suppose," Berta said. Mariela was more curious than her. She had always done better in school, especially in the sciences and math.

Mariela shifted her weight in the bow, repositioning herself. The skiff rocked a bit. "Aren't you a bit curious, you know, about them?"

Berta held her hand up and waved it. "Nope, no, absolutely not. Let's not talk about it anymore, okay?" That was enough talk. Who started this conversation anyway? Mariela was starting to make her mad.

Mariela smiled at Berta. Berta noticed Mariela had taken off her rain hat and now the sun streamed onto her hair, casting it with red highlights. Mariela fidgeted with her life jacket, which was fastened atop her raincoat. "I'm taking all this stuff off. It's too hot." Mariela unzipped her life jacket and set it down on the bow and then sat on it. "There, now my butt won't get sore." Mariela also removed her raincoat and laid it down beside her. "I don't see the jug," she said.

"I don't think we're near it yet," Berta said. "The creek is up the shore a ways." Berta cocked her head. The birds were lively today. Mariela had been right about using the small electric kicker. The quiet electric motor allowed her mind to keen in to the world around: ravens chortling in the trees, the splash of a jumping salmon, the clack of rocks on the shore. She loved moments like these. Moments when she could almost see clearly, when her sister was right there.

"You know," Berta said, "I heard about a woman who disappeared out fishing one day. She was by herself and they never found her body, only her skiff. Then one day, three or four years later, she turned up in Seattle walking around on the street. Someone saw her there. A relative, I think. They recognized her and picked her up. She's in the nuthouse in Anchorage now."

"So how did she get from Southeast to Seattle? That's a thousand miles," Mariela asked.

"I don't know. Maybe it was *them*, you know. That's what they do."

"Yeah, I know. They make people disappear. Drown. The—"

"Shush," Berta said. Did she hear it right? Had Mariela said the taboo word out loud? She had. They had broken the taboo. Should she offer something? They were supposed to make an offering. What did they have to give? Rotten bait? That wouldn't be good. Her lunch was in the small cooler. Peanut butter and jelly on Wonder Bread?

Just then, Berta spotted the creek running down the hillside. "There's the creek. Follow the creek with your eyes, straight out, and then look for the white jug." She turned the skiff out from the beach and squinted into the sunlight. She couldn't see anything.

Marilea pointed, "There it is."

"I don't see it."

"Gee, your eyesight's getting bad," Mariela said. "Turn a little more to the left and head that way, toward that log. See the log on the other side."

"Yeah, I see the log."

"Stay straight, heading for the big log, and then you'll come right up on the jug."

Berta kept the bow pointed toward the log. "Maybe someone pulled it already. This is farther out than I remember where Ole and I set it last." Finally, she spotted the jug and turned the skiff slightly. "I see it," she said, heading toward the jug. "I'll pull aside it, and you grab the jug and pull it in."

Berta slid the skiff over next to the white jug, but the electric motor didn't have enough stamina to keep them on course and the current drifted them back a bit.

Mariela leaned over to reach for the jug.

"No, wait till I get a little closer," Berta said. "The current's pushing us too strong." She tried again, making another run at the jug.

Mariela reached out and grabbed the jug and the line attached to it, pulling it into the skiff and started coiling the line. "I think we've got a few crabs. It seems heavy."

Berta smiled. "Good. Crab for dinner." She cut the engine and went to the port side of the skiff to help Mariela pull the line in. Hand over hand they coiled the rope into the skiff until the large round pot came to the surface. Berta grasped the pot and heaved it into the skiff. Dungies, clicking and clacking atop one another, filled the pot. She smiled, "Whoo hoo, *gunalchéesh*, thanks."

Berta stuck her orange-gloved hands into the pot and began to pick out the crabs, throwing away any that were already dead. She put the crabs into a five-gallon bucket.

"I better rebait it. Ole wants me to check this a few times while he's gone." She took a plastic bag from the bottom of the skiff, reached in, and grabbed a small halibut head, minus the cheeks, which were good eating—the best part of the halibut. She hooked the head on a small hook inside the pot and then latched the pot door closed.

Berta stood, wobbling in the skiff, and went to the stern again and started up the big motor. It sputtered to life. "I'm going to reset it out a ways from this spot. Try a new spot. Okay?"

"Okay," Mariela said.

Mariela flung her ponytail from front to back, reminding Berta of herself at that age. She liked having Mariela with her. She liked it a lot. Berta steered the skiff to the spot. This spot seemed right. There wasn't a Fathometer on the skiff, but she figured it was about fifty feet or more. She had enough line so that was good. "Throw the pot over," she said to Mariela.

Mariela stood up in the skiff and threw the line over. The heavy pot flipped out into the green water, splashing and then sinking fast with its own weight.

Berta watched the shore to get her bearings for when she had to come back and retrieve the pot in a few days. Let's see, out about one hundred yards from the broken spruce, near the large mossy boulder. She turned back to Mariela and her brain registered alarm. What the heck? Don't! Lean! But Mariela leaned too far to the left. It happened fast. Mariela's eyes widened, her mouth formed an "O." Mariela's red boots caught in the line.

Berta leaped forward, but she caught her own foot on the edge of the bench. The bucket of crabs spilled and the crabs clacked along the floorboards. She continued to fall and hit her chin on the seat-bench in front of her. Blood drops spattered on the aluminum floorboard. She looked up as Mariela plunge into the water. Mariela screamed. Water splashed.

Berta wobbled to her feet. The skiff rocked. She steadied herself and stood up in time to see top of Mariela's head sinking with the crab pot to the bottom of the bay.

"Mariela! Oh, god, oh Jesus. Jesus Christ!" She leaned over and grabbed the white jug. The jug bobbed madly, as if Mariela struggled below. Then the jug pulled out of her hands.

By itself, the skiff slowly swung around in circles, the pot-line swinging closer to the prop. Berta fumbled to the back of the skiff, grabbed the throttle stick, and maneuvered the skiff to where she could reach the jug again. The jug bounced out of her hands. Then the jug moved farther away as if a halibut, not a crab pot, tugged the other end of the line. She ran the skiff next to the jug on the starboard side, where she could reach it with her right hand. "Mariela! Mariela!" She motored close to the jug again, then got on her knees in the bottom of the skiff, braced herself, and leaned farther and farther, reaching her arm out. Her elbow grazed the cold salt water. Her back arched and stretched. The skiff rocked and she nearly lost her balance.

That's when she saw it, something red bobbing a few yards away. "Eeyee!" Mariela's boots. She motored the skiff over to the red object and picked it up out of the water: a small plastic bailing bucket someone had fashioned from a gallon jerry jug floated atop the water. She picked up the bucket and cried. To her left, the white jug still bobbed wildly in the water.

She sat down in the skiff, the sun streaming on her face, tears sticking to the salt spray on her cheeks. The jug bobbed about, and then ceased. She put her hands to her face, wiping away the snot and the crab juice with her orange glove. On the bow Mariela's life jacket, the one she saw her take off to sit on, wasn't there. Mariela's raincoat, the long green one, was no longer lying in the bow either. Where was she? Where was she?

Mariela was gone. That much was sure. She'd been gone a long time. For the past forty years she'd gone to Seattle to look for Mariela, to see if she could see her in the crowds of faces. Maybe Mariela would be sitting on a bench waiting for a bus. Or maybe holding a black umbrella when it flipped inside out in the wind.

They were kids when they had climbed in that crowded skiff— something stupid that kids do—and the skiff tipped over. Why? Had someone laughed at the boat? Did someone brag about how many kids they could fit in the skiff? There were six of them in the small skiff. They were rowing across the other side of the harbor. Had someone dared say the taboo name? They weren't far from shore. They could have walked. They could have swam, couldn't they have? Everyone drowned. Everyone. Except one: herself. She was twelve years old, too, like Mariela, her sister. They were ten minutes apart when they were born. Ten fingers, ten toes, ten minutes. She had been born last. She had been saved. Someone had pulled her to safety. All she remembered, though, was afterward she searched the beach with her father, finding only one of Mariela's red rubber boots. Her father was so distraught he kept calling Berta "Mariela," turning to her, studying her face, as if he could somehow see Mariela was still alive. Eventually, all the young bodies were found . . . except Mariela's.

At first, in Seattle, Berta searched for a young girl about twelve years old. As the years went by, she looked for an older Mariela. Now, after all these years, after Mariela's drowning, after her cousin Dieter's drowning, and Uncle Friz and his wife, Netta, had drowned, when Berta searches Seattle for Mariela, Mariela with Berta's same smile, Berta's same long, dark hair with reddish highlights, her same brown eyes, Berta knows she's only searching for herself. But, always, she looks at down at the feet. She searches for red boots flopping on the sidewalk. Red rubber boots dancing in puddles. Red rubber boots stumbling over the sidewalk curb, or boots dripped with vanilla ice cream. Red boots like a small buoy she will always cling to.

Date: 2010s
Recorded by Tooch Waterson
Speaker: Tova Agard

Can I Touch Your Chinese Hair?

Long ago, back in Distant Time, before time was time, before there was a *me*, before there was a plot and arc, before I discovered I had a spine and a text and illustrations and maps, there was the creation story. When I was in college, I would go walking around at Pikes Place in Seattle and tourists would ask to touch my hair. Just like when I was doing tours in Alaska.

Can I touch your hair?

At first, I let them touch my hair for a dollar, but it didn't make me rich, it made me poorer, so I decided to trade stories. *You can touch my hair if you tell me a story.* In the beginning, I got some lame stories, some really bad ones, but not all. Camille was the first person I let touch my hair in exchange for a story. Camille was from Utah and she was Mormon. She'd always wanted to be an Indian, to touch an Indian, to kiss an Indian, and low-and-behold, here one was. I was a girl, but I think that intrigued her. So she told me a story of how her father was an asshole. I know all about asshole fathers. She told me how she had to wear granny-style dresses and how her father had always told her to be submissive to men. She was supposed to have lots of children. One night, at sixteen, she snuck out to go to a party with a friend. Her father caught her and locked her in the hall closet. She hates the smell of boots, she said. For that story I let her touch my hair and when I did, leather scent dusted my pages.

What kind of person are you?

I took a poetry class at UW and the professor asked what ethnicity I was? Actually, she said "What are you?" When I said "Sámi" she gave me a blank stare, and I know she was trying to think of something to say . . . there was a long pause, even longer than I'm used to. So I said, "You know, indigenous peoples from Scandinavia?" "White Indians?" I didn't want to say the "L" word and I don't mean lesbian. I tried talking around the word. I went over the tundra and down to the lake and back up and around again. I stood up and circled that professor a couple of times. I pounded a drum and nearly fell over in a trance and finally I said, "LAPP. Have you ever heard of a Lapp? Laplander? People recognize that name. Yes, I'm a dumb-short-ragged person. That'd be me." But, you know what? She didn't know what a Lapp was, either. And I was struck silent. How else was I going to explain who I am, or was, or will be? The conversation pretty much fell off the dock, and I made some kind of an excuse to leave the room. The next day I saw the professor in the hall and she said to me, in fact she blurted it out: "You're all over the internet." She was thrilled. I was real. I was true. I wasn't lying. Google made me real. She was smiling and so excited and I said to her:

"Do you want to touch my Sámi hair?" and she did. I let her touch my hair and when she did, I reached up and held her hand there and she curled her fingers through my hair. It felt good. Very good. I said Let's go to your office, and she led me down the hall and around the corner. We went inside her office and she locked the door and pulled down the shade, and I said, No, leave the shade up, so she pulled it back up again. And she took an Indian weaving off the wall and laid it on the floor. I don't know if it was an authentic Indian weaving from India or the Americas or if it was from China, but that's okay because I am all those fibers anyway. And she didn't let go of my hair the whole time.

Can I see your card?

I think they always mean they want to see my BIA card or my tribal card or maybe my green card, but I always pull out my DNA card. Usually I have to take the card out whenever I cross a border like whenever I go from Southeast Alaska to Anchorage, or when I go to a meeting, or when I have to stand up and say something publicly. Sometimes I take the card when I go into the grocery store. I had it laminated. It's a custom card created from a study of our Sámi DNA, a diagram that looks like a sun. We are people of the sun. I have the U5b1b proof laminated with my smiling face in the center of its universe. It's proof I was born from those people. Heck, I'm a born-again Sámi or maybe I'm a Sámi born-again. I hate the church reference. They persecuted us, tried to destroy our culture. The missionaries did the same thing to my Tlingit relatives. You must be born again to enter the KINdom. So maybe Christians need a card, too. Proof they've gone down on their knees and checked the box, something about blood-of-Jesus quantum. Check. Check. Check.

What's a Sámi?

My mom and I learned how to make an oval drum. I'm learning about all the symbols on the drum now. We have to research the information at museums in Scandinavia because when the drums were confiscated, they put them into museums and now we have to ask permission to touch them. We have to use gloves when we touch them. They're afraid of our oils, our fingerprints, our D . . . N . . . A . . . our Sámi motif: mtDNA haplogroup U5b. Sounds like a punk rock group, eh?

You look exotic. What kind of Indian are you?

I'm the kind that comes from a detailed phylogeographic analysis of one of the predominant Sámi mtDNA haplogroups, U5b1b, which also includes the lineages of the "Sámi motif" was undertaken in thirty-one populations. The results indicate the origin of U5b1b, as for the other predominant Sámi haplogroup, V, is most likely in western, rather than eastern, Europe.

Can I touch your Indian Hair?

The researcher promised it was a non-invasive form of gathering biological information. It's just dead skin. With 99.999 percent accuracy he yanked my hair, pulling the strands, stuffing them into a plastic Ziploc bag. Right then and there he analyzed the root bulb, told me a story of Y-DNA, linking me to Asia and a story of haplogroup I, linking me to Europe, and of U5b1b connecting me to the Berbers. Even though it was a complicated story, full of tricksters and fornicators, it was a good story so I let him touch my hair again. This time he didn't pull it out. Instead, he leaned in and sniffed my hair. He said it smelled like a New Year, or maybe gunpowder.

Do you want to touch my Chinese Hair?

Well, we don't know if we're Chinese but we might be. We had a relative who worked in the canneries in Wrangell, Alaska, who came from China. Maybe he intermarried with our family. Maybe I have Chinese cousins.

Do you want to touch my creation story?

This story began with a young woman, me, who went off to college to study ology to become an ologist. She learned everything she could about Greeks so she could understand the colonizers' Western worldview like why she had to memorize the birth of Zeus and not the story of how Raven stole the sun, or how the Wind Man created the tundra for her Sámi people. She specialized in over four hundred ology stories: heliology, phycology, trichology, odonatology, nephology, and more. But even today she resists stories with beginnings, stories with a middle motivation, and an end that makes sense, a story so clear you can see a salmon egg on the bottom of the stream. Warning: *These stories are not fairy tales. These stories are not for children.*

Date: 2000s
Recorded by John Swanton
Assisted by Tooch Waterson

Big Jon Keats

"Big Jon Keats brought the first wave of cannery workers from Masset, British Columbia. But instead of working at the cannery, he worked at the meat department at Harbor Market. That's where I met him."

The cop stuck his finger in my chest. "Jorma, did you work at Harbor Market, too, or were you a bad boy and just shoplift there on occasion?"

"No sir," I told him. "I don't shoplift. And I work at Hammer's Hardware, but you know that already. It's Wrangell. Everybody knows everybody's business here."

"So," the cop questioned, "Did you notice anything different about Mr. Keats?"

I laughed. "Didn't you ever notice him walking around the town like he owned it—his black top hat on his head. Jeez, he was huge."

"Yeah, I noticed, kid. People say you two hung out together."

"We didn't *hang* out. I talked to him once in a while and went to his matches."

"Matches?"

"Yeah, he wrestled in Petersburg mostly. That ultimate fighter stuff. Jon is . . . he was wicked. He was so big he could flip a sea lion. That's what it looked like to me anyway, like he was hunting."

"Yeah, that's right," the cop said. "I think I saw his fight poster downtown on the drugstore window."

"Yeah, I'd show up at the fights and me and the guys would be cheering, and Jon would smile, like he was licking his lips."

"You two ever get in a fight?" the cop asked, looking me over.

"Hell, no. I'm not stupid."

"He ever threaten you?"

"No, but . . . he liked to tease." I almost broke into a smile. When I first met Big Jon, he came at me from behind the counter with two fistfuls of live dungies and put them on the floor. The crabs clicked around at my feet, and I jumped back. He laughed and said, *Kid, which one for lunch? They're all good.*

"When Jon smiled, he'd flash those long teeth, sharp bicuspids, and they'd glint, you'd swear it."

"Was he a killer?" the cop asked.

My eyes widened and I didn't know what to say, so I didn't say anything. I kept thinking about the way he tossed his opponents onto the mat.

The cop rephrased the question. "I mean, do you think one of his opponents could have fought with him outside the ring?"

"No, Jon wasn't like that outside the ring. Although I wouldn't cross him. Ever."

"Sure he never shoved your skinny white ass in a dumpster?"

"No."

"Maybe you made fun of his face."

"His face?"

"Don't give me no crap," the cop said. "You know, the birthmark on his face."

I once stood at the counter when a tourist walked in, and she took one look at Jon and stood there, staring. He had to ask her twice what she wanted. Jon had some of those dark brown marks on his arms too. They were hidden under his clothes most of the time. The one on his face covered the left cheek almost completely and then went down the side of his neck a bit.

"No, I hardly noticed it."

"No? Right," the cop said, shaking his head. "Well, we know you were on City Park Beach Saturday night."

"Yeah, what about it?" Near dusk, I'd been sitting on the big log out in front of the main shelter. How much I wanted to tell the cop, though, I wasn't sure.

The cop leaned back in his chair. "Here's the deal, Jorma. You were the last one to see him."

"Maybe his friends saw him last," I said.

"Friends? Those guys at the cannery?"

"Yeah, them. He came to town with them. Jon told me he was from Masset, BC. He's Haida."

The cop tapped his pencil on his notebook. "I already went to question them today, but they've all left. Gave the cannery short notice and left town."

"Well, the season's almost over. The cannery will be going on its fall schedule."

"Yeah, we get all kinds in here, from the Ethiopians to the Natives . . ."

I cocked my head. I thought I'd heard the cop say "Natives" as if it was a bad word. Those same slurs have been slung at me and my friends at one time or another. I came out light-skinned, with my dad's Native features and my mom's Finnish eyes. My blood quantum card says I'm Alaska Native but some see me as not *Native* enough. But that only happens when I go to visit friends in Juneau.

I shrugged.

"Your friend Clay says you told him you saw Big Jon Keats on Saturday," the cop said.

I cringed. "Clay said that?"

"Yeah, your buddy. Your *girlfriend*."

I wanted to say, *Fuck you, you Idaho flunkie. Can't get a job in Anchorage so you work in a small town until you get enough arrests and make a name, then move on. You don't know anything about the people here.* I thought this but said nothing.

"Well, kid, Earth to Jorma," the cop said, holding his hands up in exasperation. "Were you or were you not at City Park Beach on Saturday night?"

I'd sat on that log smoking some weed, watching the sun go down. It must have been late, because it finally got dark. Then I saw a big shadow walking down the beach and knew, by the shape of the head, that tall top hat, that it was Big Jon. He didn't see me. I don't think so anyway. But I saw it happen. Yeah, I did it. I'm guilty of not stopping him, of not running and grabbing his legs, of not trying to wrestle him down and keep him from walking out into the water.

"I was sitting on the beach," I finally said, "watching the sun go down."

"Just sitting. Maybe we could do a drug test, kid, and see what you were sitting with."

"Come on," I said, which came out like a whine.

"Tell me what happened."

I sighed. I didn't know if there was a law against watching someone kill themselves, but it had been weighing on me for two days now.

I began, "I went to Harbor Market to buy halibut and they said Jon hadn't showed up for work. They were worried, so someone suggested I go up to his house and see if he was there. Me and this other guy from work went to his apartment. He wasn't there. That's when the head butcher called the cops."

"So how'd you end up at the beach?"

"I was upset Jon was gone, so I drove to City Park and got out to walk my dog. I have a black lab."

"I don't give a shit about your dog. What happened then?"

"Like I said, I was sitting on the log and it was dark out but not really dark dark. I saw Jon walking down the beach toward me. I kept real still on account of his size and all. I didn't want a big wrestling giant to get spooked."

I figured I had to tell the truth. "Big Jon turned toward the ocean before he got to me and walked out into the water until his big head went under."

"You certain it was him?"

"I saw his top hat. I could see the shape of it in the dark and he was wearing a white T-shirt and dark pants like he always did. I could see the white shirt."

"Did he take his clothes off before he went into the water?"

"No."

"You know kid, we've got divers now looking near the beach and boats going along the shore. If you're lying and he's on the ferry to Skagway or home to Masset, then you're going to have to pay us back for the search. Or if we find his body, there'll be an autopsy."

"What if you never find him?" I said. Somehow, I didn't really expect them to find him. It was what it was. Big Jon was gone, like a lot of people who disappeared around here and never came back.

The cop clicked his recorder off. "Well, we might want to talk to you later, when we drag the body up. For sure, he'll be a floater soon."

The cop cocked his head, looked down at his notebook, then jotted something down.

"Did Big Jon know how to swim?"

"I dunno," I said, then thought about it. "Once, I did see him and two of those cannery guys coming from the pool early in the morning, about 7:00 a.m. I was riding my bike to work 'cause the cruise ship was coming in early that day, one of those Sunday ships. Big Jon nodded at me as he came down the steps. So maybe, yeah, they might have been swimming in there." What did I know? It wasn't like I hung out with those guys from Masset. What I didn't tell the cop, though, was that it was before the pool was opened. The sign still said "closed." It didn't open on Sundays until nine.

"So maybe he can swim," the cop said. "I wouldn't have figured a guy with a lot of friends like he had to off himself."

❊

I left the police station at dusk. They'd kept me there for two hours. I was shaken. I didn't know Big Jon well, but he was always nice to me and the guys. Gave us good deals on prawns.

I walked down Church Street, down the hill, to the city's cement dock. The sun dimmed to a pale gold behind the clouds and it started to rain. "Summer" was iffy here. Rain or sun, and rain usually won. I sat on the bull rail and hung my feet over. I wasn't afraid of heights. The only thing I was afraid of was staying in Wrangell forever, never going to the Outside, never going to Seattle, never finding a good job. Mostly, I was afraid of being the same as everyone else in Wrangell. Big Jon gave me hope there were different people in the world. I wanted different.

That's when I saw them. There were about a dozen. The one in front was leading them toward the cement dock. I'd grown up in Wrangell, and I was always told not to say anything bad when you saw a pod of killer whales swimming near the beach. When I was a kid, Grandma Liv told me whenever I saw a killer whale, I was supposed to head up to the treeline and stop playing by the water. Maybe she thought they might think I was a seal or something floundering around.

Now, the killer whales' breath misted the dusk, creating a cloud of vapor. They swam below me nearer to the pilings. From my height, I could see their sleek black-and-white bodies moving through the water. They lingered for a bit. The large one's tall dorsal fin rose out of the water like the top of a submarine. He moved out in front of the others, not lifting his nose completely out of the water, but I could see he was watching me.

I reached into my pocket and took out my Altoids tin and grabbed the last joint from the box. The pod moved back and forth along the front of the dock. Must be a ball of herring in here, I thought to myself. Then, before I lit the joint, I stopped. The large whale blew again. I put my lighter down on the rail beside me and put the joint in the palm of my hand. Ah, what the heck, I said to myself. I crumbled the joint in my hand.

I swung my legs back over the rail and stood up, locking my feet beneath the cement rail. I leaned over as the large whale turned and made another pass in front of the dock. I held out my hand and let the pot fall. It scattered in the water below. The killer whale blew again, his air rising up and filling my own lungs. I inhaled his big warm breath, smelling of salt, fish, and sea.

The killer whales turned, the big one with his towering black fin led the others down Zimovia Strait toward Prince of Wales Island. Maybe they would be stopping at Hydaburg, maybe head toward Haida Gwaii to Masset. And on the way, the pod might circle a rock island filled with sea lions like a pack of wolves. And the big killer whale, the one with the big top hat, will sneak up on a sea lion and toss it down into the sea.

Date: 1990s
Recorded by John Swanton
Assisted by Tooch Waterson

The Man Who Saw the Light

In the real world, there are always competing elements. In Sven Bolstad's world, it's fire and water. It wasn't as if he'd never considered this before. But for most of his life, he hadn't considered the consequences of anything he did. He sold custom fishing tackle that he himself created, working for Dammen Outfitters. He was a public servant and an important one, too. He was on the Ports and Harbors Commission and the Fire and Police Commission at the same time. And last October, he'd been elected port commission chairman, a paying position. Plus, he was the most successful drug dealer in town.

In a town the size of Wrangell most of that knowledge was of public record anyway, even his dealing. Ask anyone where to score some weed, coke, maybe painkillers. "Oh, that would be Sven or one of his six cousins." He had more experience with importing drugs to Wrangell than he had with *Roberts Rules of Order*. Those rules were confusing. Mostly because there wasn't an order to things. There was no evolution, no scientific method, and there certainly wasn't a god zapping and abracadabra-ing people into behaving. There were only random acts of chaos. All one had to do was look around Wrangell to discover that truth.

Of course, he never told anyone about these views, preferring to keep his theories to himself. After all, no one would have elected him commissioner if they knew he didn't give a shit about their ordinances. He didn't give a shit about their petitions. He didn't give a shit about their laws. He was a public servant because he loved center stage. Wrangell was the perfect place to be a "big fish in a little pond," as they say. He held this truth close, as if it were the last joint in his pocket. That is, until he had his first religious experience.

He'd been commissioner for one year exactly. The first meeting after the October elections had let out. He'd met new assembly members, new port commissioners, police and fire commissioners, the new parks and recreation committee, and the school board. He'd watched them being sworn in, professing to keep the laws of the state of Alaska, the US of A and, of course, their little borough, their little island. The new ones to town didn't know what they were getting into, always thinking they were going to change something, make the town better. Hell, Wrangell couldn't get any better. This town was Camelot, a perfect haven for Soapy Smith when he wanted to escape the heat in Skagway. A perfect spot for Seattle Mafia vacations and the antisocial hermits who lived on Back Channel. As one of Wrangell's political fathers had once said, "It's a dirty little town, and we're gonna keep it that way."

Sven walked up the Drug Store Hill to Church Street. Church Street boasted a church for nearly every denomination. Missionaries had first come to Wrangell in the 1800s to save the Natives. Funny thing, though, they were still here trying to do the same damn thing, coming into town in droves every summer, setting up cowboy- and Hawaiian-themed Bible summer schools. He didn't need saving, nor did anyone else he knew.

The meeting had given him a headache from trying to smile and nod while thinking, *You fucking weirdo new-to-town greenie geek with an environmental degree in your spanking new Carhartt pants trying to fit in. It won't do you any good to try and change us "backward" folks. I know you're thinking that about us. Well, wait fifteen years or so and, if you're still here, we might accept you as one of us. Maybe.*

He shrugged, pulled his hood over his ball cap, and slogged through the rain. The rainwater rushed like a muddy waterfall down the hill. Ah, crap, he'd forgotten to wear his boots. His shoes were soaking through.

At the top of Drug Store Hill, Sven's chest tightened. He coughed into his wet hand. The October storm season was in full swing and the weatherman called for seventy mile-per-hour gusts tonight. His doctor had suggested he take a walk now and then, and so he did. Once a month, he'd walk the few blocks down the hill to the City Hall near the water. He lived at the very top of the second hill.

Tonight, he'd practically snored through the discussion about whether or not to extend the cement dock another fifty feet. What did he care? Spend the money. Spend, spend, spend. The City Council wanted to extend the dock so they could accept large cruise ships into their deepwater port. What was the point? The ships weren't coming no matter what they did. There would be a few here and there. Some would schedule landings and others would drop out. Lately, only the smaller ships were consistent, and those old folks never spent any money in town anyway. Not even with the Stikine River playground in Wrangell's backyard. In order to get cruise ships here, they'd have to hijack the ships on their way to Sitka, the Paris of the Pacific, out on the ocean, and drag them all the way in here to the Inside Passage.

Yes, it was as if their town was transparent. That's what his grandma had said the landotter village was called, "Transparent Village." So, maybe folks were afraid. Maybe, Earp was right about Wrangell's wild and strange reputation. The town did still have a wild nature, despite the fact you could buy cannon balls and gurdies, and re-cork the bottom of your troller on dry land now. The best thing, though, about the town was that it was deemed the "friendliest town in Alaska." Everyone waved at everyone else. Well, take that back, his ex-wife didn't wave at him. But people would always want to stop and talk in the grocery store and chat on Main Street. And, they were always telling stories. Sometimes they were doozies.

In Wrangell, the myths remained, dancing around campfires and whispered over pizza and beer. Sometimes it was a story about who was sleeping with the neighbor. But the old stories were the best. Then there were stories about Thomas Bay, Anita Bay, up River, all the weird things that happened around here. As a kid, he and his friends used to tell landotter stories outside while camping. That subject was always taboo to talk about while around adults, especially the oldest ones, even his Norwegian grandparents. Sometimes he'd hear them laughing about trolls, but then they'd catch him listening and change the subject. He never knew why his Norwegian grandmother had married a Tlingit man. Back then, it was more common for a white man to marry a Native woman. His family teased him about being a Tlingwegian. Norwegian or Tlingit, it didn't matter, they shared the taboos. He used to dare himself and whisper the creature's name in the dark while playing hide-and-seek. Maybe that's when he decided there were no consequences, no order. Nothing seemed to happen. His friends would get mad at him, though. He played along. He and his friends would run into the house before the landotter people heard them and came scampering out from their stump holes. That was the most daring thing he and his friends could think of besides running around shooting each other with BB guns. He still had a BB rolling around in the back of his eye somewhere from when Karl Agard had shot him.

❁

The fifty-mile-per-hour winds shook the tin roofs on the small box houses. It was then, as the gust kicked his back, that Sven jerked himself away from watching where his feet were and looked up into the hillside. On Mount Dewey, a large glow emanated from the trees above the next row of houses. He stopped for a moment, puzzled, and leaned next to a metal railing keeping him from falling behind the back of the drug store. He blinked. In the light, shadows shaped like large men swayed back and forth. It reminded him of a dance he'd seen, as a kid, when he and his family had visited Hoonah. His mom had taken him to a clan memorial. All he remembered was being able to stay up all night listening to people speaking a language he couldn't understand and there was a lot of singing, dancing, and food. He remembered a men's dance, and the drumbeat had been stuck in his head ever since.

Now, on the hill above him, the dancing shapes and the light changed from yellow-gold to red, then white hot. It spit up a large spruce like a tongue of fire. What the heck? His head spun and he stepped forward to cross the street, not taking his eyes off the hillside. He intended to take a side street up to the highest level of houses above town, but he couldn't seem to catch his breath and his skin felt flush despite the cold rain.

Sven stepped out onto Church Street and didn't hear the car swishing toward him. A pair of mooned headlights hovered toward him. He slipped and fell as the moons bore down. He rolled his body back toward the sidewalk and the car drove past, splashing a small tidal wave of water, covering him. He jerked his head up trying to catch his breath in the foot-high puddle of water. Red taillights turned the corner and headed down the same hill he'd just walked up.

"Jesus Christ," he said, spitting muddy water from his mouth. Through the horizontal rain, the famous statue of Mary grinned at him from St. Rose of Lima's yard. He got up on his knees and then staggered up like a drunk. The brightly lit red cross on top of the Presbyterian Church steeple burned a hole through the horizontal rain. He wobbled, wiped his face with his hand, and straightened his ball cap. Water dripped down from the bill of his hat. He patted himself on the chest and sloshed through one large puddle to the other side of the street. His feet were soaked. Breathe. Breathe. He inhaled then coughed. Maybe he inhaled muddy water?

He headed for the red glowing cross on the Presbyterian Church. They'd have a phone. He'd call one of his cousins for a ride the rest of the way up the hill to his house. Crap. Goddamn heart, goddamn storm. His shoes sloshed up the cement steps leading from the sidewalk to the double wood doors of the Presbyterian Church.

The lights were off in the manse next door where the minister, S. Hall Young III, and his family lived. Sven turned the knob on the right half of the set of doors and opened it. He stamped his feet onto the mat and shook himself like a wet dog. His soaked jeans stuck to his skin, and his shoes muddied the floor. He took off his hat and shook his sleeves. He arms ached and his heart still beat rapidly. He tried breathing in and out, but he couldn't get a full breath.

"Christ," he mumbled, heading down the small entryway. To the right, the sanctuary doors were open, but the room was dark. Voices floated in from the left side of the hall, toward the kitchen. He'd attended many weddings and funerals here so he knew the layout: Jesus to the right, donuts to the left. He opened the door to his left and peeked inside. Two men and five or six women sat around a round table. Some of the women he recognized: Mrs. Johnsson, Mrs. Sarrel, Evelina Halko. Bibles were stacked on a table covered with a plastic-flowered tablecloth.

"Hey," Sven said hoarsely, trying his best to speak. He swayed at the door.

Reverend Young hurried to him. "Mr. Bolstad, what's the matter?"

Reverend Young led Sven to the table and sat him down at a chair. Mrs. Johnsson lifted her fat hand to his forehead. "My, my, son, on a cold night like this, you're burning up. You've got yourself a fever."

"You're soaked," Reverend Young added. "Let me help you."

Sven nodded as they undid his raincoat.

A young man with a guitar sat and stared at Sven.

Mrs. Sarell, another woman in the flock, brought Sven a cup of coffee. Sven took the cup in his hands. His hands shook. He sipped the coffee. "I saw . . . I saw the light. I came in because the light, up there." He pointed toward the wall behind them.

Mrs. Sarell, noting the large crucifix on the wall, clasped her hands and said "Hallelujah."

"Oh my," said Mrs. Johnsson.

The guitar guy strummed his guitar.

"No, no," Sven stammered. "There's a light up on the hill. Something's weird. Something's burning." He wasn't about to tell them about the dancing shapes. They'd think he was crazy.

Mrs. Johnsson mumbled something to Mrs. Sarell about it being Sven's soul that was the only thing burning.

"Christ," Sven mumbled back. "I mean, Jeezus." Sven shut his mouth. He couldn't find a swear word that fit the situation. He wanted to say "Fuck you all, you holy rollers." But, he'd figure they'd only lay hands on him and try and cast out his demons. But maybe not, they were Presbyterians, though he wasn't sure what Presbyterians did since he'd never actually been to a church service. By the looks on their faces, he figured his demons were here to stay.

Sven put his hand to his mouth and coughed. The group stared at him as if they were waiting for some explanation other than seeing a light. He said, "I was coming from a council meeting, and I looked up at the clearing on Mount Dewey and saw a light. It was glowing up there. And I don't think it was a fire. No one would be out this time of night. It's goddamn October." Sven paused and then said to the wide-eyed women, "Shit. Sorry ma'ams."

Mrs. Sarell waved him off. "Thank you for apologizing but I am married to a retired logger, you know."

Sven nodded.

Young said, "A fire? I agree. Not in this weather."

Mrs. Johnsson moved closer to Sven and sniffed.

Sven shook his head, "No, I'm not drunk."

Young turned to the parishioners. "I'm going outside to see if maybe I can see it."

Sven looked around the room. He wasn't about to stay here with these people. He said to the reverend, "I'll show you where to look."

The rest of the group followed. They put on their hats and coats in the foyer and headed outside. As Reverend Young opened the door, it whipped from his hand, slamming against the railing. "My, it's gusting now," Young yelled.

Holding their hats tight to their heads and trying to stay balanced, they crossed the street to the sidewalk on the other side. It'd stopped pouring, but was still raining. Sven pointed to the hill above the glowing red cross.

The guitar man whistled, "Wow, I see it. What the . . ." He stopped himself.

Young said, "St. Elmo's fire, maybe? Ball lightning?"

"No," Mrs. Johnsson said, "I seen ball lightning many times out fishing and it's not that."

"Maybe lightning struck a tree or something?" someone else said.

"Maybe, but the fire is . . . there's something in it," Mrs. Sarell said.

"Looks like people dancing," the guitar man said.

"People have been dancing again lately," Mrs. Johnsson said, "trying to teach the kids that Native stuff. Or maybe they're witches. There used to be witches here years ago and those shamans."

"What?" Mrs. Sarell asked.

"Could be those Natives," Mrs. Johnsson said.

Sven raised his eyebrow. His heart beat rapidly again. The wind flipped a nearby stop sign, bending it sideways and back again, rattling it hard. They stood for a few moments more holding onto the metal railing to keep their balance. The red cross above the church blinked on and off, on and off, as if it was keeping time with his heart rhythm. Suddenly, Sven recognized the pattern. He'd been a boy scout once and had learned Morse code. What the hell, it couldn't be . . .

The light on the hillside burned dimmer and then went out. Nearby, a tree cracked and thudded to the ground.

"Let's get back inside," Young said.

And, that's how he found himself inside the Presbyterian Church sanctuary on an October night on his knees with Mrs. Johnsson and Mrs. Sarell patting him on the back and handing him a Kleenex.

His concept of chaos ended with church every Sunday at 11:00 a.m., with the call to worship, the prayer, the hymns, the confession and more hymns, the word, and finally the prayers. He loved the Presbyterians. They even had the service spelled out on a wooden board telling everything they were going to do. He knew when to stand and when to sit down. There was order. Thanks to the Presbyterians, he now had the comfort of knowing the "shit wasn't going to hit the fan" anytime soon—or so he thought.

After a few months of attending church, he went to the doctor because his heart arrhythmia was gone. There was no fluttering or tightness or flip-flopping, either. The doctor asked if he'd been doing anything different, but, of course, the doctor already knew. Sven had given up drugs and drinking. He'd told his cousins he wasn't going to be dealing anymore. Nope. No more of that stuff. He'd found a new life, a new order. In fact, he'd even started to catch on to orders of the day, main motions, amendments, and debates. He even read through "Title 14: Harbor and Port Facilities, Chapter 14.01: General Provisions" while having his morning coffee.

All that changed, however, with one phone call. The phone rang before 11:00 p.m. in February of the following year. It was during the ten days when the Stikine River wind howls down the valley across the flats and into town and the chill factor dips to ten below zero and everyone stays at home.

"The church is on fire," the guitar kid's voice squeaked into the phone.

Sven threw on his turnout gear and jumped into his truck.

Cooper, another fireman, was already there spraying a hose on a full blaze. "Someone saw an explosion," he yelled to Sven.

"Furnace?" Sven asked. It was always the furnace, or the woodstove. That's the way it seemed, anyway.

Several hours into the next day, and after the fire died down, the air grew colder again without the heat from the fire. The church remained standing but the stained glass windows had blown out and the inside of the church was severely burned. Sven stood inside the church.

It's back. It's here. He could feel it. Chaos. It filled him and warmed up his feet, despite the broken windows and the cold wind whipping around in the darkness. A floodlight from outside beamed in through the windows. All around him he was washing in the blood of smoldering charred wood and brokenness.

Later, the dim winter afternoon light cast no hope on the burned church. Townsfolk had begun to gather to help clear out the wreckage. Sven helped carry out a few of the icons from the church to the manse next door and then headed back to help with cleanup. Reverend Young shuffled through the rubble, holding a small cloth against his face.

Cooper kicked over a pew and found a small section of pipe and held it up. "Looks like a pipe bomb."

Sven walked over. "What the heck?" A bomb? Who would want to do that? Why? His chest tightened. His breath caught.

Several other firemen gathered to examine the object.

Young said, "We've had trouble since—" he paused, then said, "lately."

"Trouble?" Sven asked. What kind of trouble? He hadn't heard of any.

"My tires were slashed about a month ago. One night, someone spray-painted something on the manse wall. And I found a torn Bible on the church steps one Sunday morning."

"Why?" Sven asked. These were good people. He was good people. It was a church for Christ's sake. It wasn't a bar or anything.

Young put his hand on Sven's shoulder. "Don't worry about it. We'll find out who did this."

The few hours of winter daylight had rotated in and out of the day while Sven helped clear the debris. Outside the church, darkness fell fast like a dark cape draping the island. Mrs. Sarell and Mrs. Johnsson stood bundled up in their parkas with scarves tightly woven around their faces. Sven recognized Mrs. Johnsson's round body, which looked even bigger wrapped up. Mrs. Sarell rocked nervously on her heels. Tears froze to their eyelids.

"I hope you're happy," Mrs. Johnsson mumbled through her scarf to Sven.

"Happy?"

"This is because of you," she said. "Everyone says so."

Sven raised his eyebrow. "Me?" What was she talking about? *Me?*

Mrs. Sarell nudged her.

Mrs. Johnsson pulled down her scarf from over her mouth and sneered, "Yes, you."

Mrs. Sarell pulled her away, "Tilde, this is not the time." She turned to Sven, "Maybe it would be best if you stayed away for a while."

Sven stood in the cold watching the two women wiggle their way down the street and stuff themselves into a car. His stomach soured. He wiped his forehead with his glove. Who did these women think they were? Were they judging him? Wasn't that against their rules or something like that?

Reverend Young walked over to him as another dump truck pulled up. He said, "We can meet Sundays in the manse until we rebuild."

"Yeah, sure," Sven said.

"The cross will have to be the first thing that functions. Everyone depends upon the light. It's a mariners' beacon, you know."

Sven said nothing but stared at the volunteers hauling away anything they could salvage for safekeeping and any materials for the garbage. Take it all away. It's all garbage.

Young nodded. "Sometimes God's plan is confusing. Sometimes, a light might not lead us to the light, but a light might be used to strand us somewhere, temporarily."

Sven said, "Yeah, maybe I realize now. There's a difference between being led and being stranded." Yes, like the old stories. There's a difference between being drowned and being saved. But maybe there wasn't. Led or stranded, either way, you're fucked.

Reverend Young went back to helping with cleanup. Sven got into his truck and drove up the steep hill to his house. At his home high above the town, he rummaged around in a drawer and found what he was looking for. In between the refrigerator manual and a pack of shish kebab sticks was a pack of Camels. He went outside on his deck in just his shirt. No coat. He wanted to feel the Stikine winds sting his hands and face. He wanted to feel the cold seep through his flannel shirt. He pounded his chest with his fist. He wanted to feel it right there. He lit his cigarette and inhaled deeply. The cherry from his cigarette glowed bright in the early morning hours still wintry dark. Sure, it would be light in a few hours, but goddamn, it would never be light enough.

Date: late 1990s-early 2000s
Recorded by John Swanton
Assisted by Tooch Waterson

The Girl with the Porcelain Face

Astri lay on the floor looking up at forty-three pairs of eyes. Her dolls, in their white gloves, silver and gold dresses, deerskin tunics, medieval gowns, bride's dresses, schoolgirl skirts, and pajamas. Her dolls with long brown and long blonde hair and short blonde and short red hair, curly and straight hair, all watched her from their stands.

Minutes before, Astri had flown down the stairs with the thrust of Evert's two strong arms. Evert Planz, Astri's husband, walked down the stairs and stepped over her. He went to the glass sliding door, opened it, and went out to his truck, got in, and peeled out the gravel driveway.

As soon as Astri heard the gravel roll beneath the tires, spitting chunks out toward their house, she knew it was okay to breathe, okay to remove her hands from clutching her swollen baby belly. Astri rolled up on her back, her arms behind her, half sitting up. She stared at the dolls who stared at her. Evert hated her dolls. In fact, now she had a dozen fewer dolls. Last week Evert had been pissed at her for ordering another doll from the Shopping Channel, so he proceeded to smash their porcelain heads on their stagecoach wheel coffee table and broke that too.

It wasn't Astri's fault she'd ordered the same doll she'd bought five years ago. The Navajo doll hid behind the Rapunzel doll up on the entertainment center, along with a dozen or so of them. She loved collecting dolls, especially the Native American ones. She had an "Eskimo" doll on a small sled with a small stuffed dog. She had an Iroquois doll, a Northwest Coast doll, an Apache doll, and a Seminole doll, even. She had so many she often forgot which one she'd ordered.

It wasn't her fault she couldn't remember things, and if Evert was getting mad about it, she couldn't figure that out either. Sometimes, she had trouble knowing if when Evert's eyebrows arched up it meant good or bad, or when he pursed his lips was he happy or sad or just strange. It seemed everyone else in the world knew those things: when to pause in a conversation, when to joke, when to know if a person was bored or uninterested, and lately, when to run.

Astri put her hands on her belly and wiggled it, trying to jiggle the baby. "You, okay, baby?" She waddled to the sink and had to rinse out a pink plastic cup in order to get a drink of water. Every dirty dish in the house piled in the sink. Astri didn't seem to notice.

She sat down on the couch and propped her feet up on the frame of the coffee table without the glass. She drank a few sips of her water and felt the wetness between her legs. She stood up and stuck her hand between her legs then held her hand up. It was red. She dropped the plastic cup at her feet.

❀

Suvi sat on the baby's grave with Astri. It had been four years since she held the silent child in her arms.

"Sometimes," Astri said, "I come here and lie on the grave and look at the sky. I don't say anything because I don't think baby Eric can hear me."

"I think he can hear you," Suvi said.

Astri pointed to the hillside behind the cemetery. It looked like it had been logged about ten years ago, but, in actuality, a mudslide had taken the mountainside down, shoving trees and mud into the new cemetery and flooding the old cemetery a block away.

"Did you know landotters can cause landslides and floods?" Astri said.

"I'd heard that, yes."

"That's what my dad told me. He said they might have did that."

"Astri, are you pregnant again?"

"Why? Am I fat?"

Astri was always a little round, rounder than Suvi. Beautiful Astri, with porcelain-like pale skin and black, black hair and dark brown eyes, eyes that never really focused and looked you in the eye. But now, Suvi saw the distant look, more distant than usual. She felt sorry for Astri being odd. The "Agard thing" townsfolk called it. No one had a proper name for it: the obsessive behavior, the inability to socialize properly, the inappropriate things they said in public. The Agard thing had been blamed on Norwegian stubborn square heads even, and over the years had been diagnosed as anxiety or depression. You name it.

Suvi saw it as the "Agard thing." Whatever it was, a few of Astri's cousins had it, and she was sure Astri's mother, Berta, had it and an uncle and maybe Karl and Rodney. But Astri had it worse than any of them.

And Suvi knew for sure Astri didn't deserve the broken jaw she'd gotten from Evert shortly after they were married, or the twisted ankle when he threw her down the stairs the first time.

"Yes," Astri said. "I'm pregnant. Two months, I think. I think it's a girl this time."

Suvi sighed.

"What? He's not going to kill this one. No."

"Are you going to leave him then?"

Astri frowned as if she hadn't considered that before. She said, "I don't know. I don't . . . sometimes, Suvi, I wish he was dead. Is that bad, wishing he'd die?"

Often, when Evert was out fishing on their boat, the *Island Luna*, Astri would imagine him with a circle hook in his hand, and the line jerking him overboard, or imagine him going out to piss in the middle of the night, still groggy, still drunk, slipping and falling into the ocean.

Suvi held the twelve-pack of beer in her arms in front of her as she walked down the Standard Oil float to the *Island Luna*. Rikka and Mina followed her with their own twelve-packs.

Mina said, "You sure Evert's down here and not up at the bar getting drunk? It is the Fourth of July."

"I'm missing the street dance, Suv," Rikka said. "I love the street dance."

"This is perfect, girls. He'll be in the mood to drink. There's a salmon opening in two days and he's been busy for a solid three days getting ready. And he likes women, Rikka, so use your charms. You, too, Mina."

"What about you?"

Suvi rolled her eyes. She was short and butch with curly dishwater blonde hair. Sure, Cooper loved her, but most men thought of her as one of the guys. Her favorite clothing were her Carhartts and her XtraTufs and a Henley shirt.

Down on the dock, she spotted Evert on the back deck of his troller, putting groceries into an ice chest. He'll see our beer, for sure. We'll be a gift from the gods. Sure enough, he whistled to them before they even got to the boat. "Where you going, ladies?" he hollered, when they got closer.

Rikka smiled big and headed for him. "Oh, we were going to go out in the skiff to drink some beer and watch the fireworks later."

Suvi was going to let Rikka do the sweet talking. She was good at that. Rikka had a way with men.

Evert said, "That's a lotta beer for the three of you. Are you sharing?"

Rikka shrugged. "Sure, you want some?"

"Yeah, come on board and have a drink with me."

"Okay," Rikka said, her voice singing.

Rikka, Mina, and Suvi climbed onto the *Island Luna*.

"Pull up a tote, ladies."

They sat around on totes, the beer on the hatch in a cooler of ice. Firecrackers popped in the distance and bottle rockets zipped across the harbor. Suvi sighed. It was taking too long. Evert chugged two down right away, not noticing the women sipping at their own beers. After an hour of talking story, Evert's words started to slur and he was red-faced. He put on some music and danced on the deck with Rikka.

He told them things like, "I love redheads and I love brunettes and you sure smell good."

Mina giggled, Rikka laughed, and Suvi tried hard not to puke.

Two hours into dancing and stories and singing and drinking, Rikka finally undid her long red hair from her ponytail and took off her flannel shirt. She sat in her skintight tank top stretching on the fish hatch. She put ice from the cooler on her face and rolled it around. "My, it's hot," she said.

Evert stared at her, his mouth open.

"You know, Evert," Rikka said, "we were going to pull our crab pot out front first, but it's probably full of dungies and too heavy. It's very hard to pull without a puller. We have to do it by hand." She stretched out her long white fingers and wiggled them at him.

Evert grinned and hopped up on the bull rail. "I can do that for you ladies. I can pull it."

"Oh," Mina said, "but it's getting close to dusk, and we're not exactly sure where it's at. Head out in front of the cement dock toward Sandy Beach. You'll see it in toward the beach in about fifty feet. The buoy's green."

"I can find it," Evert said.

He jumped down on the dock then turned toward them. "You girls will be here when I get back? We can cook up some crab. Have us a party."

"Oh, sure," they sang together. "Hurry back."

"Here," Rikka said, handing him a couple of beers, "take these with you. For the road."

Evert grabbed the two beers and staggered down the dock toward the girls' skiff.

Suvi called after him. "It's the little Lund on the second finger there." She hated the thought of loaning him her boat. It was hers. But what the hell. Every time she thought of Astri, she couldn't help but grit her teeth.

Evert didn't look back. He waved his hand wildly over his head, then tried to skip, but stumbled and then righted himself.

Suvi looked at Rikka, who looked at Mina. They said nothing.

❁

Evert got the skiff up on step before he even left the harbor. He zipped past the harbor office, past the breakwater, toward the cement dock in front of town. He turned the skiff out toward Sandy Beach and started to head across. It wasn't dark enough yet for the big fireworks show to start, so Evert figured he had a half hour or so. A bottle rocket zoomed over his head, landing in the boat. He reached over to grab it and let go of the outboard handle. The boat spun, tilted, and dumped Evert out of the skiff.

"Fuck," Evert yelled as he hit the cold water. His unzipped life vest popped up near his face, covering his line of sight. He tried paddling but his legs were like two driftwood logs, and he felt heavy. He swished his arms around, keeping his head above water when the skiff came around in a circle again and he tried to duck, but it was too late, the prop struck him in the head, slicing his skull. He started to float away.

❁

Evert was face down in the water. Someone on the dock yelled "Help!" and pointed to the skiff going round and round.

Karl Agard, Astri's brother, and his best friend, Cooper, were drinking on the cement dock where a crowd had nearly filled the dock waiting for the fireworks to begin. Dusk had turned to dark and everyone awaited the signal firework that would start the main fireworks show. Karl heard someone yell for him, something about an empty skiff spinning in circles out front. In these parts, everyone knew what that meant. Crap! Sometimes he hated the Fourth of July. Someone was always doing something stupid.

Karl and Cooper headed down the summer float beside the big dock, where several skiffs and runabouts were crammed in any available space. Karl found a small runabout with the key in it and started it up. They raced over to where the skiff went round and round and stopped it, pulling it against their boat.

Karl recognized the skiff as Suvi's Lund. "Shit."

"Someone must have stolen Suvi's boat," Cooper said to him.

Karl agreed. Suvi wouldn't be out here alone this time of night. Although there were dozens of Lunds, Suvi's had a big sunglassed Elton John sticker on the cowling.

Karl tied up the skiff to the boat and told Cooper to keep an eye out for anyone or anything. He was going in. He took off his jeans and, in his underwear, jumped in. He plunged through the green water and then came up for air. He swam around in the dark water until he spotted something floating on the surface. He swam toward it. When he got closer he saw it was a life jacket. He reached for it and tugged. Attached to one arm of the life jacket was a body floating below the surface. He turned the body over. It was Evert. He pulled Evert by the shirt, dragging the body over to the boat, where another rescue boat was already tied up to theirs. Cooper and an EMT rolled the body over the gunwale, flopping Evert into the boat. Above them, a blast exploded and a huge red chrysanthemum firework showered down upon them. The celebration had started.

❁

At Wrangell City Hospital, in the long-term care wing, Astri bent Evert's fingers back and forth, stretching them like the nurse showed her how. "Look what I brought," she said, his hand still in hers. She nodded to his bedside stand. "It's my new Indian doll." Really, it looked like a mixture of Athabaskan and Alutiiq. She didn't know and she figured the manufacturer didn't either, since it didn't come with a booklet.

Astri smiled at the doll on its stand. The doll's unyielding face, with full lips and painted-on eyebrows and eyelashes, stared back. It had a turquoise pendant and fake fur surrounded her cape.

"I like this one. It has a dream-catcher. See?" A small dream catcher hung from the doll's hand, feathers hung off the dream catcher.

She let Evert's curled hand drop on the bed. She lifted the doll over to him and then touched the doll's face. "It's porcelain. Like me," she said, touching her face lightly. "And her." She nodded at the floor. On the floor in a small car seat sat a chubby dark-haired, green-eyed baby girl with porcelain-like skin.

Astri put the doll back on the table. "I'll bring more. They make me feel good. I think you'll like them."

She stood up and bent down, picking up the car seat by the handle. The baby grinned at her. Astri leaned across the bed and kissed Evert's forehead. "Sweet dreams," she said as she left the room, closing the door behind her.

Date: early 2010s
Recorded in Sitka, Alaska
Recorded by Tooch Waterson

Two-Spirited

Two hundred and fifty years after they invaded her land, she held them hostage. They paid for a fifty-dollar tour and she was the Indian taking revenge on the tourists who come by the thousands on cruise ships. Tova walked to the other side of the van and heaved her small body up on the seat. For the past three summers, Tova had been getting paid to talk, which is what she liked to do anyway. Alaska Adventures had set rules about what guides could talk about. "Keep it simple," Marvin said. "None of your political crap, okay?" She'd agreed, but after work Tova and Marvin would argue politics over spicy crab rolls at the Island Pagoda, which could get hot since Tova hated labels and Marvin was ultraconservative.

Tova had friends from all walks of life, and Marvin was one of her "most difficult" ones. Marvin was older, had a son in high school and was married and divorced and remarried again. He struggled with the tour company he'd started after the pulp mill closed down and he'd lost his job. For many families in Sitka, Alaska, tourism was the angel that saved them from bankruptcy. For Tova, sometimes it was a pain in the ass.

Six days a week Tova heard her own canned voice say, "Old Sitka was established in 1799 by the Russians. The Russians established a trading post here until 1867 when Alaska was purchased by the Americans for $7.2 million." Over and over again, she'd hear her voice drone on. Yet, for Tova, greeting tourists was deeply ingrained in her heritage. Her great-great-great-grandparents were present at First Contact in the 1700s, the first to see the People-from-under-the-Clouds, the white men, as they sailed into Lituya Bay. Her clan members bravely ventured out to La Pérouse's ship. Onboard, they were given their first taste of alcohol, sugar, and rice, and they saw their reflections in a mirror for the first time.

Now, Tova shut the van door and turned around in her seat to address her passengers. She took a deep breath: this was the part she liked most. Marvin had approved her request to introduce herself in the Lingít language prior to beginning her tour. If the tourists focused on her introduction, it would keep them preoccupied and, quite literally, out of her hair. People always wanted to touch her hair. Maybe they wanted to "get in touch with an Indian." She could probably make money selling off locks of her hair. For this job, she had to keep her hair up in ponytail and dress in the required black slacks and a shirt with the company's logo on it. Her hair was long and thick, hanging down to her butt, so long she had to fling it aside in order to take a pee. Sometimes, her hair would wake her up at night yanking at her scalp, and then she'd have to pull it out from under her and put her hair in a knit hat in order to go back to sleep. She often slept in her Pippy-style hat, flaps around her ears.

As far as introducing herself in a language no one heard anymore, Marvin knew how she felt about the Tlingit language revitalization, which is why he didn't grumble when she asked to include a bit of the language in her tour. Though introducing herself in this manner was proper Tlingit protocol, the real reason she liked to introduce herself in Lingít was once the tourists were in her van, they *had* to listen to her speak. Nowadays, it was hard to find a *place* to be able to speak the language. And besides, on her tours, there were no elders around to tell her she wasn't pinching the letters correctly. "*Ch'a aadéi yei xat naay.oo. Lingít x'éináx Lugán Shaawát—*" Tova started to say.

A loud man from the back of her van said, "Shut up and speak English." Someone else laughed out loud. Tova sighed. Typical. People often responded rudely when they first heard one of the twenty sounds she could make that weren't found in any other language in the world. Tova said, "*Dleit ḵaa x'éináx̱, Tova Agard. Yéil naax̱ x̱at sitee. T'ax hit áyá x̱at. T'aḵdéintaan áyá x̱at.* Sámi *ka* Hawaiian *ka* German *ka* Norwegian *ka* Irish. Suomalaiset *yádi áyá x̱at.*"

Tova looked in the mirror toward the back of the van. Loud-Man's wife nudged him. Loud-Man turned toward the window. Tova remembered people when she gave them "Indian names." She'd done this since she was a kid as a way to remember their faces. She loved the human face, the way each one was different. She loved the thin craggy ones, the fat plump cheeks, the sallow eyes, the zillions of noses, the colors of skin.

Today, she had a full vanload of tourists. They entrusted their hard-earned vacation to her expertise. In her traditional language, she said she was a Raven and a Snail whose people came down river up above Yakutat, and her grandparents were Teiḵweidí, Bear people. She also said her people were Suomalainen, Sámi, Hawaiian, German, Norwegian, and Irish. Her passengers heard her say, amidst the Lingít, "Heinz 57," and everyone laughed. Afterward, Tova gave an English translation and Loud-Man said, "Finally." His wife, Quiet-Woman, told Tova to ignore him. *Yeah, right,* Tova thought.

After everyone in the van introduced themselves and said where they were from, Tova got excited because Loud-Man and the family in the back said they were from Israel. In college, she'd learned about the Hebrew language revitalization techniques. Tova said, "Cool. We learned about the Ben Yehuda's club in college." No one else, apparently, was excited to talk about it, so she decided to drop the subject.

Seated directly behind Tova was a couple from India with two children: Saffron-Man, Bindi-Woman, and Masala kids. In the middle seat sat an L. L. Bean Couple from California and a young Japanese woman wearing a Tilley hat: Tilley-Hat-Chick. Behind them sat a woman and man: the Furry Folks. Furry-Folk-Man and Furry-Folk-Woman bundled themselves in fur coats, clunky boots, gloves, and scarves despite the fact it was an Alaskan midsummer day and sixty-five degrees outside. And in the back, the twelve tribes of Israel squished onto one bench seat: Loud-Man, Quiet-Woman, Uncle-Aaron, Cousin-Ray-Ban, and Little-Greps. Tova made Cousin-Ray-Ban move up to share the seat with the Furry Folks and asked if Uncle-Aaron wanted to come and sit up front with her. He did. Uncle-Aaron crawled through the narrow passage, opened the van door, and hopped right up on the seat as if he was nineteen not ninety.

Now she had a vanload of happy tourists who'd spent a few hundred dollars on the cheap-economy-buster cruise deals currently being offered by the cruise lines—See Aluska: The Land of the Last Frontier.

Tova started to say, "Welcome to Sitka. We've been here for ten thousand years—" She was going to tell them about her matrilineal culture, how the Tlingit are organized by two moieties—eagle and raven—when Loud-Man informed her that her people couldn't have been around that long: He had never heard of them. Tova shook her head. She reached her hand up to her bottom lip to fiddle with her labret, but the labret wasn't there. She and a handful of Lingit language learners had had labrets pierced beneath their lower lips as Tlingit women once did. She often touched the labret to remind herself of the power of her words, to watch what she said. She sighed to herself—this was going to be one of those days.

Tova recalled her first tourist venture at ten years old, selling garnets to the tourists back home on Wrangell Island, a 120 miles from Sitka. She had to tolerate people who felt comfortable pinching her cheeks and calling her Eskimo. Tova wasn't Eskimo, of course, she was Tlingit, among a few other nations. She was Sámi, too. But at that age she didn't know what that meant. Eventually, she'd convince the tourists she wasn't Eskimo but Tlingit, but they couldn't pronounce it anyway. A kling-what, they'd say.

Tova would complain to her mother, but her mother would tell her to get back out there and sell garnets or they wouldn't be able to visit Disneyland that year. And her father would tell her to be a "Good Indian," using his same line over and over. "You know, kiddo, there are only a few of us good Indians left."

Those days were as ancient as her ancestors who pulled spruce roots with their teeth for basket weaving. Her father had disowned her nearly ten years ago after she'd told him she liked girls better than boys. She remembered her own Grandma Berta accusing her mother, "You should have made Tova wear dresses when she was little—and more pink."

Sometimes Tova wondered if her life was being run by a trickster. After all, she was a gay Indian with freckles, green eyes, and lighter skin than her brother.

Tova drove the van out of the parking lot to the small outer drive and then turned toward Lincoln Street, the street that went through town. She did her routine, pointing out shops, the hotel, the Russian Orthodox Church. "Here in the center of town is the Russian Orthodox Church, built in 1848 and burned down in 1966 and then rebuilt." After they drove the couple blocks through town, she headed over O'Connell Bridge. Once they were on Japonski Island, she pointed out the harbor, the university, the US Coast Guard Boat Station, the large Native hospital, the airport, the Coast Guard Air Station. She turned the van around at the airport, which was technically the end of the road, and headed back to town.

Tova drove the tour van back over the bridge to Totem Park, parking by the big white converted school buses the competitor used. She walked her tour group into the thick forest. The pine-needle path crunched beneath their feet, and the sun filtered in through the hemlock and spruce. She let the tourists touch the wood and taught them to identify the ovoid shapes and the faces carved into the pole. "Kootéeya," she told them. "Totem pole." In unison they said, *koo-tea-yuh.*

Tilley-Hat-Chick stepped nearer to Tova. "I'd like to get a photo of us together by this totem pole, if that's okay with you?"

"Sure," Tova said. She was used to this. She liked to say visitors to Alaska had been shooting at the Tlingit for two hundred years, but she didn't say it out loud this time. Tova sidled near Tilley-Hat-Chick. LL-Bean-Woman held up Tilley-Hat-Chick's camera. "Smile," the woman said. Click.

LL-Bean-Woman handed the camera back and Tilley-Hat-Chick said, "Everyone back home won't believe this . . . a white Indian."

Tova kept on smiling. Karma. After all, she *had* given them unofficial Indian names in her head. Probably, when they got back home to their comfortable worlds, they'd call her the "White-Indian-Tour-Guide." But people were more than color—they were shapes and landscapes like her Northwest Coast art: slants, squares, ovoids, circles, horizons, mountains, and valleys.

Tova asked Tilley-Hat-Chick, "Where did you say you were from?"

"Oh, Australia," the Japanese Tilley-hat-wearing woman said, walking away with her camera in hand.

What Tova hated most about this business, though, was she had to be charming in order to get the tips. For a job, the pay wasn't much at all: the tips made the job worth it. Yet if the tourists didn't like what she said, she wouldn't get any tips. And besides, she had a potty-mouth, so it was hard to not let "fuck this" and "fuck that" slip out.

And every now and then she wanted to do a rain dance, or play with a starfish on the beach, taboos that would incur the wrath of Raven and he'd pull down the clouds and let it pour. Sometimes, she needed a break. Once, her mother told her that in some indigenous cultures, gays were thought to be "two-spirited." Sitka was like that: one spirit in the summer and one in the winter. But whenever it rained heavily, her tour numbers would be thin. She'd get half a van because the tourists would either be on the ship complaining about the rain, or they'd all be snuggled up in Centennial Hall watching the renowned Russian dancers. Those days were very nice . . . and quiet.

Today, though, it was sunny. Today, everyone loved Sitka. Tova led the group along the park's trails, stopping to photograph the totem poles. They circled around to the narrow wooden footbridge spanning the river. Her group followed her across to the center of the bridge. Tova leaned over the rail and pointed into Indian River at the salmon spawning below them. Furry-Folk-Woman plugged her nose, "Eeewww, can't you do something about these fish, at least when the ships are in town? I mean, this detracts from the visitor experience, don't you think?"

Little-Greps made a loud sound, a tone somewhere between a fart and burp, then said, "Pee-ee-yoo." Quiet-Woman bopped him on the head and whispered something to him. Little-Greps rolled his eyes.

After they crossed the bridge and visited the Russian soldiers' graves, they crossed back over the bridge again and walked back to the park's cultural center near the parking lot. Tova took them inside the building where they saw a wood carver and a raven's-tail weaver at work. Then, she herded them into the tiny gift shop where they grabbed postcards, books, T-shirts, and hats.

Tova pulled several books from the shelves and turned to face the group. She cleared her throat. "Hmmm. These three books are the most reputable books about the Tlingit culture. Some of those tourist books are inaccurate." She set two of the books down on the counter and opened up the third one. "This one, on page 127 . . . there's a photo of my great-grandmother."

The LL Bean Couple and Tilley-Hat-Chick scrunched in beside Tova as she set the tip of her finger on a photo of her great-grandmother. LL-Bean-Woman nodded to the cashier. "It's a good thing your ancestors intermarried. You are so pretty. You girls really are." LL-Bean-Woman patted Tova's cheek. Tova turned to the Yup'ik girl behind the counter and mouthed, *Oh . . . My . . . God.*

Out in the parking lot, Tova loaded her group back into the van. She drove out the road toward Old Sitka, the first Russian settlement, which was at the end of the road, seven miles away. As she drove, she wanted to point out her own house, which was actually her cousin's, but she didn't. *Stick to the tour,* she heard Marvin say in her head.

As they passed the 35 mph sign, Tova sped up the van and began her talk. "Next, is our grocery store where you can park and watch whales lobtailing from the parking lot and eat chicken and jo-jos. Our food gets shipped up here on a barge from Seattle."

Tova drove on past the grocery store and pulled into a narrow parking lot next to the beach. Everyone remained inside the van. "And of course, you've probably already noticed we have our own Mount Fuji, but we call it Mount Edgecumbe. It's a dormant volcano. The last time it blew up was on April Fools' Day, in the mid-70s, when one of our local tricksters, by helicopter, dropped a hundred rubber tires inside the crater and lit them on fire. Everyone woke up in the morning to a smoking volcano."

The tourists laughed and Tova pulled out of the parking area and drove slowly along the narrow highway curving with the shore. For the rest of the drive Tova gave them the rainforest talk, the bear talk, the raven talk, and the no-we-don't-have-any-moose talk and the yes-we-have-a-post-office talk. Now and then Tova wondered what the hell she was doing here, the same job she'd had since she was a kid. She was thirty years old and she'd finished her master's degree, but, by the time she came home from Fairbanks, the job she'd wanted at the Park Service was already taken. Sure, she could get minimum wage jobs, but she had a master's degree in Indigenous Knowledge Systems, which meant she'd learned how indigenous people had survived invasions, survived HUD housing, survived Indian Health Service, Native Corporations, logging, environmentalists, public schools, and even college. What was she to do with a degree like that, except piss people off?

What Tova really wanted to do was get paid to talk, which is why the tour guide business in some weird way still fit her. She'd rather recite her poetry, though, and travel around hob-knobbing with other poets. In college, she dreamed about life after school, like the kids from the smallest of villages. Driving this van wasn't one of them. She was just being a "good Indian" like her father always told her to be.

On their way back to town, someone looked for the igloos. Another wanted to see a reservation. Tova politely told them what they wanted to know. Saffron-Man asked Tova about Tlingit customs, if they still practiced them. Tova told them about the koo.eex', the feast for the dead, which is held a year or two after a death. Tova said, "We still have forty-day parties after a death, use traditional medicines, eat traditional foods. Some of us still stomp our feet rather than clap our hands. Clapping hands is Western practice," she said. "We still believe in the landotter man and certain taboos like not bragging, not saying out loud you're going hunting."

Someone grumbled from the back seat. "Yes, any more questions?" she asked, turning down the lower road, heading toward the tribal house. Since most tourists asked to see their famous Russian dancers, Tova tried to steer tourists to the tribal house to see the Native dancers, a more authentic experience since there wasn't a single ethnic Russian in the Russian dance troupe. There were probably more Russian/Tlingits in the Tlingit dance group.

"This sucks," Little-Greps said as Tova stopped near the tribal house. Quiet-Woman squeezed his shoulder. "Oww," Little-Greps yelled.

Loud-Man grumbled. "Yeah, I want my money's worth."

Tova took another deep breath, "Well, Sir, I've taken you around town, did the tour you paid for. If you want your money's worth you might not like what I have to say, what I have to show you."

"Try me," he said.

"Does anyone else want a *real* tour?" she asked.

Quiet-Woman spoke up from the back seat, "I'd like a real tour."

"Sure, me too," Tilley-Hat-Chick said.

Saffron-Man and Bindi-Woman smiled. "Yes," they said.

Uncle-Aaron nodded. "You go ahead, young lady, we have plenty of time. Give us our money's worth."

Tova raised her eyebrows. "Oh, all right." She steered the van away from the sidewalk. She took the same route back through the narrow street, back up to the highway again. Along the highway she drove a few hundred yards and then turned the van up the hill to her cousin Roan's house, where she had rented a room.

"Pēśába . . . wee," the little girl said.

First things first. Tova pulled into the driveway. Tova invited everyone in for a bathroom break and a drink of water. Afterward, the tourists packed themselves back into the van again, but Tova was still inside. After a few minutes, she walked outside. She had changed her clothing into her regalia: she wore her bright blue *Fry Bread Power* T-shirt, the one like Thomas Builds-the-Fire wore in the film *Smoke Signals*—

a knock-off design from Superman with a bright yellow shield on a blue background. Also, Tova had slipped on her Carhartts, her favorite pants with holes worn in the ass. Beneath her canvas pants, though, she wore her thin, and equally threadbare, long underwear. She had put her silver labret back in her lower lip, and her long hair was now out of the hair tie, hanging loose down to her knees. She wore comfortable shoes that didn't make her feet hurt, and around her neck was her bear claw necklace she wore whenever she wrote poetry.

Tova opened the driver's door, swung her hair in front of her and hopped in. She turned around to face them. "Ready?" she asked.

"Ready," the group said in unison.

Tova stayed turned around in her seat:

Ch'u aadéi yei xat naay.oo. Lingít x'éinàx, Lugán Shaawát yoo xat duwasáakw. Dleit kaa x'éinàx, Tova Agard. Yéil nuux xat sitee. T'ax hit áyá xat. T'akdéintaan áyá xat. Sámi ka Hawaiian ka German ka Norweigan ka Irish. Suomalaiset yádi áyá xat. Karl Agard yoo duwasáakw ax éesh. Mina Laukonen yoo duwasáakw ax tláax'. Teikweidí dachxan áyá xat. Kachxaana.aakw dax as een.aa áyá. Sheet'ká Kwáan yei xat yatee. Gunalchéesh.

In English Tova said,

Please forgive me if my words offend you. My Tlingit name is Puffin-Woman. My white man name is Tova Agard. I'm a Raven from the Snail House, the T'akdéintaan clan. I'm Sámi and Hawaiian and German and Norwegian and Finnish and Irish. My father's name is Karl Agard and my mother's name is Mina Laukonen. I'm a grandchild of the Teikweidí, the Bear People. I was born in Wrangell, Alaska, and I live in Sitka. Thank you.

After she spoke, the tourists were quiet. She turned the van out of the driveway. In front of them, the volcano came into view again, and Tova said, "See the volcano out front? There's an old story about incest between a brother and sister and the shamed sister lives in the volcano. The volcano has a real name: *L'ux*, which means 'Blinking Top.'"

"*L'ux*," Uncle-Aaron said, smiling at her.

Tova smiled back. That word was hard to pronounce. "And we sometimes get earthquakes here in Sitka. Some of us still believe there's an Old-Woman-Who-Lives-Underneath, and if she gets too hungry, if she isn't fed enough fat, she'll shake the fault line."

"What kind of fat?" Bindi-Woman asked.

"How would you do that?" LL-Bean-Man added.

"Good questions," Tova said. "The fat is our stories. At least that's what I'm told. We have to keep making them up, keep telling new stories, or she gets mad."

"Ah, I see," Uncle-Aaron said. "You don't want anyone to forget. That's good . . . don't forget." Uncle-Aaron's voice trailed off. He turned his head and looked out the side window. No one else said anything, their breaths falling into Uncle-Aaron's silences.

As Tova drove them around town through back-street—the Indian village—she pointed out houses: "That's my cousin's house, and my aunt's house. And that one, the one with the rainbow flag, is my ex-girlfriend's house. And that other one, the one with the blue trim, is my other ex-girlfriend's house. And that's my ex-father's best friend's house—he disowned me because my father disowned me because I'm gay. And that's my uncle's house and my other cousin's house," she said pointing here and there.

Next, she drove them through the HUD housing and the other two housing projects. She said, "The Natives get the woods where we're out of sight and the rich folks get beachfront, places where we used to smoke our fish. Do you think we can cross their fancy yards to have a bonfire on the beach?"

Next, she drove them to the large bronze statue of Lord Baranof in the center of town. She pulled the van over. "And here we honor a tyrant, the beginning of our cultural genocide. And when the city erected it, before the unveiling, someone had chopped off the statue's nose in the middle of the night. They had to postpone the ceremony and do repairs. For many of us, it's like . . . it's like having a Hitler statue in a Jewish neighborhood."

Tova drove through the parking lot around the statue and then turned the corner toward the harbor. "And on the right is the harbor where my cousin shot himself in the stomach down on his boat."

Tova drove about a half mile. "And down the road a bit," she said, pointing to a small trailer court on the beach side, "is where my cousin lives. Whooo! Hooo! We get to live on the beach. Cory lives in the little silver trailer." She turned the van into the potholed trailer court. The van crept by a silver-sided trailer buckling under the weight of the mossy roof. "He has fetal alcohol syndrome. He works stocking shelves at the grocery store and repairs outboard motors."

Tova pulled out of the trailer court and turned left. Her passengers had been quiet for a while. Maybe she shouldn't be giving them the "real" tour. Marvin was going to be mad, really mad. She drove the highway until she turned down another small road. She slowed the van down next to a shuttered gray house. "And a while ago, right in this house—see, no one lives there anymore—is where a white cop murdered one of our Seagull Women: Cousin Kirsti. The cop shot her and then killed himself. Kirsti, my cousin, was his ex-girlfriend, and I guess the cop was pissed because she broke up with him. So he waited and must have planned it because, months later, he killed her. They can't sell the house. I don't know if it's because of the seagulls or the ghosts. I don't know," Tova said. "The seagulls still gather on the roof during every storm. The gulls, they're our clan members. And I'm worried, 'cause it's been raining a lot since Kirsti died."

Tova headed toward town again, this time going the other direction. She passed a large shop with whirligigs spinning in the wind. "In this shop, they're selling Native products made in Canada or China."

Next, they passed a large cement and brick building. Tova turned right at the building and slowed. "And on your right is where you can get a good state job working with the Filipinos and all the other immigrants in town, especially if you have specialized skills: wipe front-to-back, front-to-back, front-to-back. It's an old folks' home, but it's not half bad because we get to feed and roll and bathe and dress *and* talk in our Tlingit language if we want. Or talk Tagalog. The residents don't care. Most of them have Alzheimer's."

Tova slowed down as the road narrowed along the waterfront. She showed them the cannery and cold storage where many of her relatives had made their livings working the slime lines and egg rooms. At the end of the road, she turned the van around, back through town, and headed toward the old Sheldon Jackson College. She pulled the van up the hill to a small parking lot. Surrounding them were old brown buildings seemed to be weighted down with age. Moss grew on the roofs. "This is what remains of the closed down boarding school where they beat the little kids for speaking their language. It was run by the Presbyterian Church. There are still some churches in town that say we're evil because we have totem poles and masks and raven worship. We can still feel the spirits here. They still haunt this place."

Next, they drove over the O'Connell Bridge, again. This time, she slowed way down, nearly stopping the van at the top of the bridge. She pointed beyond to the roof of the large Native hospital. "And, on the other side of the bridge is the Native hospital, and if you live here long enough you'll get to see a Native kid commit suicide by jumping off this bridge." She pointed to the right, over the edge. "I knew a kid who jumped from here one winter. He lived. But there was a girl—" She decided she didn't want to talk about it and slowly moved on.

"And over there is one of the only remaining boarding schools in Alaska. They take the brightest kids from the villages and educate them. Often those kids don't go back home."

Tova turned the van around and swung out onto the main highway again, heading back over the bridge. She drove past the town center, the hotel, and the four-way stop. She drove past a large grocery store. "And, on your left, is one of the grocery stores that lock their Dumpsters to keep out the problem people who used to Dumpster dive there and get some pretty good food. And, now, they donate the food to the bear sanctuary. Those are the problem bears that keep getting into our garbage cans. I have trouble with that one 'cause both the people and the bears are my relatives."

Finally, Tova pulled into the parking lot where the lightering vessels—the small boats—were shuttling tourists out to their ship, which was anchored in the bay. She put the gear into park and leaned back in her seat. No one said anything. She opened the van door and got out and then went around the van and opened their doors. Outside, her passengers mingled around near the van and then she said, "One more thing. I think we need an exit song. Follow me." She began to walk around the van and they followed. Tova started to sing, "*Tsu héidei shugaxtootáan . . .*" She turned to them, and they stopped suddenly behind her. "Sorry, but we have to sing the song four times. That's the sacred number: four. Sing with me."

"Okay," Quiet-Woman said, "we'll try."

"Come on," LL-Bean-Woman said, tugging LL-Bean-Man.

"*Tsu héidei shugaxtootdan yá yaa koosgé daakeit haa jeex' a nák has kawdik'eét' ei, hei hei hei hei, Yei hei, yei hei, hei hei hei hei,*" she sang. She didn't want to tell them it was the only Tlingit song she really knew all the words to besides "Twinkle Twinkle Little Star." She didn't have a drum, and besides she would be the first to admit she was a terrible drummer. So she sang while the tourists followed her around the van, trying their best to scrape the strange letters across their tongues, slick them down into their throats, and spit them out the sides of their mouths—"*Tsu héidei shugaxtootdan . . .*"

After four times around the van, she stopped. The other guides and their passengers stood around their buses staring at them. She thought she saw Marvin in the crowd, standing back, his eyes wide. She said to her group, "You just sang, *Today we will open the container of wisdom that has been left in our care.*"

After a few seconds, Bindi-Woman opened her purse and was fidgeting around in it. Loud-Man handed Tova a hundred dollar bill. "Good job," he said.

The others surrounded her, thanked her. Someone handed her a ten; another, a twenty. The Masala kids gave her five dollars each. "*Gunalchéesh,*" she said.

Tova busied herself stuffing the bills in her wallet when she looked up at the sound of a foot hitting the ground hard, not once, but several times: thunk-thunk-thunk-thunk. She looked beyond LL-Bean-Man and LL-Bean-Woman to Loud-Man who walked forward, arms against his sides, stamping hard. Uncle-Aaron and Cousin-Ray-Ban were behind him, stomping their feet. Quiet-Woman pulled Little-Greps forward and then stood—clomp, clomp, clomp. Then the Furry Folks moved forward, flopping their boots on the ground—ka-thump-ka-flop-ka-thump. Tilley-Hat-Chick snapped a photo while stomping her feet.

Soon, Tova's entire tour group surrounded her, stamping the pavement. Over and over they stomped, staring right at her. Tova blushed. "*Gunalchéesh*, thank you."

And at that moment, Tova felt the crust of her skin shifting, the surface of her two selves sliding past each another, her energy radiating outward. She looked down at their stomping feet, as the Old-Woman-Who-Lives-Underneath grabbed hold of their fault lines and shook them all from ten thousand feet below where they stood.

Date: 2000s
Recorded by John Swanton
Assisted by Tooch Waterson

Muskeg Swallows Restaurant

Knut and Charlotte were having their usual breakfast in their usual place on the Loop Road at the airport's River Flats Cafe. They'd met there in 1973 when Charlotte first moved to Wrangell. She'd gotten a waitress job at the River Flats. She was only twenty-five years old then, and she'd heard about Alaska pipeline jobs. Since she had to go to work after her trucker husband was killed in a jackknife on I-5 near Seattle, Charlotte hopped the ferry in Seattle and headed north. Charlotte only made it as far as Ketchikan though because that was the ferry's first stop. She left after a week because it rained so much, even more than Seattle. So, she figured she'd try the next town—Wrangell. By then, she figured she'd better get used to the rain, so she stayed.

Knut was from a prominent old Wrangell family, the Dammens, and had just finished taxidermy school. He had returned home to take over his dad's business, Dammen Outfitters. The day Knut came in the diner, Charlotte thought the look on his face, as he ordered cream shrimp on toast, was one that wondered what she was made of. If she could have guessed, which is what she liked to do, she'd have figured Knut for a doctor or something. He had nice hands. And she wondered what lingered beneath those gray-blue eyes and broad shoulders.

When Knut told her his name, she thought he was saying "eye-of-newt," like an ingredient in a witch's brew. Or maybe he was referring to "squirt," an old childhood nickname. At that time, she wasn't quite used to hearing the Scandinavian names.

Eventually, she married Knut, quit waiting tables, and went to work at Knut's family business. But she couldn't figure out *why* she married Knut. Maybe it was the family name. Everyone in town enjoyed wearing their various Dammen Outfitters slogans: Dammen and Damn the Women, too. Get your Goods Dammen. Dammen the Authorities. Buy a Gun from us Dammen Folks. Animals are Dammen here. Dammen All.

But he smelled like gun oil and that wasn't as bad as smelling like whiskey like her late husband, Leo, did. Charlotte didn't want to marry Knut, but she didn't want to be serving greasy, double cheeseburgers all her life. She would rather have gone north. She'd never been to Koot's in Anchorage to dance on the sawdust floor nor ridden a funboard on Yakutat's beaches. The farthest north she'd been was Juneau. She and Knut had only one child, a daughter, who was off at college in Fairbanks studying environmental engineering.

Really, Charlotte had wanted to be a world traveler. Maybe take photographs for a magazine. She wanted to wander like a monk in the temples of Angkor Wat in Cambodia. She wanted to eat *hangikjöt* at a cafe in Reykjavík, Iceland. She never knew how she was going to do those things anyway. Life had gone by and she was sixty years old. And Knut, he wasn't the intellectual type, unless you were talking about salt gradient in salmon or the epoxy used to shape the fake nose of Sitka blacktail.

Knut ordered his eggs over easy, whole wheat toast no butter, and a small orange juice as he did every Sunday for the past thirty-five years. Charlotte sighed audibly. She held the menu in her dainty hands, turning it over and over.

The waitress said, "Look honey, the menu hasn't changed. What do you want?"

Want? thought Charlotte, *I want something different.* "I'll take the French toast with strawberries and whipped cream. And bring me a big cup of coffee."

Knut stopped sipping his coffee. "Char, you don't like strawberries. They don't agree with you. And coffee? Since when?"

Charlotte shrugged. She didn't tell him nothing agreed with her lately. Strawberries, cream certainly, Knut's boxers on the floor, the way he left the toaster plugged in with crumbs all over the counter. There were some things, though, that did agree with her. She smiled and took a sip of her water.

"What?" Knut asked.

Oh, nothing. She didn't answer him. She was a daydreamer. It bothered Knut that she could sit for an hour looking out at their garden. When he tried to probe her about what was on her mind, she never really told him. Well, take that back. Once, she told him she was thinking about the wonders of the wood frog. There is something mystical about frogs. The wood frog can survive in the Arctic. It can freeze in the winter and thaw out in the spring.

Knut had guffawed so loud she figured she'd always tell him half-truths from then on like "Oh, Knut, I'm thinking about heading to Harbor Market for prime rib on special." Or, "I was thinking about sending my friend Henna a card for her birthday." Really, she was thinking about meat, more or less, since she'd met Henna's younger brother, Tero, who was ten years younger than herself. She blushed whenever she thought about him.

No, they had never had any real contact, except the way his hand brushed hers at Henna's house six months ago when Tero was visiting. Charlotte had asked for her coat to leave and when Tero handed it to her, their hands met. Ever since then, she'd been thinking about that vibration. Was it static in her coat fabric? For a second, Tero's eyes had held hers. She'd never held a gaze like that with Knut. It was as if the ground wobbled a bit.

Charlotte and Knut's breakfast came and the waitress set it down in front of them. Charlotte's strawberries and cream were piled high. She scooped a gob of cream and put it in her mouth. "Mmmm," she murmured, almost purring. And, that's when she felt it, the feeling of being sucked into a vacuum cleaner. It was different from her hot flashes. She smelled it too, damp like rotting spruce trees, a smell she actually liked.

Just then, the booth's bench seat shifted. Knut seemed to sit a bit crooked. She was going to tell him to straighten up when he slunk to the side even more, tilting sideways.

Charlotte shrugged and took another bite of cream, scooping up a big slice of strawberry. *Whump! Crack!* Knut's eyes widened and she turned. The window in the booth next to them had cracked all the way down like a jagged bolt of lightning.

"Earthquake?" she asked Knut.

"Maybe. I don't know."

The room shifted again.

"Should we leave?" Charlotte asked, wiping her lips.

"No, it'd be worse out there," he said as the ground gave way around the parking lot. Their parked car slid into the crater. "We'll be safer in here than on the road."

The restaurant wasn't really crowded yet, because the crowd was still in church singing hallelujah Jesus or crossing themselves. Charlotte had never been a church person and, even though this moment had the possibility of becoming an emergency that might need prayer, she didn't know any prayers.

The room did seem to tilt a bit, Charlotte thought, and the hanging lights swung. Just then, a scream bellowed from the kitchen and something crashed. The waitress ran out, her mouth open, the scream leaching out half cried. Before she got to the door, the floor tilted and the diner dropped like an elevator going down.

Charlotte took another bite of French toast. Outside, mud and water rose to the windows. She chewed and looked out.

Knut grabbed his coat and stood up, hanging on to the back of the bench seat. "Come on, Charlotte, let's get out of here. Something's happening."

The waitress, still on her knees, her hand on the counter, tried to get up. She yelled, "We're sinking!"

Charlotte grinned as Knut held out his hand to her. She said, "I'm not going."

"What? We'll be safer outside."

"I'm not going." She started to cut into a piece of French toast when the room tilted more. Knut's glass of orange juice sloshed and slid off their table.

Knut's knuckles turned white, gripping the back of the bench seat. He gritted his jaw and spoke through his teeth, "Get going. Now!"

Knut had never been firm with her like that, so she knew he was stressed. But, she also figured it was the knight-in-shining-armor syndrome he'd always had, since he'd always assumed he'd rescued her from a life of drudgery. Trying to rescue her again, she supposed.

"No," she said. "I'm eating. Wait till I'm finished."

Knut huffed and turned around. He put one leg out and heaved his large body up the incline. "Suit yourself," he said, starting to walk uphill. He clung to the tables until he got to the front door. The waitress was trying to open it. Knut reached around her and jerked the door open. Mud and water poured in, wetting them to their knees. He reached up and pulled on the jagged concrete now at waist level and pulled himself up onto the parking lot. Knut lowered his hand to the waitress, who grinned, offering her hand. He pulled her up like a big halibut being lifted onto a boat deck.

The cook, Mrs. Johnsson, and another waitress emerged from the kitchen yelling at Knut. Knut bent down and helped them up into the parking lot.

Knut walked along the edge of the broken concrete over to where she sat, which was now below him. He put his hands on his hips. Charlotte shook her head. She licked her lips and grabbed for the maple syrup jar wobbling on the table. She poured it on top of her French toast. She forked a bit into her mouth. "Hmmmm."

Now, no one else remained in the restaurant. Charlotte's coffee tumbled off the table and rolled downhill. The building went *woompf* and sunk farther. Sirens howled. She could no longer see the parking lot. Surrounded by mud and water, the restaurant darkened and took on a musky scent. Suddenly, a window in the back of the restaurant gave way and mud and water poured in.

Charlotte swept a piece of French toast through a puddle of syrup as the ceiling broke through near her, tumbling sheetrock chunks into the mud. A fireman hopped down in all his gear. He stared at her sitting there. She'd always loved firemen. He clopped over in his boots and grabbed her by the arm. Her legs stuck in the muck, but the strong fireman dragged her over beneath the hole. Someone tossed a rope down and he tied the rope onto her waist and told her to hold on. He motioned someone above, and tiny Charlotte went up easily.

Up, up, up to the daylight Charlotte went. Up, up, up to the typical rainy, soggy, wet Sunday morning. Up, up, up to the flash of cameras. Up, up, up to Knut's face, his eyebrows pressing his eyes to narrow slits. Up, up, up to what she didn't know, nor did she care. Charlotte smiled. This would be something to write home about when it was the spring equinox and she was in Siem Reap eating *lok lak* and *pau*. It was something to think about when she was bicycling to the gates of Angkor Wat, when she sat on the sandstone and laterite bricks with her notebook in her hand, when she stood in the center of the five lotus towers, where she would feel herself being lifted by herself.

Date: 1990s

Recorded by John Swanton

Assisted by Tooch Waterson

Year of the Fire Dragon

One breath from Shen Lung's mouth to spread the fire in the Presbyterian Church. Cooper was Lung Tik Chuan Ren, a descendent of the Dragon. He was a dragon. All it took was one breath like his brother had said. One breath.

Cooper stood in the dark with a lighter in his hand. He could do this. He didn't want to think about it. He poured a can of fuel along the inside back wall of the church on the woods side. He was crouched down between two pews when the stained glass window, depicting Jesus on his knees praying in a garden, shattered and a pipe bomb rolled in. What the heck? Who?

Every part of his mind screamed "Run!" but he didn't. Luckily, he was on the other side of the church next to the organ. He crouched down and covered his head.

The bomb exploded and Cooper's ears seemed to blast into his head, as if inside a firework. It was a familiar sound, a familiar smell, a familiar red flash. He raced for the fire extinguisher near the double doors to the sanctuary and then stopped. Next to the doors, he closed his eyes and blew out a big breath of air.

At once, the fire burst through the sanctuary, eating the wood benches and swallowing the wall hangings.

"Burn, burn," he said softly, watching the Bibles ignite.

Goddamn Mr. Young, preaching about the old evil ways of the Natives and the Chilkat blankets, the ermine hats that floated out eagle down feathers when you shook your head, and the dancing and singing and the Tlingit language. In a week Mr. Young planned to have a bonfire at City Park. He was going to burn evil things, just when people were starting to carve again and starting to learn songs and dances. For months now, Young's sermons kept getting more radical. Then someone, he didn't know if it was Young or not, mentioned something about burning the evil stuff like they did in Kake in the 1920s. Holy crap. Wasn't there something about inherited trauma he'd seen on the news? Sperm and eggs and stuff like that could pass on fear and trauma. He was a fireman. He knew about trauma. He'd seen his friends suffer over the years, and they weren't even born when they burned the evil stuff in Kake, when they took kids away, when they made them stop dancing and drumming.

The church set the date for the burning. It was a sign. The idea had jumped around in his head like a hot spark out of a bonfire. Sure, he didn't know his mom's language, nor had he ever been to a ceremony for the dead, but he was tired of people joking about dumb Indians and smart ones and Stupid Finns and big-headed Norwegians, and the dirty Lapps, the Chonky and Chink, and the skanky women who were trying to be loved. Those things were as good reasons as any he'd told himself, as he slipped the lighter into his pocket.

Suvi, his wife, went to the Presbyterian Church once in a while. Suvi had told him about the sermon young gave after Kirsti had been murdered in Sitka. It still angered him to think about. Young preached about the consequences of loose women two days before Kirsti's memorial. Loose women? Who in the hell says that these days?

Sure, he'd been over to Kirsti's place a couple of times when she lived on the low road. Kirsti was sweet. He was a married man when he did that, had been married to Suvi for quite a few years and they had two kids. But Suvi was different. She liked girls too. He knew that about her, and he still loved her. Love was love. What did it matter?

He'd fixed the screens on Kirsti's windows and put a new element in her oven. She was a nice girl, and he thought he might be in love with her, but he could not leave Suvi. Suvi had claimed Mr. Young had yelled out, "Keep thee from the evil woman, from the flattery of the tongue of a strange woman." Suvi said she feigned a headache and got up and left. He was proud of Suvi always sticking up for folks.

Things were weird now, though. Kirsti was dead. It still sounded strange when he said it, when he thought it. Kirsti's dead. Over the last few years since she died, spring was arriving earlier, the sea had risen nearly forty inches, there were more butterflies in the summer, and the Dungeness crab were decreasing. There were more weird things. Since she died he'd been having dreams about dragons as if they were real. Whenever he was stressed he'd dream of them. He'd done that all his life. That's how he knew he was under too much stress: he'd fight a dragon and kick the shit out of his sheets. His big brother Dewie used to scare him with a lot of talk about dragons. When he was little, Dewie told a tale of four dragons that flew from the sea into the sky—how they made it rain.

Now, Cooper stood in the church, watching the fire. After a minute, he decided he'd better head through the kitchen and out the back door. Dewie would be jumping into his turnouts soon and heading over. Cooper laughed: Dewie, the pyro. Dewie the dragon. He'd always thought Dewie had the problem with fire. Well, maybe it wasn't exactly a problem. What it was, though, he didn't know.

Once, when they were kids, his friend Karl Agard told him to ask his big brother Dewie about the town fire. Cooper was impressionable and looked up to Dewie. He was five years younger than Dewie—his mother said he was an *oops*. Cooper was born in the year of the Tiger: He'd thought that was stupid. He'd never seen a tiger before, only the big lynx his uncle had shot one time. He wanted to fight dragons. Be the hero. Funny thing, Cooper could remember the fire. It was as if he was walking with his mother and brother that night. But he knew it couldn't be true. His mother was six months pregnant with him when the town burned down. She would always talk about that night, cross herself when she told the story. She told the same story over and over again, how the fire chased her out of the house. How it seemed to think and move around the town, burning building after building.

Cooper had once asked his big brother Dewie if he'd started the town fire. There were rumors, of course. No, Dewie had said, it was a dragon living in the back of stores: the furnace dragon. The night of the fire, when their mother was escaping from their store up to St. Rose of Lima, Dewie said he'd seen it sashaying down the alley with its long tail and breathing out water along with fire.

❁

Cooper walked out the back door of the Presbyterian Church into the night toward the treeline. Someone had beat him to it. He didn't see any cars rushing away. He stood next to a hundred-year-old spruce, ears still ringing from the explosion, trying to sense a shadow or listen for a snapping twig. Most of the church lot was cleared, had been cleared for a hundred years, since about the time John Muir showed up in town when they were building the manse.

Dewie had also told him that, when Mr. John Muir built the bonfire on Mount Dewey, it was really a dragon and Muir didn't want to tell anyone about it. What if it a dragon did live up there? Dewie had said dragons get hungry in the winter and come out of hiding and that's why there's a lot of house fires in the winter. When the dragon is starved, that's not good, especially if the dragon remains at a temperature above the fire point of the fuel gases. Give the dragon oxygen and the dragon inhales and the gas is heated and expands. Dewie warned Cooper to watch out for puffs of smoke sucking back into a room beneath a door frame. Also watch for dragons on the ceiling moving up from a couch, spreading its tongue along the ceiling. Dewie was full of shit. Mostly. Maybe. But his advice had kept him alive all these years. Maybe it was time to retire from fighting fire. Maybe he was testing the fates.

"Why are you a fireman, Dewie?" Cooper recalled asking his brother once.

"Because I want to fight dragons," Dewie had said.

To Cooper, that made sense. Cooper had seen what dragons in basements could do. Cooper remembered the dragon furnaces Dewie had told him about. He'd seen a dragon in the back of Hammer's Hardware. Its eyes glowed orange. Dewie snuck him into the back of the store and there it was, roaring. Huo Long, Dewie called it.

Cooper knew what woodstove dragons and hot-bacon-frying-pan dragons could do, too. One December, a few days after Christmas, he and Dewie were called to a fire. It was an address they knew but no one used street names. Typically, a fire location was announced by referring to the house next to it or the informal names of the neighborhoods and the roads—the blue house next to the Dammens or the small yellow trailer next to the Johnssons. That time, it was Karl Agard's cousin, who'd recently gotten her own place. Now, four days after she'd moved in, her small brown tarpapered house was on fire out at six mile on the loop road before the pulp mill   second driveway on the right.

That time, the woodstove dragon coughed out sparks on magazines and kindling set too close. Cooper had stayed with Karl until they found his cousin's charred body. She was twenty-two years old. When they found her, Cooper tried to pull Karl away, but Karl looked anyway and then bent down and puked all over the charcoal-smeared snow.

Cooper always thought there were too many house fires in Wrangell, despite the fact the fire department held woodstove safety classes and handed out free smoke detectors. Then it occurred to him that maybe the dragons weren't starved. They were pissed off. Someone had offended them. The dragons were mad because the white folks used to cut up the bodies of dead Chinese workers and salt them and stuff the body parts into big barrels and put them out on Deadmans Island—the small island at the mouth of the Stikine near the airport. Over the years, about a dozen or more barrels had accumulated on the island. It was Suvi's grandmother, Grandma Tova, who protested and demanded they bury the Chinese dead in the cemetery like Christians. This was history he didn't learn in school. He'd heard it from the old-timers: it must be true.

Grandma Tova was a young woman then. She went down the dock and yelled at them. A river scow was sitting there with two barrels ready to go to Deadmans Island. The young men had died of a severe flu that swept through town. Grandma Tova had two other ladies with her. One was a Japanese woman, but the men in the skiff didn't know that. The women made them haul the barrels up to the cemetery and bury them properly. And Cooper's great-grandpa, Captain Jinks, had helped conduct a ceremony.

No one came from China to get the barrels on Deadmans Island though—not that Cooper knew of. They disintegrated. Probably there were a lot of bones and spirits running around, which was why no one ever went there.

❁

The fire trucks pulled up, and the firemen ran hoses to the church. Cooper walked to his truck where it was parked on the back street, got in, and drove around to the other side in front of the church. He hopped out, already in his turnout gear. Dewie stood there, spraying water on the church along with a dozen or more volunteers. The fire shot up out of the windows and the water fell equally hard against it—fire and water competing in the natural world of elements. Cooper watched his brother desperately trying to stop the fire from rising up through the roof to the red cross, which had now gone out in the church's tower. The urge to jump in and help no longer pulled him toward the heat.

Babies dream inside the womb, his mother had said. Maybe it's like trauma DNA. His mom was a smart woman. His dragon dreams chased him a lot lately.

A memory or a dream?—a red chrysanthemum firework exploded and he felt its heat. The fire went through him as if performing a dragon dance. He kicked and moved with it, pressing against his mother's belly. Gongs chimed as he rose and fell and twisted with the "whirlpool," the "cloud cave," and the "dragon chasing the pearl." In the dream or not a dream, the dance ended with a burst of firecrackers, and at that moment, Cooper knew he was alive.

Date: 2010s
Recorded by John Swanton
Assisted by Tooch Waterson
Speaker: Mina Agard

Daughter of the Tides

I'm sitting on a log watching the tide come in. I've got about another hour, so there's enough time to tell you a story. It starts like this: When I was a teenager, I was impatient, and I couldn't wait for the berries to ripen, so maybe it was the blueberry leaves I ate. I loved to pick the blossoms off and eat them. I ate the leaves too. But I suspect it might have been the spruce tips, those unripe needles hanging off the end of the spruce branches I picked sooner than nature intended. I know, I know. I've heard the story: Raven turns himself into a spruce needle and falls into a young woman's drinking cup and she becomes pregnant with him. Raven did that so he could get inside the Head-Man's house and steal the sun, moon, and stars, and bring daylight to mankind. Maybe that's how it happened, but somehow, I found myself pregnant at sixteen years old.

My friends swirled a ring attached to a string in the air around my belly. Someone said, if the string moved in a circle, it meant I'd have a girl. Back and forth meant I'd have a boy. I watched the power in my swollen belly sway the string back and forth and they shrieked, "It's a boy! It's a boy!"

I said, "I think it's a girl." At that age, tricks lurked in sweaty basketball players' jerseys and on the backseat of a Plymouth Fury. I rubbed my belly. "You are a girl," I said to my swollen mound. At Doc Heggan's office, he listened to the heartbeat: rapid and strong. He claimed the fast heartbeat indicated it was probably a boy. I said, "No, it's a girl." It was.

When I held Tova for the first time, she opened her eyes and looked up at me as if to ask her mother-child if I was, in fact, her mother. "Whose daughter shall I say that I am?" she asked. I told her, like me, she's a child of seafoam and a child of Raven. When Tova was six months old, I let her feel the cold sea water, let her clasp bull kelp in her hands, put it in her mouth and taste it. I pointed out the killer whale pod hanging out in front of town. I told her how to talk respectfully to them. I set Tova in the dirt and let her taste rocks. She tasted the salt water and the earth, taking it inside her.

As Tova grew, she showed amazing feats: she read at three years old. She loved conversations with elders. She could make her own blueberry pancakes in the shapes of dinosaurs when she was only four. Often, she'd tell me things only grownups could know, like how slack tide happens when the direction of the tidal current reverses.

Tova loved to swing from tree branches, ride her bike, and camp outside all summer, living like a typical Alaskan child. But she knew and I knew she was far from typical. Her Grandma Berta said I should've made Tova wear dresses and more pink, but we live in Southeastern Alaska on an island, and it's cold here year-round. Grandma Berta thought the lack of dresses and exposure to the color pink made Tova want to kiss girls instead of boys. But my raven-child likes the color black, I argued: all ravens do. I was always defending Tova's sense of freedom and exploration. "She's of a curious nature," I said.

Eventually, though, Tova's dreams outgrew the four walls of my house and the island we live on. She was ready, much too soon, to leave my nest. So I let her go—she doesn't really fit in with island folks—the people who find it intellectually stimulating to peel the labels off their beer bottles every Friday night. "Go," I told her, "Jesus wasn't welcome in his hometown either."

So, Tova left on the blue-canoe—our ferry—and sailed "Down South." I didn't hear from her for a while, but one day she called me and told me she was going to school and working with head trauma patients in Seattle. "They throw shit at you," she laughed. "And they swear all the time and they bite you, but I get to hold their hands. And I tell them I can see their spirit. I know who they really are. It calms them." I held the phone and sighed, knowing she gets the cosmic joke too.

Tova wandered from Raven's territory into Coyote's, and after Coyote mentored her a while, she called me and said she missed the water and wanted to come back home. So I paid for a ticket, and she rode the blue-canoe back home again. Tova walked up the ferry ramp with a shaved head. What was left of her long dark hair was dyed pink. I felt her pink prickled head. "Indian warpaint," she told me, laughing.

Tova explained to me that Isaac Asimov, Rumi, Sherman Alexie, and Kurt Vonnegut traveled with her in her backpack. At home, she pulled out her carving tools, long underwear, and address books crammed with the names of fellow tricksters she'd met along the way. She had journals overflowing with handwritten notes and poems—lots of poems.

After a while, Tova's hair grew out, and she started wearing her traditional dress: Carhartts and a long-sleeve thermal T-shirt. She lugged her backpack around town, telling everyone her stories while she whittled on yellow cedar, carving feast dishes and dance masks. She read her poems in coffee shops, to elders, to kids, to friends, and at Shakes Island tribal house for tourists. The local tribe was so impressed they wanted Tova to read her poems at the November ceremony to celebrate Indians. She told me, "Gee, we Indians get a whole month to be remembered."

So, tonight, I went to hear her read her poems at Shakes Island, thinking I'd be the only one clapping with my feet. I was watching the crowd when she was reading one of her poems—the one about being a *civilized Indian*. She was making the crowd squirm, their Indian expectations withered. She's too pale. She's too literate. She's too young. She's not an elder.

Tova read her poems: one about being a snail. One about killer whales. Another about working in the fish cannery. And one about being, or not really being, an American. As she was reading her not-really-being poem, she paused, and then tried reading again, but her voice faltered. In fact, it kind of squawked. Her eyes fluttered and she looked out at the audience and smiled. I almost jumped from my seat and ran up on the stage, but I couldn't stop staring at her.

Her long black hair fell forward into her face, and when she raised her head, a beak had grown from where her mouth once was. Her dark eyes were small and round and the hair around her face turned to slick black feathers. The force of a hundred gasps in the room—mine included—created a draft that raised her up off the floor. Tova flew up through the smoke hole and out into the sky. Afterward, her poems fluttered from the podium, falling like alder leaves to the floor.

I ran outside after my changeling, leaving the spectators' mouths gaping open, choking down their golden orbs, stories they didn't quite understand. I knew it would take a while for their brains to untwist their long-held worldviews, to adjust to such trickery where women shapeshift into birds, windows into smoke holes, and philosophies into poems. I left them wondering whose daughter she really was.

Outside, I followed the shadow of her wings down the road to the beach. She circled over the beach and landed on a yellow cedar log— the kind of log killer whales were created from. I didn't approach her, but I was thinking of Tova's birth, how her watchful eyes looked up at me. She sat on the log picking off broken limpets and dried seaweed. I waited as the tide swirled and spiraled around the log, coaxing it from the sand. The log rolled trying to gain its balance atop the water, unsure whether or not it was a log or a war canoe. And with the She-Raven on its back, the log floated out beyond the islands. I watched until the log got smaller and smaller until it was no more.

❁

Now you have the story, for what it is. As you can tell, indigenous people are Chekhov-like: our stories don't necessarily end when or where you want them to end. Sometimes, Raven is still the trickster, waiting with us to see where things go, how they end up. So, imagine yourself here with me. I pick off some spruce tips and share them with you. We sit down on a rock near the tideline. We take off our shoes and socks and put our feet in the cold water. We chew on tart spruce tips and watch the tide swirl around a patch of bull kelp. We watch. I'm unshaken and at the same time I'm amused because I know Raven will be back someday. Maybe, when the north wind blows. Maybe, when the tide comes wandering back. Maybe, when a pod of killer whales swim near shore. Or maybe, as soon as I tell you another story.

Date: 2010s
Recorded by John Swanton
Assisted by Tooch Waterson

House Falling into the Sea

Charlie Edwin knew it was going to be a strange year when he found a three-headed dandelion blooming in mid-October. Charlie sat drinking his coffee in front of the picture window at his home on Petroglyph Beach. His dog, Ossa, an old Australian shepherd, sat beside him. Charlie was Wooshkeetaan, Eagle, from the Shark House. He is called Aan gux—the keeper or backbone of the land. His mother was from Hoonah, but he'd lived in Wrangell all his life. His father was Kaawdliyaayí Hit: House Lowered from the Sky. Here, Charlie lived among people from the Sun House, and the Dogfish Intestine House, and the Norwegians, the Finns, the Sámi, the Filipinos, and even the Chinese and Japanese. There were Vikings, wizards, bears, siyokoy, dragons, and Susanoo.

The best thing, though, about living in Wrangell was living among stories. He practically lived at the coffee shop. Their stories lived there, and at the gas pump, and the work float, and at Shakes Island, and among the petroglyphs beside his house. Since Jesse, his wife of many years, had died, he began to spend his time among rocks, wandering with his thermos of coffee along the beach. He knew exactly where the Raven stealing the sun story was carved as well as the spiral and the killer whale. But he worried lately about the beach and the erosion happening all along Alaska's coastline.

The previous winter, an ice floe broke loose from the Stikine in March. Early breakup, they called it. He didn't believe it. But, the large sheet of ice came round the corner, then along the shoreline, and smashed into his beach. The tides were higher these past few years and the storms stronger. In fact, the sea had eroded the shore so many times he had to move his house back two times in the last twenty years. It wasn't just Wrangell, though. It was Shishmaref, Sitka, Tenakee, Newtok, villages on the Ninglick River, and more.

Charlie sat down in the wet sand, tucking his raincoat under his butt. He held his thermos in his gloved hands and took a big sip of coffee. The gulls circled overhead, which made him feel comforted, since Jesse had been a seagull. She was T'akdeintaan. Some people called her a kittiwake, but she was old school and claimed she was a seagull. He looked up and screeched back at them.

Every morning since Jesse's death, he'd made a point to check up on the rocks.

Someone had to. Someone had to take care of them. Jesse used to clean up the beach. She'd pick up Pepsi cans and white plastic grocery bags. Now it was his turn, he supposed, a sad turn. But he'd take it. He'd take anything that would still connect him to Jesse. He'd started by trying to sit among the rocks, but he couldn't ignore the garbage. Once he'd found remnants of a small fire and a pile of beer bottles. Another time, a roll of butcher paper that people use to make rubbings of the petroglyphs lay wet and soggy on the beach. He even found orange letters sprayed across a petroglyph and it wasn't even something profound: the numbers 1995. That really pissed him off.

These were his people's petroglyphs. At least that's how he thought of them. He often had words with the tour guides and the town fathers when they'd claim they didn't know who carved the petroglyphs. They were his ancestors. He knew this. It was as if the white folks were saying the land around here really isn't Tlingit territory because they weren't here first. You migrated here and so did we.

Sometimes he had to stop the tourists from defacing the petroglyphs. At first, he simply stood on the porch with his rifle in his hand.

That's when the cops got involved and told him not to scare the visitors—they don't call them *tourists* anymore. The government had made the beach a state historic site and all that did was bring more people there. Some protection.

One day the government sent his nephew Johan to talk to him. "You're in trouble, Uncle, for telling folks there's a limit per day and they can't go down there."

Sure, he'd done that. It was clever. He was the first one there in the morning, standing on their newfangled platform and boardwalk telling the tourists the place was closed for renovations, or they had reached their visitor limit already, or that they had to go to the imaginary ticket booth in town and get a ticket. They always believed him. Who'd think an old man like him would be a liar.

"You are sooo lying, Uncle Charlie," his nephew Johan had chuckled.

Now Charlie looked up at the typical clouds shrouding the mountains. No, he didn't mind local folks coming down to the beach making petroglyph rubbings. He loved to see little kids tracing the spiral petroglyph with their fingers. He'd tell them about the cycle of salmon. He used to help the kids find the petroglyphs they wanted. Then he'd supervise them. That was before it became illegal to make rubbings. Now, they have fake ones on the platform tourists can make rubbings from. I suppose it might be for the best. But, this past summer, someone had spray painted a genuine petroglyph with blue paint. It had been there nine thousand years, maybe ten thousand. Probably wasn't kids because all the kids he'd met on the beach really liked the glyphs.

Charlie took another sip of his hot coffee and then remembered he'd stuffed a breakfast roll in his raincoat pocket. He took it out, ate some, and shared a piece with Ossa and a brave gull hopping on a rock nearby.

The clouds darkened, moving a sheet of rain toward the shore. He supposed he'd better head back inside. Besides, the beach was clean today and the man in the green state uniform would be showing up soon. After the blue paint incident, Charlie was pretty mad, but he'd always been told to think about his words first before saying anything.

He didn't know what he was going to say yet, but something had to be done. He just didn't know what.

Plus, he didn't think the local government or the State of Alaska was used to Natives speaking up about things, especially in Wrangell. Recently, his niece, Sarah, got the city to say the Tlingits were here first. She had to keep writing letters to them, put stuff in the paper, and finally, she called the governor. The city used to say Wrangell was the first settlement in Alaska, established when the white people built a fort. They forgot all about the Tlingits who'd inhabited the island for thousands of years.

Then, in the 1970s, the lawyers left Wrangell Tlingits out of the land claims. He and his friends went to all the meetings, went to DC, and still they forgot. Said *oops* and went on giving out their land to other tribes. They now called Wrangell Natives "the landless." Without the land we are nothing. Without the rocks we are nothing.

He stood and walked among the rocks as he headed back home. Ossa followed him, sniffing seaweed along the way. He shook his head. He wasn't landless; a strange concept for sure. He could have claimed this beach instead of the state owning it. Maybe, claimed Farm Island at the mouth of the Stikine River instead of the white farmland and his relatives who now own it. His dad had hunted and fished there. That river was in his blood. *Stikine* meant "Bitter" or "Silty Water," not Great River like the touristy types called it. Hell, it was silty and could be very bitter. The river had even taken a few of his friends' lives. One fell off a riverboat, the *Madeline Rose*. And, one winter, another friend went trapping and was found dead stuck to an ice floe.

Charlie nodded to the river water, mixing with the green ocean in front of his house. Respect that river. Respect the rocks. He was nearly to his house when he turned back toward the beach. A small man walked among the petroglyphs. He thought he recognized him and yelled, "Morning, Mr. Lee." But the man didn't look up. That's when Charlie remembered old Mr. Lee had been dead a few years. He and Mr. Lee used to have coffee at the gas station and bullshit about old times. A long time ago, Mr. Lee had said the townsfolk didn't want the

Chinese buried in the white cemetery. They used to cut them up and shove them into barrels and salt them. Then someone was supposed to let the Chinese government know so they could come get their countrymen. Mr. Lee said he didn't know if anyone ever did, but he was never going to set foot on Deadmans Island, that's for sure.

The man bent down and rubbed sand off a rock, the spiral petroglyph—Charlie's favorite one. The man crouched there staring at the rock. Finally, Charlie turned back and headed up the beach to his house. The tide flowed inward, already lifting a log from the beach. Soon it would be pitching waves onto his front porch.

Last week, Johan had come to visit. He asked Charlie about moving the house back again. Charlie had said, "I'm not moving back. I'm old. I won't be able to see the petroglyphs if I move to where you want me to, anyway. And, I'll be too close to that damned road."

❦

Charlie and his friend Nillan Hetta sipped their coffee and looked out the window.

"The big tides are coming. Lots of bad weather," Nillan said. "You ready?"

"I'm ready."

"I like your plan, but you're a crazy son-of-a-bitch, you know that?"

At 3:00 a.m., four days later, on a November night, the black dark folded over the island and the wind howled. No one could hear Nillan rolling the bobcat off the back of his lowboy trailer and driving it down the beach. The bobcat heaved the rocks into Charlie's house. Charlie had torn out the two by fours on his front door to make it bigger, and then eventually the wall, and most of the walls inside his house. Nillan drove up a makeshift ramp and set the rocks down in Charlie's living room and in what was once his bedroom and kitchen.

The previous week, Johan and two of his buddies had come over and put in Styrofoam floats beneath the house. They didn't think it would hold forty petroglyphs, but some of them wouldn't be able to move, anyway. They'd pile in what they could. Now, the house sunk down a bit, but the large logs beneath it held. After all the rocks were loaded, Nillan put the bobcat away and drove home in the dark.

Waves thrashed the front of the house, like a truck in a carwash, smashing into the large window. The tide stuck its tongue under the logs and lifted Charlie's house as if it were a piece of candy to be eaten. The house rocked, and then lifted, bobbing on the sea. Charlie sat inside on his recliner, the only piece of furniture he saved, holding on to a two-by-four post. Ossa, big as he was, jumped in his lap. Ossa whined. Maybe this wasn't such a good idea.

The current shoved the house out hard and it thumped. What was that sound? Charlie cringed as he felt the rock scraping the floats beneath him, but it didn't stop the little house from floating. The storm surged and the wind blew. Out his front windows, the night was so dark he couldn't see anything. Hanging onto the skeleton frame of his house, he went to the living room and then the bedroom looking out the windows. Through his bedroom window, the faint outline of the shore swept by. He was moving fast. Real fast.

Charlie sat back down in his chair, trying his best to take sips of coffee from his thermos. That's when he heard it. He'd heard that sound before, a howl spiraling by. Nillan, who worked for the Forest Service, had once taken him to Garnet Ledge to show him the destruction left by one of those winds. No one believed Nillan when he'd reported something like a tornado had torn through the trail, making a swath through the trees, so he'd shown Charlie. Charlie remembered the giant spruce and hemlock toppled as if they were sticks.

Now, the house spun around. The wind knocked the kitchen window in. Glass crashed onto the petroglyphs. The house moaned and creaked with each wave that hit it, slopping over the logs. Beneath him, the floorboards wobbled and a large piece of the float gave way and popped up from beneath the house. One corner of the house sunk down. A piece of float whipped up and hit the roof hard. The house shook.

"Shit," Charlie said to Ossa, who now quivered at his feet. The house rocked and rolled on the waves as he hobbled over the rocks, clamoring on his hands and knees to the corner of the living room where water seeped in fast. The wind howled and the house twisted again. Finally, the house stopped twisting and then went up and down as if riding huge waves.

Charlie looked out the living room windows and, this time, he was face to face with the white froth of a wave ten or more feet high. "Christ, the size of the waves," he said out loud.

He kneeled among the petroglyphs, his hand clutching a two-by-four post, and hung on for what seemed like hours. Waves and wind bellowed through the house. The house tilted and cracked with a splitting sound. Charlie fell sideways, hitting his head on a rock.

Water, waves, and wind roared through his ears as if he had an inner ear infection. He woke to Ossa licking his face. He blinked, trying to adjust his eyes to the darkness, and then reached out and felt around. Beneath him, it felt solid. Should he move? His back hurt. His arm was on fire. He reached to touch his arm, feeling a big gash, sticky with blood. It was then he realized the ground wasn't bending like the floorboards in his house. He was lying on a beach on a small piece of his living room floor. He sat up. He could see the airport lights. He was on Deadmans Island.

Crap. He hadn't made it far. The wind had picked him up and slid his house on the waves to the small island. He could make out sand around him and a rocky beach. He stood and patted his dog. Ossa dripped water. The old dog stank, plus he limped, but his tail still wagged.

Charlie pulled his Bic lighter from his pants pocket. He walked along the shoreline, clicking his lighter to find his way, discovering pieces of his house: a wall with sunflower wallpaper, a log from the float beneath the house. There, a piece of his roof. Over there, a small refrigerator banged against a rock. He stepped over a rock. Parts of his house scattered to the treeline, where he found his recliner upright as if waiting for him to sit in it and flip the television channels. Maybe he could change this channel.

Rain pelted his face. He rubbed his hand across his partly bald head. He'd always dressed in layers, so he took off his flannel shirt and tied it up like a hood. He walked a few steps farther and his foot clunked against a rock. He bent down close to the rock touching it. "What the hell," he said, feeling the spiral in the rock at his feet. The spiral, he knew, was the symbol for new beginnings in many cultures: Maori, Hawaiian, Tlingit, and Finnish.

He tried to adjust his eyesight, but it seemed the darkness had swallowed up the beach. Maybe he had a head injury. He couldn't tell if a rock was a petroglyph until he touched it. He clicked the lighter on again to be sure. Floorboards from his house surrounded them. "Well, Jesse, I've done it now." He didn't know, really, what he did. Or at least the consequences. But it would make a good story, anyway. He stepped around the petroglyphs sunk into the sand. They were stuck, too, like he was.

Charlie sat down and rested for a minute next to a glyph. He flicked his lighter again and traced the Raven stealing the sun glyph with his finger. "Well, Raven," he said out loud, "I guess we'd better build a fire."

Up near the treeline, Charlie fumbled with his lighter. His hands were becoming numb. His thumb barely worked, but eventually he lit it again. He fashioned a small torch from a stick and moss and lit it. Moss covered stumps, stones, and roots, so he couldn't see where the graves or the ghosts were. Were the barrels still here? Were there graves? Markers? He'd never been here. Never wanted to go here, really. With the torch held out to the woods, he said *Chaa addei yei xat naay oo.* Please forgive me. It was one of the few Tlingit phrases he knew. In English, he asked the island's dead to forgive him for trudging around.

Charlie gathered wood from the small stand of trees and found a dry spot under a tree and built a fire. The rain softened to a light mist. The fire lit up the beach and Charlie sat by the fire rubbing his hands over Ossa's hair. He stopped in mid-pet, seeing a shadow walking along the beach. It looked like a small man or a child. Mr. Lee?

The person stopped near the spiral rock and bent over. The person never looked in Charlie's direction, in the direction of the fire, but instead kept tracing the spiral pattern over and over. Charlie knew what he was doing, as he'd done the same thing many times, pressing his finger into backbone of the spiral, letting his mind wander to a centered place in a spiral galaxy, our Milky Way. The man faded away in the early morning light and the fire died down to white ash.

Date: Any day now
Recorded by John Swanton
Assisted by Tooch Waterson

The Dead Man Who Swam Away

He awoke from the dead at around 5:00 p.m. It wasn't an extraordinary time to come alive. He smelled mashed potatoes and baked halibut. His mouth was raw and he coughed. That was the first thing he did.

Evert Planz looked around his long-term care room, at the mauve drapes and the hard chair in the corner. He raised his hand only to find a contorted tree branch, but it was indeed his hand. He felt a pillow between his knees and he tried to turn but his back seemed fused in place. What the hell. Had he been dreaming for a long time, maybe days? Shit. How long he had been lying there?

He wiggled his toes and moved his leg slightly, and the thing that was once his foot, the small, thin childlike wedge, moved out from beneath the orange bedspread. His yellow toenails had been clipped, but they were still too long. His toes pressed tightly together like one giant toe. He lifted his head up. After all this, he was exhausted and fell asleep

Evert awoke again as he was lifted and moved to the side. A warm washrag wiped his bottom and then someone flipped him like a fish onto his other side. He groaned. No one responded. He groaned again. No one responded. He raised his head. Two nurse aides—one at the sink rinsed something, and another shoved a chair around. They didn't look at him. And he couldn't cough again. He tried but his chest heaved and a jagged pain tightened his torso.

Fuck. They think I'm still sleeping. He rolled his eyes back and laid his head back down as they walked out of the room and shut the door. It was dark outside. The aides had forgotten to shut the drapes. A small light shone on his headboard and an FM radio played on the nightstand beside him. The lyrics chimed in his head: "Wake me up before you go-go. 'Cause I'm not plannin' on going solo." He tried to sing with them, but only made strange burbling sounds.

Mom? My mom? She had come to see him for a while but had stopped. He was remembering. And Berta Agard and Hilda Johnsson came to pray with him, to cast out the devil. They laid their soft hands on him. He liked their soft hands. If he could have gotten an erection, he would have. Maybe their hands did have healing power. He was awake, really awake.

Again, another memory came back to him: he was undressing Yelena. She was the Russian mail order wife of the minister of the Free Church. Then he remembered his wife, Astri. He was married. So where was she? Did she visit him? He had no memory of any visits. She never came to see him. Well, fuck her. He tried to lift his leg. He wanted to go down the hall to the nurses' station and call that bitch Astri and tell her he was coming home. How long had he been here? Maybe he was divorced or something. He didn't sign any papers, though. Well, not that he knew of, anyway. Besides, with this goddamn tree hand, he couldn't have.

The rain pelted the window. It was a hard rain and, when Evert looked closer, he saw mud splatters on the window. Maybe the pond out back was overflowing. Then the radio announcer interrupted the music, telling people where to evacuate because the town was flooding. Flooding. Holy crap. Flooding? The mud splattered the window hard. He jumped. Or thought he jumped. The announcement was followed by a loud ringing sound, an emergency broadcast. In a serious voice, the announcer told people go to Mount Dewey or the reservoir hill behind town. Vans would pick up people at designated areas, the airport, the school, the library, Shoemaker Bay, and Wrangell City Hospital.

"Christ," he mumbled, sounding only like a baby's bawl. Surely he would be the first on the van, their miracle, their poster boy for healing. He tried to move his foot again and it came popping out of the covers. He wiggled and moved to the side a bit. Progress. He was actually doing it. It *was* a miracle. Since his arms were already bent strangely, he used them to lift himself up on his pillow, almost sitting up now. Beneath the door, muddy water poured in. The lights glowing around the doorframe flickered and went out. The bed lamp zapped and the radio buzzed off.

Evert sat in the dark. He opened his mouth to yell but only coughed. He coughed hard this time. Someone would hear it. He spit phlegm on the bed. "Fuck, fuck, fuck." The words sounded like a dog's bark.

Then he tried to cry out for his wife, Astri, but only whistled, "Eeeee, eeeee."

A generator started up. Emergency lights flooded the hospital. After a few minutes, the generator sputtered and died. The lights dimmed but remained on. They can't do anything right in here. Those goddamn smashed peas and pureed beef, those Filipino nurse aides.

One small emergency light came on above his bed. Outside his room, people sloshed around, beds clanked in the hall. Under the door, a dim light moved across like a searching flashlight. Over here! Over here! But wait, the hospital staff didn't know about the miracle yet—that he could talk and walk, that he was awake. Awake! He heaved his legs to the side. The blanket fell away from the bed onto the wet floor, sinking like a worn-out magic carpet. His legs bent at an odd angle. A fluffy white brace covered one hand.

In his room, the water rose to the bottom rung of his bed. He could crawl or wade to the door. He could do it. He set his bent legs down on the floor. The cold water numbed him almost immediately. He was like a ninety-year-old man. His hands were useless. He tried to raise his feet to walk but he could only shuffle. He moved slowly toward the door, the water to his knees. He bent far over, almost in half so he faced the water. He heaved his arm toward the doorknob to turn it, but his hand clunked on the knob. He couldn't wrap his fingers around it.

Evert flopped against the door. "Help, help," he barked. He flung his body at the door again. Nothing.

Evert leaned against the door and closed his eyes. He was so tired. He didn't want to close his eyes again, to return to that dark, dark sleep. He opened his eyes. He raised his arm once more and hooked his curved hands on the doorknob. He moved his whole body in the direction of the twist and the knob turned, then flung back. He did it again. This time, the door opened slightly. Water rushed in, pressing against his legs, and he nearly went under. He leaned against the doorjamb, his head bent down, his nose nearly touching the rising water.

He tilted his head at an odd angle, like the hunchback of Notre Dame. A nurse waded by the doorway with a small child slung over his back. "It's me," he wanted to say. Seeing Evert he frowned. "Sorry, Evert. Forgive me?" The child began to cry and the nurse moved through chest-deep water toward the large sliding doors, which were broken open.

An outboard motor idled outside. A rescuer yelled, "Johan, over here." The nurse headed left with the child held above him in the rising water.

The small floodlight near the nurses' station dimmed further until it finally went out. "Noo," Evert cried. Was he ever going to get out of this room? Despite the darkness, he knew the direction of the doors: Straight ahead. With all his strength he pulled the door open farther. The water was higher now, rising faster as it rushed into the room. If he could just get to the boat, he thought. He heaved his body through the water, moving his crooked arms back and forth. They wouldn't do what he wanted them to do. He moved like a deadhead log with limbs sticking out, bobbing along with the tide. Near the front doors, he tried to stand up, but the water pressed against him. As he shuffled toward the front doors his arms and legs weighted down. Near the door, the water deepened and he fell and rolled on his back. He floated outside.

He was free. The miracle. He would survive. Evert pushed his legs down trying to find a bottom to stand on. His back cracked again and he sunk. The current dragged him under and that's when he remembered the night he drowned. In his mind, he pictured Karl, his brother-in-law, always helping pull bodies from the ocean, pulling him up by his hair. The women, it was those women. He'd been partying with a couple of girls. They'd gotten him drunk. He was going to pull a crab pot or something for the women that night, the Fourth of July. Red chrysanthemum fireworks blasted above him, and sparks fizzled down into the water beside him.

Evert saw the red lights again. Fireworks? He came sputtering up to the surface of the cold, muddy water. A big EXIT light still glowed. The wind howled like the pack of wolves he once saw running through town when he was a child. The stern of a white skiff motored about fifty yards in front of him. For a few moments, he floated on his back. He tried to swim again but he couldn't. He tried to yell for them, but only the same seal bark came out from his throat. He felt a sudden force of water, like a river beneath the surface of the muddy water shove him forward, and before he knew it he was being carried away by the current down the hospital hill toward the highway. No! Stop! In a few minutes, he'd be out in the Pacific and they'd never find him.

The skiff moved toward him and Evert took in a small but painful breath. It motored closer and he could see it was Cooper Lee and another man.

"What the hell?" he heard Cooper say. With some difficulty, Cooper and the other fireman rolled Evert over the gunwales into the boat. "Must have floated out here like a goddamn log."

Evert expected a warming blanket, a cup of coffee, or something, but they put him in a newfangled plastic rescue bag that felt like a space blanket. But at least he was starting to warm up. He wanted so much to hug them and to thank them. His arms ached, but at least he was out of that hospital. He was a miracle, a goddamn miracle. Why weren't they excited about it? Cooper put his hand on his chest, leaned down, and looked him in the eye. Yes, it's me. He didn't say it out loud, but he'd thought it. He'd been in a coma for god's sake. He'd swallowed water. He stared back at Cooper, too exhausted to cry out for Astri or grunt like a sea lion, too exhausted to move.

Cooper said, "Okay."

The other guy said, "Do it."

Cooper gave a hard tug at the blanket and Evert heard a zipper. He wanted to shout, but water bubbled from his mouth and the bag zipped closed. Why were they zipping the blanket all the way up past his face? He couldn't feel the cold anymore on his limbs. Maybe he was going to be okay. Yes, everything was going to be all right. He gritted his teeth. He would try to forgive Astri. She would see he was a miracle. He was. He was a real live miracle, and he would thank those lovely praying ladies with their softy praying hands.

Date: Sometime in the near future
Recorded by Tooch Waterson
Assisted by Tova Agard

The Flood Story

It rained and rained. A young woman stood with her baby, water rushing around her feet. She held her breath, and, as she submerged, she turned to stone. A house fell off its pilings near the harbor. A husband and wife rolled off their bed and out the door and transformed into logs. All around, the island sloughed and fell into the sea.

Gulls floated on logs, deadheads bobbed, tree roots stuck up like giant tentacled monsters. The river took over the ocean, turning it into mud and whirlpools. The logging roads, once high in elevation, became the island's beaches. Melted glacier water rushed down the Stikine, not stopping for Wrangell Island in its way. Bicycles, swing sets, boat trailers, and chest freezers twisted, spun, and flipped. A small truck tumbled and rolled off the highway. The current seized it, shoving it toward the sea. It crashed against the post office before it got there. And, when the water receded, it became the story of the fleeing couple: a rock shaped like a truck, a woman cocking her head out the window.

It rained more. In the future, a large rock will be sunk deep in the yard of the rebuilt Presbyterian Church. It resembles a man pointing up. They say that's the Man-Who-Saw-the-Light. Nobody remembers what light he saw, though. Some say it was an alien spaceship. Some say a huge forest fire in Canada. Some say it was God. Some say John Muir played god, pointing the way to Glacier Bay.

It kept on raining. Rocks tumbled into human shapes. Strange out-croppings appeared on the cliffs, like faces carved in the mountain: a Roman nose and chin. One large saucer-shaped rock balanced across a precipice as if it hovered there. Petrified trees stood in unusual places. Beach sand scattered on mountaintops. And on the beach there now sat a large cairn, resembling a man pointing in the direction of Seattle. Scientists speculated about these phenomena, but the stories told of a great flood and the Shakes Glacier melting and the Stikine River and all the other major rivers in Alaska overflowing their banks. The LeConte Glacier became a twenty-one-mile-long valley with a gravel wash. The Stikine Icefield transformed into a huge outwash plain with remains of a buried forest.

People lived in the hills for a long time. They rebuilt in the higher elevations, where they were shrouded in the clouds draping the moun-tains. The original size of the islands became a distant memory. They say it all started happening the year Raven came down the Stikine dur-ing one of the switching seasons—the seasons when everything gets messed up and weird.

Raven came to collect our stories, they say. He came in the form of a young man from upriver. Raven found a white guy wandering around town, John Swanton, and hired him to help. But, of course, the white guy got the author credit. That's the way it's always been. At least, that's how the story goes. The stories were everywhere, and Swanton became confused. The people in Wrangell walked around talking story in the restaurants, in the coffee shops, in the post office, in the den-tist's and doctor's office, on the Reliance float, Heritage Harbor, and at Shoemaker Bay parking lot. Stories were whispered among lovers and drawn as glyphs on their skin.

❈

"See what the animals are doing?" Tooch said. "Do what they do." This is how he was going to teach them: by example, by doing. This was how the elders did things. Just watch, they'd say. Sometimes that was hard to do.

Swanton followed Tooch, who was trailing several black bears up an old deer trail to the top of a mountain. When they lagged behind, the bears would turn as if to wait for them. The rain poured down, muddying the trail. On the way up, Swanton stumbled and fell, landing on his knees. The large bag he carried in his hand slipped and tumbled off a cliff into the rushing water below.

"Leave it," Tooch said. What did it matter? Over the years Swanton had mailed dozens of notebooks to the Smithsonian. Occasionally, on Swanton's instructions, Tooch had mailed them himself. But so far they hadn't published a book. Sure, Swanton had spent several lifetimes collecting the stories. But they weren't really his stories. Swanton would get credit for John Muir marrying a tree, for a boy who lit the town on fire.

"But the stories, how will I remember all those stories? That bag had all my notes, tapes, reels, CDs, even that digital tape recorder of yours."

Tooch shrugged, and then tapped his own head. "They are in here," he said, and then pointed to Swanton's head. "And in there."

Tooch then picked up a small pinecone. "And in here." He tossed the pinecone into the brush. Tooch turned, leaving Swanton staring down at the water.

Swanton sighed and then followed him up into the alpine. The brown river water below met with the green ocean, like two competing elements. Beside them, the bears groaned, their black fur grayed, and, at once, they became stone.

"See," he said to Swanton, "the stories are already telling themselves."

Someone would carve a totem pole to remember this story. Someone would hike up here in the future and point out the rocks.

"Come on," Tooch said. "Let's build a shelter." He didn't feel cold; he usually didn't. As the story goes, Raven was created because his mother swallowed a rock. Tough. You had to be tough to live here, to survive this. Swanton looked ragged.

As they gathered wood for the shelter, they were joined by a few dozen others: the lost and bedraggled who wandered up during that same day. There on the mountain, they built a few small shelters from spruce and hemlock and huddled that first night as the rain kept coming down.

The next day, several men went hunting and later returned with two deer.

Swanton kept talking about rescue, as if someone out there would come sweeping in like a hero and whisk them away in the middle of a disaster. He should've paid attention to history. Swanton left the camp and wandered back and forth and back and forth along the mountaintop, walking to the alpine lake and back to their camp again.

"What's the matter?" Tooch finally asked.

"Do you think we'll be rescued?"

"I think we've already rescued ourselves."

"No, do you think someone's coming for us," Swanton asked, "to check on the communities, I mean. The government."

"Government?" he said, nearly choking on the word.

"Yes, the United States government."

Tooch frowned. "I don't think we need the government."

"Well someone will eventually send someone," Swanton said, "and, if we're way up here, how can anyone find us? We should be on the beach."

"But what if the water rises further? You don't want to be down there with the current. Besides, there's nothing left."

Like two lone spruce trees on the mountain they stared at the water below, only a mile or so down to the logging road, which was now the shoreline. Swanton said, "Yeah, but I need to go home. Get back to Seattle at least."

Tooch shrugged. "Well, I can't stop you, but it's not the best thing to do. Don't you listen to the oral traditions about waiting forty days and forty nights?"

"No, I should pack up and head down to the road," Swanton replied.

"Suit yourself," he said. "I can walk you down part way."

❀

Two Tlingits in a large canoe found a white man walking on the beach.

Swanton waved madly at the canoe. He had a small pack strapped to his back and wore a rain hat and a raincoat too small for him. All these days walking the beach road, he didn't find the bag with the notebooks in it, and it seemed he'd looked everywhere. Probably at the bottom of the ocean by now. It was heavy. More important to get to safety. More important to get home.

The canoe approached the beach where he stood. When they landed he explained he needed help. They seemed willing. The two young men held the canoe steady and he maneuvered himself in. Swanton sat in the middle. "I can't thank you enough. I had just about given up hope."

The young man behind him spoke up. "Well, good thing for us, too," he smiled. "My name is Jorma Agard and up there is my friend Henry Turrpa."

He nodded. Did he know these young men? He'd met so many people over the years and years he'd lived there. "I'm John Swanton. I was living in Wrangell and when the flood came, we all headed to the hills. See that beach? It's really a logging road. All this," he pointed to the water, "is fresh river water down this far. It's amazing isn't it?"

"Yeah," Henry said, "but I wouldn't call it amazing."

"I know you," Jorma said. "I'm from Wrangell. Your friend, Tooch, recorded one of my stories. It was about a killer whale."

"Oh," he said, remembering the transcript. "Big Jon Keats. Quite a tale." This kid was Tova's brother. Tova, the enigma. Tova the storyteller. Tova the story. How was he ever going to make sense of this? Who would believe him? Maybe losing his bag wasn't so bad after all.

"Hey, it really happened," Jorma said.

Yeah, I suppose. He chuckled as Jorma pushed the canoe out farther with his paddle. The two men started to paddle away from the shore. He thought about Tova. Where was she? Did she survive? He asked, "Where's your sister, Tova?"

"She's gone."

"Gone?" Did he mean she was dead? Or, god forbid, drowned?

"She's not dead. She and her friends are . . . are going to save people. She's helping out. In her own way."

That was good news. And surely help would come. But until then he had to take care of himself. "Where are you headed?"

"We're out hunting," Jorma said. "There are about twenty of us up there at the top of Rainbow Falls Trail. You?"

"We're up past the reservoir area. Are you going north or south?"

"West, sort of," Jorma said. "We heard there were some deer left on Zarembo, that you could get access to the roads from the backside. The front side—the lower elevation roads are all underwater."

He felt a surge of hope and sat straighter. "Great. I can go as far as you go."

Henry huffed, almost laughed. "Then what?"

"I'll walk."

Henry pointed. "Ummm. These are islands. I thought you knew that."

"Yes," he replied, "but I've seen lots of boats, skiffs, even a small ship or two going around. No one's got close enough for me to holler at except you. I'm sure there are others. I have fire starter, and I can eat from the land. I've been doing that for a couple of weeks now."

Henry looked back over his shoulder at Jorma and then shrugged.

The men paddled across to the other side of Woronofski, where they camped for the night. In the morning, they headed across to Etolin and canoed what remained of the shoreline over tops of submerged spruce trees. They camped on the beach again the second night. The third day, early in the morning, they made the crossing to Zarembo Island when Jorma sighted a ship with his binoculars.

"Shit," Jorma said.

Swanton turned sharply to the right, trying to see Jorma behind him. The boat rocked. "What's wrong?"

"It's the Navy," Jorma said. "The *Dewey*, a patrol boat. She used to be the *Tempest*, years ago. But she was refurbished for this mission. A PC they call her. We've seen her before."

"*Dewey* as in Mount Dewey? I used to go hiking up there."

"I don't know," Jorma said. "Dewey as in a Navy admiral, I think."

"Why the Navy?" Swanton asked. What was the Navy doing here? Maybe they were sent to help out.

"Yeah, they came up from Seattle," Jorma said.

"Yeah, like in the good old days," Henry said. "Navy rule. It's martial law now, and they're patrolling."

He held the side of the canoe tightly. There was hope again. If they came from Seattle they might be already heading back there. "Well, drop me off and they can take me south."

Jorma shook his head. "I'm not going near her. *Dewey's* got a 25mm auto-cannon aimed at us, probably right now, and .50 caliber machine guns, grenade launchers—the whole bit."

That didn't sound good. But he had nothing to worry about. He wasn't looting. There was nothing left to loot anyway. "We didn't do anything," he said, almost pleading.

Jorma said, "No, but we're Natives. Didn't you notice?"

He shrugged. "What's that got to do with it?"

"Like I told you, this flood blew us back into the Stone Age." Jorma shook his head. "No, not the Stone Age, but it's like we're still at First Contact, and they don't trust us."

"And, we don't trust them," Henry said.

"I'll vouch for you," Swanton said. "Take me there."

"Hey," Henry said, "they've been rounding up Natives like they did the Japanese and taking them to camps for their 'safety' like they forced the Aleuts. Anyone who had slanted eyes had to go. Anyone with a BIA card is rounded up."

"But now it's worse," Jorma added. "It's anyone they *think* is Native, too."

"Well, I wouldn't want to risk that," he said.

Henry said something to Jorma in Tlingit.

Jorma was silent for a minute and then said something back.

"Okay," Henry said, "here's what we can do. We'll drop you off in this cove on the backside. We'll continue on down the shore and tuck ourselves up where the logging roads meet the ocean."

"But, what if they don't see me? Sure you can't take me close to the ship?" He didn't want to risk being stranded again.

"It's going to have to do. We have to go," Jorma said.

Henry said, "You stay on the beach. Hold up something white and they'll see you. They'll be going right past you. Right over top of where Bushy and Shrubby Islands used to be."

Jorma said, "Do like they do in the movies. Make them think you're a friendly."

"Aren't you friendly?" Swanton asked. These young men seemed friendly.

"Define *friendly*," Henry said.

"As friendly as they're going to be," Jorma said.

Swanton said, "Well, I have a white T-shirt on."

"That'll do," Henry said.

Swanton stood on the shore as the men canoed away, heading to the logging roads on Zarembo. He took off his white T-shirt and stuck it on a piece of driftwood. He waved it in the air. Nothing. What if the ship didn't see him? He'd be doomed. He'd die out here. He sat and watched for about a half hour as the ship came closer. When the ship appeared, it headed right for him. He stood up and waved his white T-shirt.

❁

In the coffee shop, some years from now, two old women sit around telling stories.

TOVA: They say the flood happened because the earth was in mourning. The earth is a woman, you know?

FERN: Yeah, I know that.

TOVA: Well, people became too violent against the woman. That's what my auntie Suvi used to say. And when they killed the woman, the tide wouldn't go in or out. Maybe it was the moon. Maybe it was the melting of the planet. They're still studying it.

FERN: But things have settled down now. I feel all right. This place feels good now, doesn't it?

(*A waitress pours coffee for them and sets down two plates of strawberry rhubarb pie.*)

TOVA: Yes, but things come in cycles, you know.

FERN: That wasn't the first flood? I mean, I know about the one in the Bible.

TOVA: No, there's the Hopi one with the Insect People, the Wooden People from Guatemala. There are lots. Ours won't be the last.

FERN: (*Raises eyebrows but says nothing.*)

TOVA: Well, things aren't really settled. The earth is now 80 percent water and humans are now 75 percent water. Reminds me, I need to take my water pill.

FERN: Yeah, those were tough times.

TOVA: Yeah, we barely made it.

FERN: Yeah, if you hadn't rounded up your aunt's skiff, we might not have gotten out.

TOVA: Before I met up with you and the others, I'd gone up to Great-Grandma Tova's to get her. My dad had fueled up the *Sea Wolf*. There were a lot of people on the boat. I begged him to wait so I could go get Grandma, and he said he'd wait for me. But Grandma didn't want to go with me. She'd lost three toes by then and she was so heavy. I was ready to drag her butt down to the dock. She said she was ready to die and lit up another cigarette. She had a DVD of Jerry Springer on the television. The generator was running out back.

(*Tova pauses, coughs.*)

FERN: (*Reaches for Tova's hand and pats it.*) I know. I've heard the story, hon. But tell it again. Stories, we should tell them a lot. I know you feel bad about it.

TOVA: Yeah, I left her. I left her there. When I headed down to the dock, I saw the *Sea Wolf* heading past the breakwater. Dad left me. That's when I saw Auntie Suvi, Auntie Rikka, and Mom on the *Ocean Maiden*. They were rounding up all the single mothers, the elderly, anyone they could. Suvi gave me her skiff tied up next to the boat and told me to round people up. That's when I found you and Sarah and Johan. You were going to head up the mountain, remember. But I think your ankle was sprained or something.

FERN: Yeah, and I was limping. You saved us, Tova. You're a Jesus. (*Waitress comes over again.*)

WAITRESS: Ladies, there's a new guy in town who's collecting flood stories. So, if you two are interested, I can give him your name. He wanted me to recommend people who could tell him stories. He's usually in here for coffee early in the morning. He says he gets up before the Raven cries. He's the first one in here. He meets me at the door for coffee. Talk, talk, talk. He sure chatters.

TOVA: What does he look like?

WAITRESS: Young, long black hair. He says he's from the Interior—Canada. Got a real strange name . . . ah . . . Stooge?

TOVA: Tooch?

WAITRESS: Yeah, that's it . . . how'd . . .

TOVA: Stories are like the planet. Everything comes in cycles.

WAITRESS: (*Waitress looks confused.*) Ah, well, more coffee?

TOVA: No, no my bladder can't handle it anymore.

FERN: If he comes in tomorrow, tell him we'll meet him here after the lunch rush. He can buy us pie.

(*The waitress smiles and nods and walks to the next table.*)

FERN: Remember when? It was after the flood . . .

TOVA: (*Just about to put a forkful of pie in her mouth. She sets the fork down on the pie plate again.*) Yeah, I sure do . . . I found Swanton's satchel. I wonder if that guy is still alive. I doubt it. He'd be ancient by now. Hell, Fern, I'm ancient. Should I give Swanton's stories to Tooch, eh? Maybe he could get them published.

✽

Swanton waved his white T-shirt. Did the ship see him? Maybe they didn't. Then the ship appeared to bear down on the island. Yes, they're coming. The ship slowed and then launched a rubber boat from the stern. The small boat made its way closer.

Swanton waved and yelled, "I'm John Swanton. Smithsonian Institution." He almost forgot the white T-shirt. He'd tied it to a stick. He waved it around in the air. He could see two sailors in the boat. One steered and the other held a rifle on him. The boat nosed up to the beach, finally landing. One sailor was a woman, the other male. Both were dressed in digital camos.

He put down the white flag. "I'm John Swanton," he said. "I work for the Smithsonian Institution. I'm an ethnologist, and I've been stranded. Can I catch a ride?"

The *Dewey* didn't look that big out in the pass, but as they motored closer, she grew in size. Once aboard the bigger ship, he noted crates and totes stacked everywhere along the stern and up on the back platforms behind the cabin. The chief petty officer found him a bunk next to several other sailors and he lay down. He fell asleep right away and dreamed of the Devils Thumb, the Witch's Tit, Ratz, and Kates Needle, their sharp jagged peaks like the teeth of the earth devouring itself. He saw falling and tumbling rock.

He awoke sweating, the room closing in. He went out on back deck. It was dark and the stars were out, which was unusual, lately, with all the rain. Two sailors walked about on guard duty. He waved and sat down on a large tote that looked like it would hold his weight. He rubbed his hands together, warming them with his breath.

One of the sailors came over. "Hi, I'm Seaman Hughes. What brings you to these parts?"

Funny, the one thing he learned while living in Alaska is that people always want to know where you're from. "I've been in Wrangell, working for the Smithsonian collecting stories. I've been trying to get home. Are you headed south?"

"No. North to Kake."

"North. Ah crap—" He paused. Why would they go to Kake? Nothing there but a small village. "Kake?"

"Yeah, supposedly the Natives there won't let us take care of their totems and all their stuff."

"Stuff?"

"Yeah, the stuff they have in museums—should have in museums. They keep them in closets. You know, the stuff they dance in."

"Oh."

"Our mission is to gather all the totems, masks, blankets, everything. In Kake, there's the largest totem pole in the world." Hughes raised his rifle as if to poke the sky. "We need to save it."

"Really?" As much time as he'd spent with the Natives, he wasn't sure that'd go over well.

"Really," Hughes repeated. "You know, since the flood, all the Natives' stuff has been damaged. We're going to take care of it for them. Plus, we're providing a safe place for the Natives. We have camps in Sitka, Juneau, and in Haines. But some don't want to go. It's weird, though, there's nothing, *nothing* in the villages. No schools, hospitals, churches. I don't know how they're surviving."

"This is their land, you know," said a voice from behind. "They were here before you came."

He looked up to see another sailor, a tall man. He nodded to him.

"Abrahamson, shouldn't you be up on the bow?" Hughes said.

"Yes, but you're filling him full of shit."

Seaman Hughes shook his head. "They won't survive without us and neither will all this stuff." He swept his hand over the back deck. "We can't lose the culture."

Abrahamson walked forward and nodded sideways at Hughes, suggesting he go away.

Hughes frowned. "I'll go up front then. I'd rather be next to the cannon anyway." He made a fake salute and walked on the port side up to the bow.

The tall man scooted a tote from the stack and moved it over near him. "Hi, I'm Seaman Jackson Abrahamson. I'm assigned to this ship."

"Assigned?"

"I'm a writer, a poet mostly. I got a job with the artist's corps. This is my assignment. Well, sort of." Abrahamson looked around and then lowered his voice. "I was forced."

"Oh," he said, "like the CCC, the Civilian Conservation Corps?"

"Yeah, like that, only they have some strict rules."

Abrahamson held out a small book. "This is one of the few books I can read from or share with the sailors: Walt Whitman's *Leaves of Grass*. Well, that's not true. We can read Billy Collins, too."

Seaman Abrahamson smiled and then closed his eyes and recited: "The eighteen thousand miles of sea-coast and bay-coast on the main, the thirty thousand miles of river navigation, / the seven millions of distinct families, and the same number of dwellings—always these, and more, branching forth into numberless branches. / Always the free range and diversity—always the continent of Democracy!"

Swanton looked the man over, wondering if he was being tricked again.

"Pretty strange, huh?" Abrahamson said. "Colonization poetry."

"You Natives tell some great stories, that's for sure."

"We call ourselves Indians where I'm from."

"What nation are you?"

"Kwakwaka'wakw. I'm not a threat. Or, so they think," he said, winking at Swanton. "They aren't rounding up any of us from the States. But up here—"

Somewhere in the dark, someone coughed.

Seaman Abrahamson looked around. "I've told you enough," he said, and added, "or not enough."

❁

Smithsonian Institution
Bureau of American Ethnology
Washington, DC

S. D. Harstead, Chief
The Secretary of the Smithsonian Institution
Washington, DC

Sir: I am submitting this collection of stories with the recommendation that
it be published in the Bureau's series of Bulletins. As you might have supposed, Dr. Swanton was detained in Wrangell, Alaska, by some unknown
influences and was weary of collecting stories. Therefore, Dr. Swanton's de-
cision to obtain my assistance was essential.

I worked in collaboration with Dr. John R. Swanton as his assistant, tran-
scribing and translating stories. Thus, I would appreciate being listed as co-
author. It's not about pride, but a matter of decolonization. Wrangell folk
are not "informants" as you call them. It's about sharing, about living on after you're dead, about what it means to be human, about what it means to
live on an island shaped like a snow goose flying to the riverflats. Further-
more, you might note that Swanton, ever the ethnologist, simply observed
the bull kelp on the surface of the sea; I saw the bull kelp attached to the
holdfast.

Yes, most of the stories were told in English, the colonizer's language, but
translations were necessary as Wrangell folk's dialect, worldview, and sto-

rytelling styles are different from standard Western worldview. This is due to the fact they live on a fairly isolated island, and, in addition, the Scandinavian and Tlingit have intermarried and coexisted for generations. As well, as it's also likely they are simply accomplished storytellers.

Unfortunately, I don't know what happened to Dr. Swanton. The last time I saw him, or rather the last time I heard his story, he was walking on the beach. Two Tlingits rescued him. You might look for him in Seattle.

In conclusion, I have taken liberty with the collected stories, *this* story. I've been around long enough to know things. After all, I did steal the light, and, at that same moment, stories were let into the world. I am bringing the light again.

Mr. Tooch Waterson
Wrangell, Alaska

❁

The outboard on the Lund sputtered to life. From the bow, Johan raised his fist in the air. "Yes," he said.

Iova held the throttle and turned the handle and the skiff. She pulled her hat down farther over her ears. She was tired. The ground wasn't a good place to sleep in this kind of weather with everything wetter than usual. For the past few days, she and her friends Johan, Sarah, and Fern had been camping on the beach and, when daylight came, they'd head off again. They followed a young black bear swimming from island to island, seeming to know a safe passage. Back in Wrangell, when they told Tooch they were leaving the island, he'd told them to follow the animals. The animals always knew.

They had been traveling for a couple days now, navigating through downed trees, logs and debris, from Wrangell to Saint John Harbor, across to Douglas Bay, past Totem Bay, and into Keku Strait up past

Devils Elbow, past Big John Bay, Dkaneek Bay. The landmarks were barely recognizable.

As they headed toward the village of Kake, Sarah sighed audibly. "You sure you heard right?" She asked Tova.

"Yeah, Kake. _Ḵéix̱'_," Tova said again in Tlingit. "They're my Grandmother Berta's people. They're known to be fierce. I heard they have supplies—food—and it's the thirteenth largest island in the US. They lost some land mass, but they're better off than other places."

"They'll take us in, right?" Sarah asked. "I used to know the health aide at the clinic. And my aunt lived there for a few years. She married a guy from there. But she moved to Juneau."

Tova licked the rain off her lips. "It's Southeast. I have relatives here."

Tova slowed the skiff, her eyes scouring the shoreline. She was right. Not all of Kupreanof Island was submerged. The small colorful square houses and the harbor were all gone. Most of the seashore of the island had sloughed off in the initial flood. A few boats tucked inside the trees.

As they neared the village, two small boats motored out from the treeline and headed in their direction. Johan waved. No one waved back.

The boats intercepted them. Tova slowed the skiff then shut the engine off as the boats sidled alongside, one on either side. There were two men in one boat, and one woman and one man in the other.

"Who are you?" the woman asked, holding a rifle.

She recognized her. "Nan, it's me. _Yak'éi yee x̱wasteeni._" She nodded to the others in the boats. "_Wáa sá iyaatee?_"

The woman smiled, "_Aaa, tlél wáa sá x̱at utí._"

The woman turned to the man in her boat, "This is Tova Agard. She's cool. I know her from college. We were in the same Tlingit language classes."

The man pointed his gun at the others. "And them?"

"I can vouch for them," Tova said. "They're friends."

"You came at a bad time," Nan said. "We're on the watch for a navy ship they say is headed this way. The _Dewey_. It's armed."

"So are you," Johan said, nodding to their weapons. "And, besides, what have you done, anyway?"

"We've resisted," one of the men said flatly.

"That's my brother, Thomas," Nan said.

"Thomas," Johan said, nodding to him.

Fern held out her hand, palm up. "Resisted what?" she asked.

"They're going around taking all our *at.óow* for safekeeping," Thomas replied. "That's what the radio says. Safekeeping. They want the totem, our carved masks, any helmets, headdresses, anything we might have. Everything we have."

"Wow," Johan whistled.

"And worse," Nan said, "they're taking us."

Tova put a hand to her chest. "Us? You?" What was she talking about? Wasn't the government supposed to save them? At least, help them? She didn't believe that, but she'd at least hoped for a rescue or help even.

"Yeah, you, me, them. They're taking Natives to camps," Nan said through her gritted teeth. "There are two or three around Southeast. They say we'll starve if we don't, and we have to have our kids in school and have access to hospitals and housing. We're going to die if they don't help us."

"What?" They weren't starving. Sure, they'd have to work to get food. They'd get hungry. But if they worked together, they'd be okay. This news didn't sound good. Not good at all.

Thomas held up a pair of binoculars searching the horizon. "Don't see them yet," he said. "First the camps were voluntary and, when no one volunteered to go, it became mandatory. Now they're rounding us up."

Nan nodded her chin upward. "Girl, you could pass for white. Or Japanese. Sure you want to hole up with us? They've already been here once a couple months ago. Said they'd be back. Said we'd better have the totems down and ready to go. Gave us some free plastic totes, and they said to gather up the *at.óow*."

Thomas lit up a cigarette and inhaled. "They want our world's largest totem. We saved it from the flood and somehow they figured we did. We floated it to the fort and dragged it back behind it. We're going to raise it when we rebuild. Like hell we're giving it to them."

"That's bullshit," Johan said.

Tova looked at Sarah, Johan, and Fern and shrugged as if to say, *Well, do you want to stay?* Of course, she wanted to stay. There'd be a good fire and maybe a bed. And there'd be stories. Kake folks were good storytellers. These were her grandmother's people.

Fern and Sarah both nodded.

"Yeah," Tova said. "We'll stay. I'm a good fisherman. And Johan weaves and he's a nurse too. He's good. He can suture, stuff like that. Fern's good with traditional medicines."

❁

In the woods beyond the treeline, the villagers had built a small fort. Large spruce trees were cut for the perimeter. Inside, there were five or six small buildings and a large one that held two hundred people or more. Tova smiled when she first saw it. There was even a basketball court set up and several kids were playing ball. Men and women were skinning deer and a half dozen smokehouses puffed smoke from out the cracks in the doors.

That night, the village held a big dinner. There were speeches in both Tlingit and English. The dancers had come out to dance when Thomas came into the large room, looking worried. The dancing stopped abruptly.

"Two of our guys spotted the *Dewey* by Portage Bay," Thomas said. "She stopped in Petersburg overnight."

A low rumble of voices moved through the room. Uh-oh, Tova thought, but didn't say it out loud. She'd been quiet all night, listening to the language she didn't get to hear as often as she'd like.

"Good news is," Thomas said, "they don't have a full crew. They didn't even have a full crew to begin with: about twenty. They stopped in Petersburg and saw a bunch of bonfires on the hills. The harbor and the canneries are gone. But we gotta thank those Vikings. Quite a few sailors got drunk with the locals and the commander hasn't been able to find the rest of his crew. The *Dewey*'s down to fourteen sailors—so I'm told."

Laughter.

Johan stood up from the floor and raised his hand. "I have an idea."

She looked at him and frowned. What kind of an idea? Johan was outspoken. Not a trait that would be respected here. But as he spoke, first introducing himself in Tlingit, people must have realized he had a future as a good orator, a good attribute to have.

Later, men and women sat around in a circle exchanging ideas. Several were experienced Iraq war veterans, some Vietnam vets, some worked for the tribal hospital. They talked about plans and strategies.

The eldest, Joseph Williams, was a WWII vet and led the discussion. They talked of diplomacy and the importance of talking things over with the government.

"I like Johan's idea," Williams said. "It's possible this might work since it's been done before."

Williams nodded to Johan.

Johan stood and motioned for Tova to stand, too. Oh, boy. She was used to talking to outsiders, tourists, but these were her elders. That was a different story. How could she explain it to the elders, how she really *did* know what was going to happen if they tried diplomacy. Didn't they remember the First Contact story? La Pérouse gave her people, her clan, the first taste of "civilization." The old men and the young ones were going to paddle their canoes out to the navy ship. The sailors will give the Tlingits rice and laugh because the elders will think they're eating maggots.

After that, the sailors will give them sugar, which the Tlingits will assume is white sand. But the "white sand" will turn into another type of death. In future generations, they'll hobble on severed legs and their bellies will sting with insulin shots. And worse, the sailors will give the young men a bottle of brandy, and the men will spin in circles, laughing on deck, spinning through her family for a long time to come.

And the commander, after taking all their *at.óow*, will inquire as to the locations of all the villages and ask if there are riches: sea otter pelts, copper and gold, and, of course, Natives themselves. After this first contact, the Tlingits will head back to shore with their gifts and the sailors will claim in their diaries they were the first to greet the savages. And if the diplomacy didn't work, she knew they'd bomb the village like they did Angoon, Kake, and Wrangell a long time ago.

Tova shook her head. She said to the grandfather, "Yeah, I speak their language. How about I go in your place?"

"You speak their language?" Mr. Williams questioned.

"Ah, yeah, I can speak their language—fluently. I can say, 'You better speak English only, you savages, because you're lucky you get to believe in our god and our schools but if you carve totem poles and eat seal grease you can't go to our schools and when you finally challenge us to go to our schools, our kids will beat up your kids for generations right into the twenty-first century when kids will spray paint around town "Kill All Natives" reminding you of the good American life: two halibut a day, free healthcare, a new HUD house, shares-or-no-shares in corporations not tribes, a laminated card, a degree for driving tour buses and working at the cold storage and canneries, where we will process your salmon up in cans, ship them out to our storehouses, and then, out of the goodness of our hearts, ship the salmon back to you when you receive our commodities."

After she finished speaking, there was silence, but only for about a minute. To someone from the Western culture, that might have seemed like a long time. To her it was time enough to close her eyes and see herself beneath a glacier, enclosed within its womb. She rode a small raft from beneath the ice, coming out at the mouth of the Stikine River. She saw herself beneath a volcano, shaking the tectonic plates, spewing ash into the air. She saw herself whipping a blanket in Lituya Bay, sending a tidal wave crashing against the mountains. She saw herself lying on her back in a trance, an oval drum beside her, the way she had once traveled, through time and stories, and cultures. Maybe she was still traveling.

She saw herself walking along a beach. There was a dead girl walking to Seattle. Kirsti. Her dress was tattered and her dishwater-blonde hair stuck this way and that.

She approached her. Kirsti looked up at Tova. "It's okay, Kirsti. I'm here. You can breathe now. Inhale."

Kirsti inhaled, taking a deep breath.

Tova touched her shoulder. Kirsti felt as solid as beach rock. Real. "You have to stay here. You're not dead. You're alive like me. You forgot, like me. Sit down on the beach."

Kirsti nodded but said nothing.

She helped Kirsti onto the beach to the sitting position. She leaned down and whispered, "Let the clouds caress your skin, the waxing moon sigh through your cells, the curl of wave rush over your thighs." She straightened then stepped back from Kirsti. "Now, stick your legs out straight in front of you."

Kirsti stuck her legs out.

"Now," Tova instructed, "move them up to your chest and hold your arms around them." Just like that the sea moved toward them. She turned around to look at Kirsti, who now had a big grin on her face.

❁

Inside the fort's house, surrounded by flood survivors, Tova opened her eyes, the image in her mind fading like melting ice. Everyone in the room stared at her.

The elder, Mr. Williams, spoke first. "Ah, I see. You are fluent, granddaughter. Maybe you should go out to meet them first, ask them what they want."

"That's right," Johan said. Johan then told the story of the *Naanyaa. aayí* and the *S'iknakadi* coming down the Stikine and how the men dressed like women and fooled their attackers.

Johan grinned. "It'll be like a Pride Week Parade. Instead of dykes on bikes and cruising for the rainbow, we'll be aunt fancys skiffing with filet knives. We'll be looking for the aggies on board the ship, make them help us."

"We'll need your best warriors, no Abigails," Johan added. "Bring me your angel with a dirty face and only half dozen or so androgynes. Two boats and our skiff. Some can hide under tarps, under the bow. Take a boat with a space under the bow."

"I see," Thomas said, laughing. "We don't want them to think we're ganging up on them."

"Right," Johan said. "If you have women who are fighters, that's great. We're going in drag. Keeps 'em thinking we're old ladies."

Mr. Williams cleared his throat then said, "Knives and small weapons."

❈

On the shore, Tova and Fern and Sarah and Johan got into the Lund. Thomas and Nan and a half dozen others got into their boats. Some hid in the bow, others under tarps. Tova smiled at Johan, at his blue flowered scarf tied under his chin. He did look good in it.

Mr. Williams raised his walking stick up in the air. "Be careful, grandchildren," he said.

Tova shoved the Lund off with her oar. She started the engine and turned the skiff parallel to the beach. She put her hand into the pocket of her hoodie and pulled a sleek metal blade from its hiding place. She raised it slightly. The young men and women on the beach nodded, raising their own knives. "*I gu.aa yáx̱ xwán*—be strong—be brave," they cried in unison.

She turned the skiff toward the ship with their signal flags flapping in the wind. *Oh, I speak their language, all right*, she thought. She'd been speaking with the slice of steel every summer at the cannery since she was fifteen years old: cut-slice-scrape, cut-slice-scrape. She knew how it felt to stick her knife in the anus, move it up through the belly, how to spread open the abdomen, rip out the entrails, scrape the backbone, and hack off the head.

This had better work. Everything depended on it, depended on them, their story; how they came down through generations, how they came down through the floodwaters, how they paddled here in the canoe, how they survived. This was their chance. Tell it again. Be the story shaking the sea. Be the story pounding on the taught skin of a drum. Be the story carved in stone.

BIOGRAPHICAL NOTE

Vivian Faith Prescott is a fifth generation Alaskan born and raised on the small island of Wrangell in Southeastern Alaska. She's a founding member of Blue Canoe Writers in Sitka and Flying Island Writers and Artists in Wrangell, Alaska with an emphasis on mentoring Indigenous writers. Vivian lives at Mickey's Fishcamp, her family's fishcamp in Wrangell. She holds an MFA in poetry from the University of Alaska and a PhD in Cross Cultural Studies from the University of Alaska Fairbanks. Her stories and poems have appeared in a variety of literary journals and anthologies including *Cold Flashes: Literary Snapshots of Alaska*, *Cirque: A Literary Journal for Alaska and the Pacific Northwest*, and *Building Fires in the Snow: A Collection of Alaskan LGBTQ Short Fiction and Poetry*. She is the recipient of a Rasmuson Fellowship and the Jason Wenger Award for Literary Excellence from the University of Alaska.